The Rancher

This is a work of fiction. Names, characters, places, and incidents are products of the author's imagination or are used fictitiously and are not to be construed as real. Any resemblance to actual events, locations, organizations, or persons, living or dead, is entirely coincidental. This work is for adult audiences.

ISBN: 9781796770971

Warning

This work of fiction contains explicit language and graphic sexual scenes.

Chapter 1

Adrian Matthews drove his pick-up truck down the highway. He was only ten miles away from the ranch. He had gone to Drew's Bar for a beer. Adrian went there at least once a week.

He stopped at the stop sign at the fork in the road. A car was coming from the right. It was moving at a normal speed, but the car that was coming from across the road from Adrian wasn't. The headlights on the speeding car were swerving from side to side.

"What the hell?" Adrian said.

Before he knew it, the swerving car T-boned the car that had the right away.

"Shit!" Adrian yelled as the cars collided. The vehicles just missed his truck by a few inches.

Tires screeched on the pavement with the sound of metal on metal. The idiot's car, which Adrian could now clearly see was a Hummer, pushed and spun the other vehicle off the road and side first into a large oak. Adrian was in shock, and then anger rose in his throat when the Hummer revved and speeded down the road like nothing happened.

Adrian slammed the gear shift into park. He jumped out of his truck to see the Hummer's taillights and the first three letters of the license plate. He ran across the road to the crashed four-door vehicle.

Luckily, it was the passenger side that was damaged and slammed against the tree. Adrian quickly opened the dented and scraped driver's side door. The airbag had deployed and was resting in the driver's lap. The driver, a light-skinned black woman, was out cold.

Adrian knew he shouldn't move her in that state, so he called out to her, “Ma'am! Ma'am!”

She didn't move, yet her chest rose up and down with each breath.

Adrian dug in his pants' pocket and pulled out his cell phone. He called 911. The operator told him that emergency responders were on their way. They asked him to try to reach for the driver's purse to search for identification.

Adrian carefully reached his arm between the driver and the airbag. He felt a strap. He pulled it over. It was a big black purse.

He got back on his cell phone with the 911 operator. “I have it,” he said as he dug past two tampons, a Snickers bar, and a bottle of Midol to look for her wallet. Seeing feminine hygiene products usually made his nose turn up, but there was no time for that. The woman was still knocked out. She could be dying.

“Hold on,” he said frantically to the operator. “I found her wallet.”

“I need her name on the license.”

Adrian looked at her license. “Faith Lauren Roberts. It says here she's from Miami, Florida.”

"Thank you for that information," the operator said. "Now, are there any pill bottles in her purse? Like prescription medications that the EMTs should know about."

Adrian quickly dug around a pack of Kleenex, a comb, a cell phone, and what looked like one of those electronic readers. "No, just a bottle of ladies' aspirin and....ladies'....monthly products," he stuttered.

It's almost midnight. What in the world was this woman thinking traveling to another state this late – alone?

"All right, sir," the operator said. "Please continue to stay on the line with me until the police and the EMTs arrive.

He looked around the darkness. There wasn't a soul in sight. Elliot was a small town in Wichita County. The only people that would be out this late on a weekday were drunks and the unemployed. He knelt down next to the woman whose name was Faith Roberts.

Poor thing was still out cold. She was lucky that she didn't have any burns from the airbag. Adrian examined her position. Her seat was leaned back pretty far. Her head was slightly cocked towards the passenger side.

In Texas, a person could smell a lot of things, cow crap, coming rain, bourbon, and freshly cut grass. But, the last thing any Texan wanted to smell was gas outside of the gas station.

Adrian's eyes widened at the smell. He quickly looked under the car. Sure enough, the gas tank was punctured, and the liquid was doing a fast drizzle on the ground. If that wasn't bad enough, Adrian heard crackling. He looked up. The sound was coming from the dashboard.

"Shit!" he yelled.

"What is it?" the operator asked with concern.

"This thing is going to catch on fire!" Adrian said. "Ma'am! Ma'am! Wake up!"

Her hand moved for a second.

"Emergency crews will be there in fifteen minutes," the operator said.

Adrian watched as a spark crackled across the dashboard. "She doesn't have fifteen minutes!"

"Don't move her. She could have injuries that you can't see."

"A worse injury than her dying in a burning car!" he shouted with anger. "If I don't move her, she'll die."

"Sir, stay on the line with me," the operator said urgently.

Adrian hung up on the operator. He jammed his cell phone in his pocket. He slung the driver's purse on his shoulder and started fighting with the seat belt.

"Come on damn you!" he shouted in frustration as he fought to loosen the seat belt.

The woman's eyes started to flutter open.

Adrian finally got the seat belt unbuckled.

The woman groaned.

Smoke was coming from the hood.

"Jesus! Come on, woman!" Adrian said as he grabbed her.

She let out a little squeal of surprise. She was staring at him in confusion.

"Come on!" Adrian said and pulled her out of the car.

She let out a short shriek and leaned to one side. She

was favoring her left leg.

Adrian didn't waste time asking her what was wrong. If they didn't get away from the car, it wouldn't matter. Adrian scooped her up in his arms and trotted across the street. There was a small ditch in their path. He placed her down in it and quickly got on top of her.

"Hey, what the hell-" she said weakly in protest.

"Just put your head down!" he yelled and covered her with his body.

A loud boom shot out from across the road.

Chapter 2

Faith Roberts lay in the hospital bed at the Elliot Medical Center. Faith wasn't sure if it could be called a medical center. It was the size of a welfare clinic. She barely remembered what happened or how she ended up here. What she did know was that some jagoff slammed into her, her eight-year-old Honda was destroyed, and she was in some hillbilly town in Texas.

A man in a white coat walked into her room. "Ms. Roberts," he began. "It's nice to see that you are awake." He was in his mid to late fifties. He was a short, balding man. What hair he did have was curly and white.

Faith just stared at him. *Who is this guy?*

"I'm Dr. Seamus Green. I attended to you when the EMTs brought you in. How are you feeling?"

"Honestly? I feel like shit," she said flatly. She had a headache, the side of her neck was sore and stiff, and her ankle was swollen under the gauze around it.

Dr. Green chuckled. "I'm not surprised, but it could have been worse. You could have come in here in a body bag. You were fortunate that you survived that hit and run."

Faith nodded. "I see. So whoever hit me just drove off."

"Looks like. The hero that saved you is talking to the sheriff now," Dr. Green said. "The sheriff wants to talk to you, too. Before he comes in, I would like to take your vitals."

"Sure," Faith mumbled. What was she going to do? She couldn't afford to buy another car. Half of her clothes were in the charred-up remains of her vehicle. Luckily, the cowboy who pulled her out of her car grabbed her purse. If he hadn't done that, she would be away from home with no money or a cell phone.

Dr. Green checked her lungs and blood pressure. He flashed his penlight in her eyes. After he was done with his mini examination, he quietly made notes in a chart.

"Is the patient up for visitors?" a cop with a thick Texan accent asked as he walked in.

The cop was wearing a brown uniform with the biggest brown cowboy hat she had ever seen. His mustache was thicker than Burt Reynolds's. The cop was tall and fat.

"For a few minutes," Dr. Green replied without looking up from the chart.

The cowboy that saved her ass was standing behind the cop.

"Ms. Roberts," the cop began as he took off his hat. His hair was blacker than black, like he dyed it. "I'm Sheriff Langford. I'm looking into your case. I need to know what happened from your perspective."

Faith swallowed. "I'm afraid I don't know much. I was driving down the road, heading to Dallas. I was approaching a crossroad, and then….it felt like my car was hit by a mac truck."

Sheriff Langford nodded. "I bet it did feel that way. You remember anything else?"

"The next thing I knew, that gentleman next to you was carrying me across the road and putting me in a ditch. Then, my car blew up," Faith said.

The sheriff nodded again. "I'll be writing up a report. I'll give you a copy to give your car insurance company so they'll have proof of the damages."

A lot of good that will do. The car was eight years old. I'll be lucky if my insurance company will give me the blue book value, she thought.

"Thank you," she said.

"Why were you heading to Dallas so late at night?" Sheriff Langford asked.

"I was traveling…cross-country," she said. "I know it was late, but I had a full tank of gas and Dallas is only two hours from here. I would have made it if it wasn't for the jerk that hit me."

"If you got kinfolk in Dallas, I can call them. Tell them what happened. They're probably worried that you haven't shown up," Sheriff Langford said.

"My family is in Florida. I don't know anyone in Texas," Faith said. "I'm on vacation. I was…just traveling."

"I'm sorry that your vacation got ruined by a drunk driver, ma'am," Sheriff Langford said.

"You know he was drunk," she said.

"That's what it looked like to our friend here," Sheriff Langford said and gestured to the cowboy next to him.

"Adrian Matthews, ma'am," the cowboy said and

tipped his black hat to her.

She gave him a small smile.

"If it wasn't for Adrian, you'd be charcoal crispy right now," Sheriff Langford said bluntly. "No one is on that road at this time of night during the week. If Adrian wasn't driving home, no one would have found you till morning. Then, it would have been too late."

Faith looked at the cowboy. "Thank you, sir."

"I'm just glad I was there," he said.

"I'm going to keep you overnight for observation, Ms. Roberts," Dr. Green said. "According to Adrian, you lost consciousness for the second time after your car caught on fire. I want to make sure you don't have any brain swelling. I can release you tomorrow afternoon. Is there anyone that you can call to come pick you up?"

"I'm afraid not," Faith said. "I don't know anyone in Texas. If you gentleman can refer me to a rental car company, I'll make my way to Dallas to check into a hotel tomorrow."

"You are in no condition to travel," Dr. Green said with a serious tone. "You have a sprained ankle, whiplash, and a concussion. You need to stay off that ankle for at least a week. Plus, you need to ice your neck and head for at least four days. I would prefer you stay closer to the medical center. I'll be able to do a follow-up on you in a few days."

"Fine. I can check into a hotel here," Faith said.

"You'll have a hard time," Adrian said flatly. "You'll be on crutches. The hotel and two motels we got here don't do room service. How will you eat?"

"I'll figure something out. I usually do," she said. Although she didn't know what that was.

"I have a better idea," Adrian announced. "There's a small cabin on my ranch. It's only one bedroom, but it's cozy and homey. You can recover there. My aunt makes mean chili."

Faith's eyes widened. Who was this guy? She wasn't going to stay with some stranger. Yes, he saved her life, but she didn't know this guy from a bum on the street. "I appreciate your offer, Mr. Matthews, but-"

"Adrian," he interjected.

"Adrian," she repeated. "I am grateful. I truly am. You didn't have to stop when you saw that I was in trouble, but I can't inconvenience you any further."

"No inconvenience for me," Adrian said. "If I know my aunt, and I do, she'll take you in like a dove with a broken wing."

"That's very sweet, but-"

"As your doctor, I would feel better if you took Adrian up on his offer," Dr. Green said. "You shouldn't be alone right now. Adrian is a good man. I've known him for years."

"I have to second that," Sheriff Langford added. "Adrian's a helluva guy. I've known him since he was in kindergarten. And you don't want to miss Aunt Bea's cooking. I envy you being able to stay out there for a while."

"Aunt Bea?" she inquired.

"My aunt," Adrian said. "Everyone calls her Aunt Bea, though."

"I see. It sounds nice, but-," she struggled out. "How could she say thanks for saving my life, but you could be a sexual predator even though the sheriff and doctor vouched for your character?"

Adrian gave her a smile that would charm most women. “I assure you, I am not a rapist, murderer, or weirdo. What I am offering you is good ole-fashioned Texan hospitality.”

“Nothing like it in the world,” Dr. Green said with a smile.

Faith looked at all three men. They were expecting her to agree. The other option was to call her brother and sister-in-law in Florida to fly out to be with her. Faith’s insides bubbled at that idea. She could hear her brother now, *I told you traveling alone was a bad idea.*

She would rather take her chances with the possible serial killer. Faith looked at Adrian. “I happily accept your offer.”

Chapter 3

The next afternoon, Adrian hopped out of his truck at the Elliot Medical Center. He walked through the doors.

"Morning, hero," Lodi, the receptionist, said. She had short blonde hair and blue eyes.

He gave her a small smile. "No hero, Lodi. Anyone would have done what I did."

"I don't know," she said with a cheesy smile. "You have a way of being around when a damsel is in distress."

"Is she ready to go?" Adrian asked.

"Yes, Dr. Green just gave me Ms. Roberts's discharge papers. Poor thang miles away from family and friends. You're doing a good thing taking her in," Lodi said. "She seems nice, but you can tell she's depressed."

"I'm sure she is," Adrian said. "One minute she's enjoying a vacation and the next minute she's injured in an accident and the driver callously drives away."

The elevator doors opened. The medical center only had three floors; the basement, the first floor, and the second floor. A nurse was pushing a wheelchair with Faith Roberts in the seat. Dr. Green walked beside the wheelchair. A candy striper was walking behind them holding a pair of crutches.

Faith was in her clothes from last night. She had her large purse in her lap along with a plastic hospital bag. Her hair was auburn and straight. She was attractive. He didn't notice it last night because of all the excitement.

"I really don't need a wheelchair," she said.

"Hospital procedure, Ms. Roberts," the nurse said. "Just enjoy the ride."

"Morning, Adrian," Dr. Green said.

"Morning," Adrian said back. He looked down at Faith. "Ready to go?"

"Yes," she mumbled.

****

After Adrian and Faith stopped at the drugstore to get her prescriptions filled and for her to pick up some personal items, they headed to Adrian's ranch.

"The Lone Wolf Ranch is five miles away," Adrian said. "We'll be there in no time, and then you can get your rest."

Faith nodded as she looked around the small town scenery. Faith didn't like small towns. She didn't really like the city life either, but it's not like there was a third option in places to live. Faith felt like she didn't belong anywhere. That's why she threw caution to the wind and set off cross-country.

"It's a cattle ranch," Adrian said. "I think you'll

enjoy it. The guest house isn't far from the main house. You'll have your privacy, yet be close to people just in case you need us."

Faith gave him a little smile. "Thank you. I really appreciate it. I don't know how I'll ever repay you."

"You're welcome, ma'am, but this is what people do around here. We help each other out when the other is in trouble," Adrian said.

"Um, your manners are appreciated, but please don't call me ma'am," she said. "It makes me feel old. I'm not a giddy young thing, but I'm only thirty-one. Just call me Faith."

"Whatever makes you comfortable," Adrian said. "So, what do you do for a living?"

"I used to be a hotel supervisor," Faith said. "I…I quit my job, and a few days later I was on the road to parts unknown."

Adrian's eyebrows shot up as he made a left turn onto the highway. "I take it that you didn't like it."

Faith chuckled. "That's putting it mildly. Let's say I got tired of nasty guests and an asshole manager who didn't think his stuff stank. After another one of our arguments, I told the manager where he could go and where to stuff the job. I worked there for five years. That was more than enough for one lifetime."

"And a few days later, you decided to go on vacation in Dallas?" he asked as he drove.

"Kind of," she said. "I had money in savings. I never had a vacation for me….for myself. I wasn't sure where to go, so I decided to go where my savings could take me. For the last two weeks, I've been in New Orleans and Little Rock. Two days ago, I decided to go to Dallas to check out the lifestyle there. I did a little research on the Internet about Dallas. I was hoping to find a job there that I liked. If I do, I'll get the rest of my things back in Miami."

"What about your life back in Miami?"

"It isn't much of a life. I couldn't keep up with the cost of living in Florida. I had mostly acquaintances than friends. I lived with my brother and sister-in-law. I paid them once a month to stay with them. It's a small amount, but I'm tired of living with them."

"I see. I hope your ordeal hasn't soured you on the Lone Star State," Adrian said as he glanced at her. "Texas is a decent place. We got our bad apples like anywhere else, but most folks are good and hospitable."

"I still have an open mind," she said in a low tone. "I did thank you for helping me, right?"

He smiled, showing his straight teeth. It was an "ah shucks ma'am" type of smile. Faith found it charming.

"Yes, but you are doing me a favor as well," he said. "My aunt hadn't had company in a while. I think she misses having another woman around. I told Aunt Bea what happened last night and that you were coming. She's been working all morning to get the place ready for ya. I think she's lonely."

"I hope she didn't put herself out."

"No. Aunt Bea didn't do anything that she wouldn't normally do if we had a guest comin'."

Adrian turned on a dirt road.

The landscaping was lush with greenery. A large white fence went for what seemed like miles with no end in sight. The truck came upon a turn-off. A large gray iron sign was over it that read, "Lone Wolf Ranch."

Adrian turned to drive under iron threshold of the sign. "We're here. I'll drive around back so you won't have to hobble through the house to the cabin."

The main house was huge. It was two stories and painted white. It looked like a ranch house you would see in the movies.

Adrian circled around the drive to the back of the home. A small white cabin came into view. Faith smiled a little. It was cute.

Adrian stopped the truck and put it in park.

Faith opened her door to get out.

"Let me help you," Adrian said as he opened his door.

"It's all right. I got it," Faith said as she gripped the handle over the door and pulled herself out. She hobbled on one leg as she grabbed her purse and bag."

"At least let me take your things," Adrian said as he rounded the truck.

"Okay," she said. She handed Adrian her bags. Faith grabbed her crutches and placed them under her arms.

"Let's go into your new home," Adrian said.

Adrian was thoughtful enough to keep pace with Faith's awkward hobbling. She had to be careful with her neck. She was wearing a soft neck brace, but it only relieved the pain a little. She hated taking prescription medications, but she had no choice. The pain in her neck was beyond uncomfortable.

Adrian opened the door for her.

Faith swayed in. The place was small, but nice. It was an open floor plan. The floors were wood. The furnishings were flowered pattern. The kitchen had a two-chair dining room table. There was a sink, a stove, and a refrigerator.

"The bathroom and the bedroom are in the back," Adrian said.

"It's nice. Very homey like you said," Faith said as she headed for an armchair. She plopped down. She had forgotten how difficult it was to adjust to crutches. She had sprained her ankle in high school. It took her two days to get the hang of them.

Adrian sat her things down on the rustic coffee table. There was a vase of fresh wildflowers on it.

A light tapping echoed off the door.

"Come in," Adrian said.

The door opened. An older woman with dark hair with strands of gray walked in. She had a chunky frame. She looked to be in her late fifties. "Howdy," she chirped.

"Faith, this is my aunt, Bea Collins," Adrian said.

"Nice to meet you, Mrs. Collins," Faith said.

"Call me Aunt Bea, sweetie, everyone else does," she said as she walked to Faith. "You poor dear. Are you in pain?"

Faith smiled at the sweet old lady. "Just a little. Nothing I can't handle."

"Did you eat lunch at the hospital?" Aunt Bea asked.

"No, ma'am," Faith said.

"You must be hungry. I can fix you a sandwich," Aunt Bea said.

"I don't want to put you out," Faith said. "I can fix a simple sandwich."

"Put me out? Nonsense. I'm sure you should stay off that foot anyway," Aunt Bea said. "Adrian, why don't you carry out your chores while I get this girl settled?"

"Yes, ma'am," Adrian said with a small smile.

Chapter 4

Two weeks later....

Faith had fully recovered from her accident. She had called her brother last week to check in. She didn't tell him about the accident because she didn't want him to worry. However, Faith did tell him that she was staying in Texas for a little while. He had told her to be careful and to have fun.

Until today, Faith hadn't been able to have fun or explore. The farthest she had gone in the past two weeks was the medical center for a follow-up appointment. For the past three days, she had dinner with Aunt Bea. Adrian and his brothers never joined them. They were out on the range working the cattle. They had spent the last five nights camping out on the property, which Faith found out was a thousand acres. Faith didn't know that large spreads like the Lone Wolf Ranch still existed. She appreciated the ranch's natural habitat. These days, it seemed like if there was a spot of land that was more than an acre, someone came along wanting to put a building on it.

Faith walked through the patio doors to the kitchen in the main house. Bea had fried fish that the Matthews brothers caught in the creek on the property. She also had fried potatoes and steamed broccoli.

"There you are," Bea said happily. "The table is set, and the food is hot on the table in the dining room."

Faith felt ashen. "I could have set the table. I wish you would let me help. I'm better now."

"Oh, honey, I have plenty of energy," Aunt Bea said. "Let's go to the dining room."

The ladies walked into the large dining room. There were two extra place settings.

"Are we having guests?" Faith asked.

"More like family," Aunt Bea said. "The boys are back. They'll be joining us for dinner, and you'll finally get to meet my other nephews."

Two tall men walked into the dining room. One had light brown hair like Adrian. The other one had thick blonde hair. They were the same height.

"Speak of the devils," Aunt Bea said with a grin. "Faith, these are my other nephews. The hunk with the blonde hair is Steve."

"Ma'am," Steve said with a nod and a big grin. Bea wasn't exaggerating. He was a hunk. Faith could see the muscle definition through his tight blue shirt. He had dreamy blue eyes. Faith didn't like men with bulging muscles, but it suited Steve.

"Nice to meet you," Faith said.

"The quiet one is Joey. He's the youngest," Aunt Bea said.

"It's nice to finally meet you," Joey said with a shy smile. Joey was slim and toned.

"And you," Faith said. "Where's Adrian?"

"He likes working himself to death," Steve answered. "He's tending to the horses, giving them a brush down and all."

"Let's sit down and say grace before the food gets cold," Aunt Bea said.

Ten minutes later, they were eating.

Faith took this time to tell the Matthews family her plans. "My stay here has been wonderful, but now that I'm better I should be moving on."

"Oh no," Aunt Bea said frantically as she looked up from her plate. "You can't leave, yet. Next month is our annual BBQ here at the ranch. You have to stay for that."

Faith doubted she would want to stick around for a hillbilly BBQ. It wasn't her style. She was used to cookouts in the backyard, and she enjoyed them. "I can't intrude on you any longer. I don't want to overstay my welcome after all," she said as politely as she could.

Faith knew that Aunt Bea was lonely. The old woman had friends, but they had responsibilities of their own. Aunt Bea had one daughter who lived in Houston. During the last two weeks, Faith had figured out that Bea's daughter didn't visit very often. She rarely called Aunt Bea. Faith really liked Aunt Bea, but she couldn't stay here for the rest of her life.

"Intrude?" Aunt Bea repeated with a hint of insult. "Nonsense. I've enjoyed having you here. Besides, have you thought about sticking around Elliot for a little while?"

Stick around for what? There's nothing here, but a few shops, animals, and grass, she thought.

"No, ma'am, I hadn't," Faith said. "I have to make a living. I need to get to Dallas, find a hotel to stay in for a little while, and start looking for a job."

"I understand all that," Aunt Bea said. "But another few weeks can't hurt. Judging from what you've told me, you need a nice long break. Just stay for a few more weeks. Give Elliot a chance. Matter of fact, you've only left the ranch once and that was for a doctor's appointment. You should go out tomorrow; look around, meet some of the locals. It's a really nice area."

"Aunt Bea," Steve began. "Don't you think you're laying it on a bit thick? Yes, Elliot is a nice place, but it isn't for everybody."

"I don't even have any clothes," Faith said. For the past two weeks, Faith had been wearing old clothes that belonged to Aunt Bea's sister. Her sister had passed away four years ago, but Aunt Bea kept some of her old clothes in the attack. They were a size too big for Faith, but it was better than walking around naked.

"We got a clothing store," Aunt Bea said. "It isn't filled with high fashion, but they have nice things in there."

"You may as well give it up, Faith," Joey said. "She's not going to let you go anywhere with the BBQ on the horizon."

Faith looked around the table at the expecting faces. "When's the BBQ?"

"Five weeks from today," Aunt Bea said. "You'll love it. Everyone in town and the neighboring towns usually come for it. Good folks."

Faith wasn't in a big hurry to leave, but she felt like a moocher. She was used to taking care of herself. When she did need help, she always repaid the favor. "I'll stay for another few weeks on one condition."

"Which is?" Aunt Bea asked.

"That you let me help out around here," Faith said. "I know how to cook and clean. Starting tonight, I'm doing the dishes."

Aunt Bea gave her a little smile. "All right, dear."

Faith felt better already. "Good. Now, if I'm going to stay for another few weeks to explore the town, I'll need a car and clothes. Can someone drive me into town tomorrow?"

"I'll be happy to," Steve said.

Faith was surprised that Steve would offer to be her chauffeur. "You don't mind taking me shopping?"

Steve chuckled. "Well, I won't be in the store with you. I can drop you off. I need to go into town to pick up some supplies."

"All right. Thanks," Faith said.

Several hours later, Faith was lying awake in bed in the cabin. She looked over at the clock. It was 9:30. She wasn't used to going to bed so early. Apparently, that was the thing in Elliot. Aunt Bea told her that people stayed up late during the weekends if the local bar was having what Aunt Bea called a shindig.

Faith decided to get up and get a drink of water. She padded to the fridge and pulled out a bottled water. As she was drinking the water, she heard rustling outside. Faith walked to the living room window and lifted one slit of the white blinds with her finger.

It was Adrian. He was pulling his T-shirt over his head. Faith's eyebrows rose as she stared at Adrian's chest. He had some muscle definition. Straight brown hair sprinkled his chest and abs. Faith licked her lips as Adrian sat down on a cement bench in the courtyard. He pulled his boots and socks off.

Before Faith could wonder what he was doing, Adrian's actions told her. He walked to the outdoor shower to the right and turned on the water.

Faith was surprised. She thought the shower in the little courtyard was for looks. She didn't know it actually worked. The wall on the shower blocked the view of it towards the main house, but it was open for anyone in the cabin to see.

Faith held her breath as she watched Adrian unbuckle his belt. She knew she should turn away, but she couldn't. For some reason, she wanted to see. She didn't know why. It's not like she hadn't seen a man naked before.

Adrian pushed his jeans down to his ankles. He was tan all over; including his member which was impressive in the moonlight. Faith's lips parted at the sight of it. It was perfect; not too little and not too long. It was partially hard.

Adrian grabbed something from the cement bench. It was a bar of soap. Faith sucked in a breath as Adrian stepped under the sprinkles of water. He stood there, letting the water wet his hair and body. He turned. He had a sexy ass. The dimples in his butt cheeks squeezed as he stretched. Then, he turned back around, wetting the soap as he did. He dragged the bar across his chest and shoulders, washing away the dust from the range.

Faith placed her hand on the front of her left thigh as Adrian dragged the bar of soap to his shaft. She licked her lips again as she watched Adrian soap his member that was now hard and bobbing under the water.

She wiggled her hips as her womanhood became moist with want. Damn, he was a good-looking man.

Chapter 5

Adrian cut the shower off and stepped out of the small area. He grabbed the white towel that Aunt Bea left out for him. She knew Adrian and his brothers liked washing up before they came into the house. It was a habit that their mother had instilled in them when they were kids. It was the perfect night for a warm shower. It was muggy out, but a good warm night nonetheless.

He dried off and grabbed the pair of blue sweatpants that Aunt Bea set out for him. He was pulling them on as the patio door to the kitchen opened. It was Steve. He was shirtless. He had on a pair of jeans. "Finally decided to come in I see," Steve said.

"Yep," Adrian replied as he ran his fingers through his wet hair.

"You missed a good dinner," Steve said as he propped his foot up on the bench. "Aunt Bea talked Faith into staying for another five weeks. She sure does like that girl."

"Seems like," Adrian said.

"I like her, too," Steve said. "She seems nice and willing to pull her weight. Faith said she wanted to help

Bea around the house in exchange for room and board."

"Steve, no," Adrian said. He knew what his brother was thinking. Steve has bedded most of the women in Wichita County that were above eighteen and below fifty. "She's a lady."

"I know that. I love ladies," Steve said with a grin.

"You love them too much. Faith doesn't strike me as the one-night stand type," Adrian said.

"Oh, I get it," Steve said. "You want her for yourself. I guess I can move over once for you. When was the last time you got your dick wet anyway?"

Adrian was about to tell his brother to go to hell when they heard a crash. The noise came from the cabin. Steve and Adrian jogged towards the door.

Steve banged on the door. "Hey, are you okay in there?" Steve didn't wait to be invited in. He turned the knob and opened the door.

The men rushed in to see Faith standing next to a small table on its side on the floor. The large ugly vase that used to sit on it was in pieces. The moonlight coming from the kitchen window illuminated Faith's horrified expression.

"I….I….heard noises outside. I went to the window to see what was going on and I knocked over the table. I'm sorry," she stuttered.

"Well, as long as you're all right," Steve said.

"I am. Thank you," she breathed. "I'll get a broom."

"Don't move. You're barefoot," Adrian said.

"So are you," she said back at him.

"I got shoes on," Steve said and headed for the kitchen.

"I thought you were in bed," Adrian said.

"I was," Faith said.

Realization registered. "Oh…we woke you up," Adrian said. She had said she heard noises. "Sorry about that."

"No…it's fine. I was thirsty, anyway," she stuttered.

Steve walked over to Faith and started sweeping up the broken porcelain.

"I hope that wasn't expensive," Faith said.

"Nah," Steve said as he quickly swept up the pieces. "It was a big piece of junk that Aunt Bea got from the antique store. If that's what you want to call it. I call it a junk store."

Steve started sweeping the pieces into the dustpan.

Adrian noticed Faith's night attire. A long-sleeved white cotton shirt that came above her cute knees. "Is that my shirt?" he asked.

"Oh, um, yes," Faith said. "Aunt Bea gave it to me to sleep in. I…hope it's okay."

Okay? It was more than okay. She looked great in it. This thought disturbed Adrian and turned him on at the same time.

"Yeah, it's fine," he stuttered.

"Yeah," Steve said with a grin as he stood up with the dustpan and broom in hand. "You look better in it than he does."

Faith smiled as she bashfully looked away.

"Steve," Adrian chided.

"Thank you," Faith whispered.

"Just being honest," Steve said. "Now, you better get to bed. We have to get an early start in the morning before it gets too hot."

"Early start?" Adrian inquired.

"Steve has offered to take me into town in the morning to get some clothes. I'm hoping to take a look around the car lot Steve was talking about. Maybe I can get another vehicle cheap."

Adrian didn't like the sound of that. He didn't want Steve around Faith. His brother was like a blood hound when it came to women. The last thing Faith needed was a horn dog sniffing around her after everything she's been through.

Chapter 6

Faith had bought some clothes at the local boutique. The woman who owned the store was an African-American named Linda. Faith was glad to see that Elliot had diversity. It made her feel more comfortable in the area. Turns out the owner of the clothing store went to cosmetology school and did hair on the side. Faith usually did her own hair, but sometimes she needed help dying her hair auburn, the way she liked it. She would need a touch up in a week or two. Faith would call on the chipper sister then. Faith had also gone to the drug store and a little shop full of Texas trinkets.

She patiently wanted on a bench on the sidewalk with her packages. Steve should be back in a few minutes. He had to pick up cattle feed from a supplier. Faith hoped that there was room in his truck for her things. To her surprise, Adrian's black Dodge truck pulled up next to the sidewalk.

He got out of the truck and walked to her. "Hey," he greeted.

"Hey," she said back. "What are you doing here?"

"I had to run into town real quick," Adrian said.

"Are you waitin' for Steve?"

"Yes," she answered.

Like clockwork, Steve's blue Ford truck pulled up behind Adrian's Dodge. Steve kept the motor running. He got out.

"Adrian," Steve said as he walked to them. "Fancy meeting you here."

"I had to come into town real quick," Adrian stated.

Steve gave his brother a brief nod. "Ready to go, Faith?"

"Yes," she answered.

"Steve, why don't you let me drive the lady back? You don't have room for her packages," Adrian said.

"I don't mind as long as Faith doesn't," Steve said.

"Oh, I don't if you don't," she said.

"Not at all," Steve said. "I'll see you two back at the ranch."

A few minutes later, Steve was gone, and Faith was riding in the passenger seat in Adrian's truck.

"Did you enjoy your shopping?" he asked.

"Yes," she said solemnly.

"Are you sure? You don't sound like it."

"Well, the stores were fine, but...I walked to the dealership. I need a new car. The problem is that I can't afford a decent replacement. The cars I could afford were complete junkers. I'd be surprised if they could make it off the lot."

"Know a lot about cars, huh?"

"Some. My brother is a mechanic. I also dated a guy in high school who was into cars. I paid attention when they worked on them," she said with a shrug. "I can't leave town even if I wanted, too."

"If you don't mind me askin', how much do you need?" Adrian asked.

"At least fifteen thousand for something half decent," she answered. "Even if I had a job right now, it will take me forever to raise it. Since I am unemployed, no one will offer me credit."

Faith was discouraged. She had no choice but to stay in Elliot until she secured a vehicle. She'd rather drop dead than to ask her brother for money. He would lend it to her, but he would never let her forget it. "Looks like I have to get a job here - at least for a while."

"Is that so bad?"

"Not bad, it's just a small town. How much money can I make here?"

"You'd be surprised. We have tourists come in from the big cities looking for hunting adventures on the weekends. You could make a lot as a waitress at the diner."

"That's a good idea. I'll think about it," she said.

Fifteen minutes later, they were back at the ranch. Adrian carried Faith's packages into the guest house for her. He was such a gentleman. She liked it. "Would you like a glass of lemonade before you go?"

He gave her a smile. "Can I take a rain check? I need to get back to the stables. We got a mare that's expecting a colt sometime today or tomorrow. I'd like to be there to make sure everything goes well."

"Oh, sure," Faith said. "If that's the case, I'm going to give this to you now. I might not see you for a few days." Faith turned away from him and dug in one of her shopping bags. She pulled out a gift box. She turned around to Adrian and handed him the gift. "I wanted to get you something…to say thank you for saving my bacon."

"Thank you, but you didn't have to get me anything," Adrian said.

"Open it," she urged. "I want to make sure you like it. If you don't, I can take it back. I kept the receipt."

Adrian smiled at her statement as he opened the box. He was taken aback by the sterling silver belt buckle. A stallion was etched into the piece. "Wow, this must have cost-"

"Not the amount of saving my life," she said. "Steve said that you loved horses and I noticed that you like wearing belt buckles. I saw it at the shop today. I thought you might like it."

"I love it," he said. Adrian leaned in and kissed her on the forehead.

It surprised both of them. It really surprised Faith when Adrian kept lingering in her personal space. She wasn't going to stop him. Adrian was attractive, and he seemed like a sweet guy. She wondered if he was going to kiss her on the lips. It had been so long since she had been kissed.

He didn't let her wonder for very long. Adrian bent his head and placed his lips on hers. He had a gentle touch. It was a feathery kiss - like Faith was a wild mare that he didn't want to spook. Before Faith could get into the kiss good, Adrian's head snapped back.

"I'm sorry," he said quickly. "I shouldn't have."

"It's okay," she assured him.

"No, it's not," he said and took two steps back – away from her. "I'm taking advantage."

"What?" she asked with confusion.

"You're far from home. You don't know anyone here. You've been through a life and death experience," he shot out quickly. "You're vulnerable right now and I…I apologize."

"Please don't apologize," she said. "It's fine." She saw the horrified expression on his face. He really regretted kissing her.

"No, it's not. I'm truly sorry," Adrian said. "I'll see you later."

Before Faith could say another word, Adrian bolted out the front door.

Chapter 7

That evening, Faith was having dinner with Aunt Bea, Steve, and Joey in the main house. Adrian was at the barn with the expecting mare. Steve and Aunt Bea chatted away as Joey and Faith quietly ate. After dinner, Faith took the dirty dishes into the kitchen.

She quietly washed the dishes as she wondered what had happened this afternoon. What made Adrian freak out so much over a little kiss. A thought entered her head that she didn't like. However, she couldn't ignore it.

Steve walked into the kitchen. "I thought I could help you dry."

Faith shook her head. "I got it. Go rest. You've been working all day."

Steve ignored her statement and grabbed a dish towel. "Actually, it's an excuse. I wanted to talk to you. Just you and me."

"Oh?"

"Yeah, when I got back with the feed, Adrian was acting strangely," Steve said. "Well, he was moody; more than usual. I was wondering if you knew why that was."

Faith didn't blame Steve for asking. Adrian was his brother, after all. Of course, he would be concerned about his brother's well-being. Faith looked down in the dishwater. "I'm not exactly sure. I....we..." she stuttered.

"Okay, take a deep breath and let's sit down," Steve said soothingly.

Faith slowly took her hands out of the water. Steve handed her the dish towel to dry her hands. They quietly sat down at the kitchen table.

"Now, tell me what happened," he said in a gentle tone.

"We got back to the guest house from town. Adrian carried my packages in. I offered him some lemonade, but he asked to take a rain check. He said he wanted to go back to the barn to be with the pregnant horse. I said okay then offered him the gift I bought him today...as a thank you for saving my life and bringing me here to heal."

"Okay," Steve said. "What happened? He didn't like the gift?"

"No, it seemed like he did. A lot. He kissed me on the forehead," she said softly.

Steve's golden eyebrows arched up. "He did," he whispered in a shocked tone.

"Then, he....kissed me. Like on the mouth," she whispered.

"Wow," Steve said as a slow smile spread across his lips.

"It stopped as quickly as it began. Adrian started apologizing and....then he bolted like he saw the ghost of Christmas past," Faith explained. "I....he looked like he really regretted it."

"I see," Steve said.

"Is it because I'm black?" she asked. The question came out before she could stop it. However, she couldn't help but think that. Adrian had looked so mortified that he was within an inch of her.

Steve looked surprised at the question. "Good grief," he said with a hint of disgust. "He must have made you feel horrible. I assure you it's not because you're black. Matter of fact, he likes women who are....cultured."

"Okay, so what's the problem?" Faith asked.

Steve glanced down at the table and looked back up at her. "Well, I can't divulge all my brother's secrets, but please know that it wasn't you. You're attractive and nice. Adrian...well, let's say Adrian had a hard time with a woman in the past. He never really got over it. Plus, our own family tragedies hadn't helped his disposition."

Faith didn't want to pry. If Steve wanted to tell her details, he would have. "All right," she whispered.

"Do you like my brother?" he asked.

Damn. One thing she has learned about Texans during her visit was that they cut right to the chase. "I think so. I mean we hadn't talked that much, but we get along. He's a gentleman, and I like that. Miami doesn't have a lot of gentlemen."

Steve gave her a million dollar smile. "Texas is full of gentlemen, honey. But, I'm glad you like gentlemen. I'm not sure if Adrian is ready to move forward concerning his personal life. However, his kid brother is available. And he happens to find you adorable. Are you willing to give me a shot?"

Faith couldn't help but feel flattered. "You can have any woman you want."

He chuckled. "Maybe, but a guy can only play the field for so long. You're a nice woman. I can tell by how you carry yourself. Would you like to go out with me tomorrow night?"

Her mouth dropped open. She couldn't believe Steve was asking her out on a date. "I…I….don't know what to say."

"No funny business, I promise," he said seriously. "Not unless you want some funny business," he said with a mischievous smirk.

She couldn't help but smile. Steve really was a charmer. It wasn't what he said, but how he said things. "Well, I guess one dinner date wouldn't hurt. I haven't been out on a date in a long time."

"Great," Steve said with victory in his tone. "I'm not Adrian, but I know how to show a lady a good time. And it might make Adrian jealous. Or I could help you forget about Adrian. Either way, I get to spend tomorrow night with a good lookin' woman."

Chapter 8

Adrian had avoided Faith for twenty-four hours. Last night, after the mare had her colt, he had slept out in the barn to avoid her. He didn't know what to say. Faith probably thought he was a jerk. He didn't mean to run off the way he did on her, but if he stayed with her for one more minute, he would have taken her to bed. He had no interest in getting tangled up with a woman again. Women were pleasant to chat with, but anything more was trouble and heartache. He had learned that the hard way.

Once he felt like his libido calmed down enough, he had gone to the main house and showered. It was nine o'clock at night. Faith was probably in bed and his family had eaten dinner by now. He had showered outside as usual and went into the kitchen through the patio doors. Adrian opened the microwave to grab the wrapped plate that Aunt Bea always set aside for him if he missed dinner. He took the foil off the plate and warmed his food. Adrian gobbled up his dinner.

After he was done, he walked into the living room to see Joey and Aunt Bea playing Scrabble.

"Evenin'," Aunt Bea chirped.

"Evenin'," Adrian said back. "Who's winning?"

"Your brother as usual," Aunt Bea said as Joey was putting down letters on the board.

"Where's Steve?" Adrian asked.

His brother looked up at him. "Out on a date," Joey answered.

"Ah," Adrian said. It was Friday night. Of course, Steve was out on a date. "I take it that Faith doesn't like Scrabble." Adrian couldn't help it. He had to know how she was. Was she angry with him? Were her feelings hurt?

"No, she likes it," Aunt Bea said as she dug in the bag for letters. "I like playing with her 'cause I can beat her."

Adrian and Joey chuckled.

"Couldn't keep her eyes open, huh?" Adrian asked.

"Nope," Joey said. "She's gone."

"Gone?" Adrian said. "What do you mean she's gone?" *Shit, did I chase her off? I never meant to do that.*

Joey looked up at him. He had a sly grin across his lips. "She's going to be out for a while I expect."

Joey knew exactly what was going on. "Out where?" Adrian asked.

"Out. On a date," Joey said with that same sly grin that Adrian wanted to knock off his face.

His brother's reply had his wheels turning. "No," Adrian said in a low tone.

"Yep," Joey clipped out.

"Where did Steve take her?" Adrian asked.

Joey just stared at him with a cutesy grin.

"Speak or I'll beat it out of you," Adrian said in a menacing tone.

"Oh, good grief," Aunt Bea whined. "I shampooed the carpet yesterday. I really don't want to scrub blood out of it. And despite his size, Joey is as good of a fighter as you are. You two will wreck the living room."

Joey was slimmer than his brother, but he could fight. Joey could give any man a run for his money just like his eldest brother.

"Just tell him, Joey," Aunt Bea said. "No reason to ruin a good evening over it."

"Drew's," Joey said.

Drew's Bar. Adrian started walking out the living room.

"Where are you going?" Aunt Bea asked.

"I'm going upstairs to get a shirt and then I'm going to Drew's. I can't leave Faith with Steve. It's like leaving a lamb with a lion," Adrian said.

"Oh dear," his aunt said with an amused smile. "You better go with him, Joey. You know how your brothers like getting into scuffs. You're good at breaking up a fight between them."

"There isn't going to be a fight," Adrian said. If Steve knew what was good for him.

"But, I'm winning," Joey stated.

"I know. That's why I'm sending you away," Aunt Bea said.

****

Joey and Adrian walked into Drew's Bar. The old country bar was packed. Some folks would come from the next town to party at Drew's on the weekends. The bar had the old Texan rustic charm. Bull horns and pictures of horses and cattle decorated the walls. The place had a big ole dance floor with sawdust and nut shells on the dining room floor. A live band was playing.

The owner walked up to them. "Hey, boys. You want a table?" Drew asked.

"Not right now, Drew," Adrian said. "We're looking for our brother."

"Oh yeah," Drew said. "He and Isaiah are with two pretty fillies in a booth along the far side of the wall."

"Thanks," Adrian said.

Joey and Adrian scaled the wall. Adrian spotted them. Steve had his arm around Faith who was smiling. Jealousy burned Adrian's loins. It looked like she was having a good time. He could show her a good time. She didn't need Steve for that.

Adrian stalked to the booth with Joey in toe.

"Evening," Adrian said, announcing his arrival.

The foursome looked surprised to see them. Isaiah was a black man who lived in the area. He was also a ranch hand on the Lone Wolf Ranch. He was with a brunette that Adrian had never seen before. She had a big nose. Adrian glanced over at Faith and Steve. His brother was smirking like the cat that ate the canary. Faith looked at him with wide eyes.

"Evenin', boss," Isaiah said. He was wearing his favorite white Stetson. Adrian didn't blame him. It was a damn fine hat.

"What are you guys doing here?" Faith slurred.

Steve had gotten her drunk. The cad. "Joey and I wanted to come out for a drink," Adrian answered. He glanced at Joey.

Joey looked like he had swallowed a bug. He knew Adrian was full of it, but he knew better than to call him out in front of everyone.

"Mind if we join ya'll?" Joey asked.

Adrian didn't wait for an answer. He scooted next to Faith on the bench that she and Steve sat on, squeezing her in the middle.

"Not at all," the brunette said. "The more the merrier." She and Isaiah scooted over to let Joey sit down.

"I'll buy the next round," Adrian announced.

They chatted and drank beer for almost two hours.

"How about a dance, Faith?" Steve asked.

Faith shrugged. "I'll try. I don't know how to do the two-step or anything like that."

Steve chuckled. "It's a slow song. You can swing it."

"Faith, don't you think you've had too much to drink to dance?" Adrian asked.

"No," she answered simply.

"Let us out, big brother," Steve said.

Adrian reluctantly stood up. He watched Faith and Steve scoot out of the booth to go to the dance floor.

Chapter 9

Steve wrapped his arms around Faith's waist. They swayed to the music that wasn't necessarily Faith's taste. She appreciated different music, but that doesn't mean she wanted to listen to it all night.

"What did I tell you?" Steve said. "Adrian likes you. He came here to spy on us. He just can't admit right now."

"It's a coincidence that he's here. You said Adrian came here all the time to have a beer or two," Faith said.

"Yeah, but he came here tonight and made a B-line straight for us," Steve said. "I saw him and Joey as soon as they came in."

Faith shrugged. *Steve could be right, but do I want to get involved with a guy who has ex-girlfriend issues?* She knew how some men were. Some men used the excuse of having their heart broken once to treat all future women in their life like shit.

"Hey, buddy," a man slurred as he approached them. He had on jeans and a hunting jacket. "Is that your wife?"

"No," Steve answered.

"Well, let me have a spin with her," the man slurred.

"Thank you, but this gentleman is my date. I'm afraid it might be rude if I danced with you," Faith said. She didn't want to dance with this middle-aged pot belly mofo. She had enough of those guys in Miami. They would come to Miami for the weekend trying to bed younger women knowing good and damn well that they had wives at home feigning for attention.

"Oh shit," he slurred. "He ain't gonna mind."

"No offense, buddy, but I do mind," Steve said. "There are plenty of ladies in here. Ask one of them to dance."

"Don't you dismiss me like some cow shit that you found on the bottom of your shoe," the man slurred angrily. The man shoved Steve so hard he rocked back. Then, he put a vice grip on Faith's arm.

"Get of off me!" she shouted.

Before she knew it, Steve swung the guy around and punched him in the face. The man hit the floor.

"Hey!" a man shouted as he came out of the bathroom. He headed straight for Steve. Before Steve could defend himself, Joey leaped at the guy like a cat, tackling him on the dance floor.

"You stuck-up bitch," a man slurred loudly as he stalked towards Faith. "All you had to do was dance with him. It wouldn't have done any harm. You started all this." He started reaching for Faith.

Before Faith could get away from the large imposing man, Adrian came out of nowhere and gave him an uppercut.

All hell broke loose. Men that didn't have any stake in what was going on started jumping into the fray.

Instead of dancing on the dance floor, people were brawling on the dance floor. A waitress who was carrying a tray of mugs was accidentally pushed. She dropped the empty glasses on the floor. “Damn it!” she shouted. The young redhead took the tray and hit the guy that bumped into her over the head.

The band continued to play like nothing was going on.

“Get out of there, honey!” a woman that Faith didn’t know yelled at her. The woman grabbed Faith’s hand and pulled her over to the side. “You’ll get yourself hurt standing to close to a brawl!”

Faith knew that. After all, she spent the first fourteen years of her life growing up in a ghetto. However, she was awestruck at how quickly this all happened. If it happened in the hood she and her brother grew up in, it wouldn’t have surprised her as much. But, a backwoods bar filled with locals? She never thought she would see it in her lifetime. She thought cowboy bar fights just happened in the movies and on TV. She was wrong.

Isaiah was in the fray, too. He kicked a guy in the face. Steve was pummeling a guy on the floor. Joey just kicked another guy in the balls. Adrian punched a guy in the face, knocking his hat off. Another guy lunged at Adrian from a booth table top. They hit the floor. A guy that Faith didn’t know jumped on Adrian’s attacker and pulled him off of Adrian. Steve went flying past Adrian and the guy that helped him and hit the floor. The man that hit Steve was about to mount an attack until Joey came out of nowhere and jumped on the guy’s back. Joey had him in a chokehold. Other men were fighting on the dance floor along with the Matthews brothers.

The drunken pot belly bastard that started it all was passed out against the wall.

Faith didn't think it was going to end, but it did, and in a way she wasn't expecting. Someone fired three gunshots into the air. Several women shrieked with fright. All the action stopped, and everyone in the bar looked to see where the shots came from.

It was Drew, the owner. He had a pistol in his hand aimed up at the ceiling. Dust from the bullet holes in the ceiling sprinkled down on top of him and a couple of patrons. Faith noticed that there were more than three bullet holes in the ceiling. How many fights did this man have to break up in the past by firing a gun?

"All right!" Drew yelled. "That's enough. Now, you gul'damn tourists get the hell outta my bar!"

"I live here," a man slurred.

"Bullshit!" a waitress yelled.

"There's never a fight in here until you assholes show up!" Drew yelled. "This isn't the first time you boys have come in here fighting with my regular customers and harassing the ladies. I should have banned you a year ago."

"We're not going anywhere!" a man yelled.

Drew pointed the barrel of the gun at him. "Oh yeah," he said through gritted teeth. "Go now or I'll pop a cap in your ass!"

The guy snorted.

"Maybe we should go," another guy said nervously as he held his abdomen.

"Don't worry, Devon," the guy who was staring at the barrel of the gun said with amusement. He had a split lip. "He doesn't have the balls to pull that trigger."

Drew quickly adjusted his aim and pulled the trigger.

Women shrieked around Faith as she jumped at the sound of the gun.

The big mouth grabbed his knee and crumpled on the floor, screaming in agony.

Every man that was on the dance floor had wide eyes.

"Anybody else wanna get shot?" Drew asked as he looked around.

Chapter 10

Adrian, Steve, Joey, and Faith were back at the Lone Wolf Ranch. Faith insisted on tending to their wounds in the kitchen. They were a little worse for the wear, but they gave better than what they got. The men who started all the trouble were tourists who came into Elliot once a month to hunt. A waitress had said that they were from Dallas. Privileged middle-aged men who thought they could treat middle-class Americans like crap.

The local men had dragged the beat-up, troublemaking tourists out of the bar and tossed them in the parking lot like they were garbage, which they were. Sheriff Langford had shown up as Faith and the Matthews brothers were leaving the bar. He had asked Drew what happened to the men that were there. Drew had told the sheriff that they got hit by a car. All five of them. He knew Drew was lying, but the sheriff had shrugged, stated that shit happens, and got back in his cruiser and drove off.

Faith had given Steve a few cubes of ice wrapped in a dish towel for his split lip. A bruise was also forming on his cheek. Joey sat at the kitchen table as he held a dish towel over his bloody nose. Other than that, he was fine.

Faith handed Adrian a slab of beef from the fridge for his black eye. "I still think ice is better for that."

"My father used steak for a black eye. If it was good enough for him, it's good enough for me," Adrian said as he slapped the meat over his eye.

"I'm hungry," Joey stated.

"Yeah," Steve said. "I'm always starving after a good fight."

"It's after one o'clock in the morning," Faith said.

"So?" the brothers said in unison.

A smile slowly spread across her lips. "Well, I guess it's my duty to cook for the men that defended my honor. What do you guys want to eat?"

"Steak and eggs," they mumbled in unison.

Faith chuckled. They were related all right. Twenty minutes later, Faith was placing big slabs of steak on plates. They all liked their meat medium rare. She had scrambled eggs on a hot plate. The boys sat down to dig in.

"You're not eating?" Joey asked as he shoved a big piece of steak in his mouth.

"No, this meal is a little heavy for me at this time of night," Faith said with a smile. She started running dishwater into the sink. She was going to wash the frying pans and bowls she had used.

"This steak is good, honey," Steve said with his mouth full. "You weren't lying. You can cook."

"Thanks," she said over her shoulder.

"The eggs are fantastic," Adrian said. "They're filling and fluffy all at the same time. How do you do that?"

Faith giggled like a girl. She started to become embarrassed by the way she laughed at Adrian's compliment until he let out a low chuckle.

"I smell food," Aunt Bea said from down the hall. She walked into the kitchen as she spoke. "Why are you boys eating this-?" She stopped short in the doorway when she got a look at her beat-up nephews. "What in the Sam Hill happened?" she asked in a high-pitched voice.

"We didn't start it," the men said with their mouths full.

"Really?" Aunt Bea said as she crossed her pudgy arms. She walked to the kitchen table.

"They really didn't, Aunt Bea," Faith said. "A drunk approached me in the bar that wouldn't take no for an answer. Then, his buddies got involved. It really was unavoidable."

"I see," Aunt Bea said with less accusation in her voice. "I take it that they were tourists."

"They were, actually," Faith answered over her shoulder as she scrubbed the bowl she had scrambled the eggs in. "How did you know?"

"That's the only time when a fight breaks out at Drew's," Aunt Bea said. "Some of the tourists that come here behave themselves – they have a good time and go back to where they came from. The others come here acting like wild coyotes. I have no doubt they deserved whatever they got."

"Even the one that will be limping for the rest of his life thanks to Drew shooting him in the knee?" Steve asked with a mischievous smirk.

"What?" Aunt Bea exclaimed. "Drew actually shot one of them?"

"Yep," Joey answered and shoved a fork full of eggs in his mouth.

"Apparently, those guys have caused Drew trouble several times before," Adrian said. "He snapped."

"Gosh," Aunt Bea said. "I hope Drew isn't going to get in trouble."

The men chuckled.

"The sheriff showed up. He asked Drew about it and Drew told him that the guys got hit by a car," Steve said.

"Langford believed that?" she asked with disbelief.

"Nope," Joey said. "But, he let it go. The sheriff isn't going to run Drew up the river over an asshole like that."

"More like it's because they're cousins," Steve said.

"Honey, why don't you let me clean up since you cooked for these carnivores in the middle of the night? You must be exhausted after all that excitement," Aunt Bea said as she approached the sink.

"Well, I am a little tired," Faith said. It was almost two o'clock in the morning.

"Go to bed," Aunt Bea said. "I can take over from here. Besides, I got to figure out what I'm going to cook for dinner since the boys are eating the steak I thawed out."

"All right," Faith said and moved aside. She grabbed a dish towel to dry her hands. "But, first, I'm thanking my heroes." Faith walked over to Joey and planted a kiss on his slim cheek.

Joey's face flushed crimson. "Awe," he mumbled bashfully.

She walked over to Steve and kissed him on the cheek.

"It was nothing, ma'am," Steve said with a big grin.

She chuckled as she approached Adrian. She gave him a quick kiss on the cheek. She made it quick because she didn't want to offend him again.

"It was our pleasure," Adrian said. "They were jerks. I'll walk you to your door."

"No need," she said. "Finish your food before it gets cold."

"Are you sure?" Adrian asked.

"I'm positive. I'll see you guys in the morning," Faith said.

Chapter 11

A few days later, Steve drove Faith into town again. Aunt Bea had called in a favor with the local dentist. His secretary had just quit and he was looking for another one. Aunt Bea asked him to interview Faith.

The interview went better than Faith had hoped. She had told Dr. Brent that she had a two-year degree in secretarial support and that she had worked at a hotel typing in guest information for five years. Two of those years had been spent being a supervisor. Dr. Brent had said that if Aunt Bea vouched for her, that was good enough for him. He had hired Faith on the spot. He had asked her to start the next day.

Faith told Steve about her good fortune on the way back to the ranch.

"That's great, but I won't get to see you as much," he said with a mischievous chuckle.

"You're such a flirt," Faith said with a smirk.

"I only flirt with good lookin' women," he said as he made the turn onto the dirt road.

"The only problem is me getting to town five days a week," Faith said.

"I'm sure Aunt Bea will let you borrow her car. She hardly drives it anyway," Steve said as he drove his truck on the road. "Days when she wants to drive, I'll be happy to take you to town and pick you up."

"Thank you," Faith said. "You guys have been so good to me."

"You know how you could thank me? By letting me teach you how to ride," Steve said.

Steve had been trying to get her on a horse for days.

"Why do you want me to learn how to ride so badly?" she asked.

"Because Adrian likes to ride," he said with a proud smile. "It will go a long way with him."

"Uh, I don't know," Faith mumbled. "For one thing, horses are big…too big. Second thing, Adrian doesn't want me. I'm not going to throw myself at a man that doesn't find me attractive."

Steve burst out laughing. "He finds you attractive, especially when you wear those Levi jeans. How many of those things did you buy anyway?"

"I got a few pairs. I like jeans. What's wrong with that?"

"Not a damn thing, honey. Your ass looks delicious in them," Steve said with pride.

"Steve," she said with astonishment.

He laughed.

"Have you been looking at my ass?" she asked with surprise.

"Of course, I have," he admitted without shame. "So has Adrian. I've caught him a couple of times doing it in the past two days."

"You boys are bad," she said, trying not to smile.

Steve glanced over at her. "Yeah, but you like it." He chuckled. "Let me teach you. I think you will like it."

"All right, I'll try it," she conceded.

An hour later, Steve and Faith were riding horses.

"You're doing great," he said.

She smiled. She actually liked it. The white horse she was on was called Lily.

"Let's let them rest for a minute. Gently pull on the reins," he said.

Faith did what he said. The horse stopped along with Steve's horse.

"Good," he said with a smile.

"Such a good horse," Faith said as she petted the white beauty. "I didn't think I would like this, but I do."

"I told you," Steve said. "You need to learn how to trust me."

Faith chuckled. "I'm starting to."

"You know, we're only a little ways from the coral that we brand the cattle at," Steve said with a smile. "Adrian is out there with the boys. Let's say we gallop out there. Show him what you've learned today."

Faith shook her head as she smiled. "I have to say, I've never figured you to be a matchmaker."

Steve chuckled. "I have layers, honey, like an onion. But, I don't stink."

They both laughed.

"Seriously, you look great. Adrian won't be able to resist you today. You look like a real Texas woman."

Faith wore a pair of Levi blue jeans and black boots. Her light brown T-shirt went great with her brown cowgirl hat. The clerk at the shop talked her into buying one. She had said that if Faith was going to hang out in

Elliot for a while, she should have at least one cowgirl hat to fit in with the locals. Faith bought it to please the woman. It wasn't expensive. Faith didn't think she would wear it, but Aunt Bea encouraged her to put it on since she was going riding.

"Oh, all right," Faith said. "But, if this doesn't work, will you forget about trying to set me up with your brother?"

Steve beamed. "It will work. This is a good time to teach you how to gallop. When the horse is in a full gallop, tighten your inner thighs to hold your seat."

Faith listened to the rest of Steve's instructions, and then they were off. Faith smiled as they galloped to their destination. Riding Lily made her feel a freedom that she has never experienced before.

They were coming up on the coral. Cattle were lingering in a fenced-off area. The men that were at the coral turned to face their direction. They must have heard the gallops of the horses.

"All right," Steve yelled. "Now slowly pull on the reins to slow the horse down."

They came to a stop at the iron fencing.

Adrian and four ranch hands greeted them.

"Well, look at you," Adrian said to Faith. "I didn't know you knew how to ride."

"I don't," Faith admitted.

"She does now. I'm giving Faith her first riding lesson," Steve bragged. "Faith, you haven't met these guys, have you?"

"No," she said.

Adrian examined her as Steve made the introductions.

The ranch hands tilted their hats to her.

Faith smiled. “Nice to meet you.”

The sound of hoofs quickly approached. They all turned to see a man with a straw cowboy hat riding hard towards them.

“It’s Jose,” Steve said.

“What the hell is going on?” Ray, one of the hands, asked. “He doesn’t run that horse like that unless something is amiss.”

The man pulled short on the reins, making the horse stop short.

“Hey, Jose,” Adrian said.

“Hola,” Jose said. He was Mexican.

“Faith, Jose owns the spread twelve miles away from us,” Steve said. “Jose, this is Faith Roberts. She’s staying with us for a while.”

“Nice to meet you, senorita,” he said. “I’m sorry to cut the greeting short, but I have to get back to the ranch. As your neighbor, I thought I owed it to you to warn you, and my cell phone is dead.”

“Warn us about what?” Adrian asked with concern.

“Coyotes,” he said with a Spanish flare. “A pack of what I estimate to be fifteen killed my bull calf last night and injured the mother. Nothing could be done. My boy had to shoot her.”

Faith winced at the news. She knew they were just animals, but she felt sorry for them when they suffered unnecessarily.

“Damn,” Jake, another ranch hand said. “Sorry to hear that. That bull calf was a fine specimen. Would have won you first prize in the fair next year.”

“Yeah. I was going to put him out to stud when he

was old enough," Jose said.

"Are you sure it was coyotes, Jose?" Steve asked. "They don't usually travel in large packs."

"Positive. Coyotes form a group when they are hunting large prey like deer, elk, and cattle," Jose said. "The deer population is down this year because of the out-of-town hunters. Coyotes got to eat something."

"Shit," Steve mumbled.

"Where were they when the coyotes attacked?" Adrian asked.

"On the east side of my property," Jose said. "The coyotes slipped right through my fence on that side."

"We hadn't had trouble with coyotes for three years," Steve said.

"I know, but they are back, and they are hungry," Jose said. "I've been riding with my son and my hands all afternoon herding the cattle closer to the homestead and putting them in my barns. They'll be safe there."

"Thanks for the warning, Jose," Adrian said with a serious tone.

"Why don't you let your horse rest before you head back?" Steve said.

"Yeah, there's a water trough on the other side there," Ray said as he pointed around the building where their horses were grazing.

"Thank you for your hospitality. Betsy could use a quick rest," Jose said as he dismounted. Jose walked his horse to the trough. Ray went with him.

"Steve, we need to gather up the cattle that are more than ten acres away," Adrian said. "The fencing on the west side of the property is damaged. Coyotes can get through it easily."

"Hell, that will take us four days. If we're lucky," Steve said. "We got over three hundred cattle out there."

"We can't take the chance of coyotes tearing through our stock, Steve," Adrian said. "If Jose's approximation is correct, a pack that size can tear through at least twenty of our steers in one night."

"I know, Adrian," Steve said. "But that's a lot of herding to do on the fly."

"We'll split up in two groups. I'll call the other four hands in. I hate to do it since it's there time off from work, but we got to."

"Once you gather the herds, what will you do if the coyotes come?" Faith asked.

"We'll set traps," Adrian answered. "We did it three years ago and got them."

"We don't have fifteen traps," Steve said. "Hell, we need more than fifteen to set. Who knows where they'll end up if they come?"

"I'll radio Joey to go to the store and pick up at least fifteen. That will go with the ten we already got," Adrian said as he pulled his walkie-talkie off his belt.

Faith noticed that Adrian was wearing the belt buckle she gave him. It warmed her heart that he started wearing it so soon.

Adrian talked on the radio to Joey.

"Well, I guess I better call my wife," Tony mumbled.

"Sorry, Tony," Steve said. "I know you're a newlywed."

"It's all right," Tony said. "My wife is very understanding. Sometimes too much so. I don't know why she puts up with me, but I'm glad she does." He gave them a soft smile.

Adrian got off the radio. "Tony, Jake, get Ray and go back home and get some rest. Meet us at the house at four. We'll ride out before sundown."

"Yes, sir," Jake said. Jake and Tony left them to get Ray.

"This sounds dangerous. Can't you call the game warden or animal control or something," Faith said before she could stop herself.

"Faith, we are animal control," Adrian said. "And the game warden's office doesn't have the manpower to send officers all over Wichita County to deal with coyotes, cougars, and rattlesnakes. That's why they give ranchers license to trap and/or kill predators that are dangerous to our stock."

"I see," she said with worry.

Adrian looked up at her on the horse and gave her a reassuring smile. "Don't worry. My brothers and I have been doing this all of our lives."

She returned the smile.

Chapter 12

Adrian rode back to the stables with Steve and Faith. Adrian called in his other men. It took Joey an hour, but he got back to the ranch with extra traps.

As the brothers packed up guns, bullets, and a change of clothes, Faith helped Aunt Bea pack enough food for four days. Aunt Bea fried chicken for the guys to eat tonight when they found a place to camp. Faith made potato salad. It was her grandmother's recipe. She had handed it down to her daughter, Faith's mother, and Faith's mother gave it to her. Aunt Bea packed fresh rolls she had made yesterday along with the chocolate chip cookies Faith had baked that morning.

Aunt Bea packed two coolers full of frozen steak, water, and sodas. She said the steaks would keep with ice for at least twenty-four hours in the Texas heat. But, the boys would have to eat it on the next night or they would spoil. The rest of the food was freeze-dried. The ladies packed other supplies like toilet paper and paper towels.

Steve split and loaded the items in the back of his and Adrian's trucks. Joey did the same with the camping gear. The rest of the ranch hands had arrived and waited outside the house with their horses ready to ride.

Aunt Bea and Faith walked the Matthews brothers out the front door and onto the porch.

"You boys be safe," Aunt Bea said to her nephews. Then, she looked out at the ranch hands. "I'm sure I speak for your wives and mothers when I say you boys be safe, too."

"Yes, ma'am," the hands said as they tipped their hats to her.

"Ray, Joey, Isaiah, Jake, Duke, you're with me," Adrian said. "The rest will ride with Steve."

"You must be very careful, you little devil," Aunt Bea said to Steve.

Steve gave her his famous million dollar smile. "The devil doesn't get got, Auntie." He kissed Aunt Bea on the cheek and headed for his truck. "Come on boys, we got the Westside, which means we got farther to drive. I got supplies in my truck to repair the fence on that side."

Steve got in his truck. The rest of the guys rode on horseback. They were off.

Joey looked at the ladies. "Welp, see ya'll later," Joey said and kissed Aunt Bea on the cheek. He went to Adrian's truck. Joey was a man of few words, but he got his point across in his own way.

"Goodbye, Aunt Bea," Adrian said. "You got the walkie-talkie just in case you need us."

Aunt Bea nodded.

Adrian kissed Aunt Bea on her cheek. He looked at Faith. "You wanna walk me to the truck?"

"Yes," she said above a whisper.

Joey started Adrian's truck and then slid over to the

passenger's side.

As Adrian and Faith walked to the truck, he spoke to his men, "We're heading for the Northside, guys."

The men mounted their horses.

Adrian opened his truck door and turned to look at Faith. He was wearing blue jeans that hugged him in all the right places. He had on a short-sleeved green shirt that showed off his strong forearms.

"Good luck," she said in a low tone. "And be careful, please."

He smiled at her. "Don't worry, Angel. I know what I'm doing." And with that, he caught her in his arms and kissed her.

This kiss was different than the first one. This one was more – sensual. Adrian's tongue slipped past her lips, dipping into her mouth. Faith's hands smoothed up his arms to his shoulders. Adrian pulled his tongue back. Then, he gave her two luscious laps on her lips. He damn near stole her breath. Faith was in a haze. It's been ages since she had been kissed like this.

His lips lifted from hers. Adrian continued to hold her in his arms as her eyes fluttered open.

Adrian was smirking at her. "Congratulations on the job," he said in a low deep tone. He gave her a quick smooch on the lips, released her, turned, and hopped in the black truck.

Still feeling the effects of the devastating kiss, Faith staggered two steps backward from the vehicle.

Adrian pulled off without looking back. She watched the truck speed away from the house as the ranch hands did a fast gallop, following behind.

Faith was catching her breath. She swayed from side

to side. If that's how he said goodbye, she would love to know how he said hello.

"Girl, get in this house before you pass out. I'm too old to be picking you up off the pavement," Aunt Bea shouted.

Faith slowly turned around to see Aunt Bea grinning from ear to ear.

An hour later, Aunt Bea and Faith were eating dinner. Faith thought this would be a good time to bring up her living arrangements. "Um, Aunt Bea, now that I have a job in Elliot, I would like to stay on in the guest house."

"I had hoped that you would," Aunt Bea said. "Technically, it's not up to me. The boys own the ranch, but I don't think they'll have a problem with it, especially Adrian."

Faith ignored the cutesy dig and continued. "But, I can't keep living here for free," she stated. "I should be paying you some sort of rent. I'm sure having an extra person here has raised your utility bills."

"Oh, honey, I wouldn't know," Aunt Bea said. "The only monthly bills I see are my personal ones and the grocery store bills. Adrian usually handles the monthly bills. If that boy isn't working in the fields, he's in his father's old office in the stables balancing accounts and writing checks."

"Oh," Faith said.

"You should take it up with him. Although I don't think he would take money from a woman he likes – a lot."

Faith looked down. She felt like a school girl.

Aunt Bea chuckled. "I'm happy about it. It's beyond

time that boy let things go and move on. You're a nice girl."

"Thanks, but-" Faith wondered if she should ask what had been plaguing her for the past few days.

"But, what?"

"What happened to make Adrian so....cautious of women?"

Aunt Bea sucked in a breath. "Oh honey, I'm not sure if I should be the one to tell you that. Adrian should tell you the story when he's ready. But, I will tell you about the scars that wounded Adrian right afterward."

Faith remained quiet, eager to hear what Aunt Bea had to say.

"Four years ago, a month after...well, after the incident that Adrian suffered, his mother, my sister, was diagnosed with breast cancer. The doctors gave her a fifty-fifty chance. Arn, the boys' father, rented a condo in Dallas so Dana could be close to the hospital for chemo treatments. Dana had such beautiful long blonde hair, but chemo took care of that. After all the treatments and a mastectomy," Aunt Bea stopped to take a long breath, "it didn't kill the cancer. My sister wanted to go out of this world with dignity. She stopped the treatments. She wasn't the same after the mastectomy. Like....she didn't feel like a woman anymore. She spent her last two weeks on earth on the ranch. She wanted to die here – at home. I, the boys, and Arn didn't leave the ranch until she passed. It was a beautiful funeral. Everyone in town showed up. Everyone loved Dana, especially Arn. Sometimes, I think Arn loved her too much, may God have mercy on his soul."

Faith knew Mr. Matthews was dead, but she didn't

know what had happened. "What happened to Arn, Aunt Bea?"

Aunt Bea leaned back in the chair. "Three weeks after Dana died – Arn – we all thought Arn was coping. Everyone was coping the best they could. Young Joey threw himself into his work on the ranch. Steve…well, he stayed at the bar, and then he would sleep it off at the motel across the street. Me… my husband died in an oil rig accident two years earlier, and now my sister was dead. Back then, I was one of the cooks at the town diner. If I wasn't working, I was at the church throwing myself into community service. And Adrian," she paused to take a breath, "had decided to take some time for himself. He went on a road trip, traveling around the state. He was in Houston when it happened."

"When what happened?" Faith asked with wide eyes.

"I…I…was at the diner one day. The phone rang. I answered thinking it was a customer calling in an order. It was Arn. He asked me to come to the house in thirty minutes. He wouldn't tell me why. He just begged me to come to the house in thirty minutes. Arn…Arn had said that he didn't want his youngest son to find him and hung up. When the line went dead, I got the coldest chill up my spine…hadn't felt a chill that cold since. I swear, Faith, I got here as fast as I could, but I wasn't fast enough. When I arrived, I called out for Arn. No answer. I went upstairs. His bedroom door was cracked. I ran down the hall and swung the door open. Arn…Arn had shot himself in the head."

"Oh my God," Faith whispered with despair.

"He was lying on the bed holding a picture of Dana

in one hand. The pistol had slipped out of his other hand. Blood had splattered on the wall and soaked the top half of the bed. To say I was horrified at the scene would be an understatement. I don't remember doing it, but apparently, I called the preacher and the police. Hell, I rushed into the house so fast I left the front door wide open."

"I…I don't know what to say," Faith stuttered. How ghastly. She couldn't imagine being in Aunt Bea's shoes on that horrible day.

"Sheriff Langford called the coroner on his way here. Joey and two of the ranch hands rushed to the house on horseback. Later, I learned that they saw the flashing lights of the sheriff's cruiser and the coroner's van ten minutes later. Joey's face…it was so pale. By the time Joey and the ranch hands got to the house, they were carrying Arn's body out in a body bag on a stretcher. No one had to tell him. Joey knew it was his daddy….and he knew what his daddy had done."

Faith remained quiet. This was one of the saddest family tragedies she has ever heard. She has lived with the Matthews for over three weeks, but in that short amount of time she had learned how close they were. The patriarch of the clan killing himself a few weeks after their mother died had to be a harsh blow.

"Believe it or not, Joey used to be a real chatterbox. But, from that day on…he changed. He's still a good boy, but he's no longer the happy-go-lucky kid he once was. Poor thang had just turned twenty-one. Steve was sleeping off an all-nighter with a girl at the motel across from Drew's. He was shocked, but for some reason it shook Steve out of his depression. I think he pulled through because the family needed him to pull through."

"What about Adrian?"

"I called Adrian in Houston. I told him....for a minute, I thought we were disconnected. It was stone cold quiet. Then he said he was coming home and hung up. Arn left notes for all of us. I don't know what he wrote to the boys, but I know what he wrote to me. He had written that he knew I wouldn't approve of what he did, but true hell was living without Dana. He asked me to look after the boys the best I could because I was all they had left now. Enclosed with the letter was a bank book. It was to an account that he opened for me. He said that he wanted to make sure I was taken care of, too. He had opened the account a week before he died," Aunt Bea said. "I don't know what Arn wrote to Adrian, but Adrian blamed himself for not being here when it happened. For some reason, Adrian believed he could have stopped him."

"One thing I have learned in life is that if someone is determined to kill themselves, they will, one way or the other. A guy I went to school with tried to kill himself, but wasn't successful. Two years later, he tried again. Let's say on the second attempt, he made sure it was a one-way street," Faith said solemnly.

"Yes. That's what I tried telling Adrian. And Arn was the type of man that when he made up his mind to do something, he did it," Aunt Bea said and shook her head. "The preacher wouldn't even let us have a service for Arn at the church. He had told me that since Arn killed himself that his soul was damned. I asked him to not tell the boys. It would be best if it came from me." Aunt Bea scoffed. "I couldn't tell them such a thing.

They had been through enough already. So, I talked them into having a memorial service here at the ranch. I said that would be what their daddy would have wanted. The preacher had refused to officiate. Dr. Green used to be a deacon at the church he attended when he used to live in Ohio. He knew enough to lead a service. However, the preacher did let us bury Arn next to Dana in the cemetery."

Faith shook her head. Someone who claims to be a man of God and to devote his life to helping others couldn't find it in his heart to comfort a grieving family after a tragedy?

"Now, I love the Lord, but after Arn's memorial, I never went to church again," Aunt Bea said flatly.

Chapter 13

Adrian, Joey, and the ranch hands had just finished eating dinner around the campfire. Adrian was going to take first watch. He thought it was a good idea that one of them stayed awake just in case the coyotes came along.

Adrian and Joey were hanging around the campfire. The ranch hands were checking the perimeter.

Adrian loved Aunt Bea's cooking, but Faith had proven that she was a great cook as well. The potato salad she made was delicious. She was practically the perfect woman; pretty, a good cook, sweet, sexy ass, and her lips were soft and yummy.

"You're thinking about her," Joey stated.

"Her, who?" Adrian said, playing dumb.

Joey scoffed. "I know you didn't ask for my advice, but I'm giving it anyway. Go for it. Faith seems to be a nice woman. Move on with your life. It's time."

Adrian scoffed. "You're one to talk about moving on."

"You're not me," Joey said. "I'm different. You're the best of the lot. You're the one that should reproduce.

Not me and Steve."

"Reproduce? Don't you think you're jumping the gun a little? I hardly know the woman," Adrian said.

"That didn't stop you from busting up her and Steve's date or flossing her tonsils before we left," Joey said simply.

"For your information, I was looking out for Faith's welfare. You know how Steve is with women. And as far as kissing her tonight…we could die out here. A pack of hungry and desperate coyotes isn't anything to trifle with. It was like a last ride type of kiss."

Joey chuckled. "Die out here? Drama queen."

Adrian rolled his eyes at his little brother. He did want Faith. He hadn't been this attracted to a woman in four years. But, could he take a chance with Faith? He got lonely sometimes, but it wasn't anything he couldn't handle. He would rather be alone than to be made to look like a fool again.

Static came over the walkie-talkie. "Come in, Adrian. It's Steve. Adrian, come on back."

Adrian picked up the walkie-talkie. "Go ahead, brother."

"We were too late getting to the Westside," Steve said. "When we got here, we found three dead steers. Tore up pretty good. Look like they've been dead for at least day, over."

"Shit," Adrian sneered. He got back on the radio. "What about the fence? Did you fix it?"

"Yeah, but I don't think it will do any good because we are not dealing with coyotes. They're wolves, over."

"That's impossible," Adrian said over the radio. "Wolves have been extinct in Texas for years, over."

"Well, you tell the wolf that Tony shot an hour ago that," Steve said flatly.

Joey's eyes widened.

The ranch hands walked to the campfire as they listened to the conversation.

"Are you sure it's a wolf?" Adrian asked slowly.

"More like a half-breed, but a wolf just the same. Tony called his wife on his cell and asked her to do some quick research. Apparently, there have been sightings in Arkansas of some sort of wolf-coyote crossbreed that has the red wolf bloodline. One dude actually got a picture of a small pack in his backyard. He sent a copy to the Arkansas Game Commission and posted it online, over," Steve said.

"That's in Arkansas, Steve," Adrian said and clicked off the walkie-talkie button.

"Well, wolves can travel, Adrian," Steve countered in a light tone. "The Arkansas border is not that far away especially for animals who are hungry and crazy as hell, over."

Adrian let the radio dangle in his hand. "I just don't believe it."

A long howl echoed in the distance. At least a half dozen howls followed behind it.

"You believe the shit now!" Joey shouted and stood up. It was rare when Joey talked loudly. When he did, shit had definitely hit the fan.

The ranch hands' eyes widened.

Adrian's body wanted to freeze, but he couldn't let it. He slowly picked up the radio. "Yeah, Steve. I believe you," he said slowly. "We just heard howling in the distance. Maybe a mile or two away from us.

Where's the rest of the herd that was on the Westside?"

"Judging from the tracks, it looks like they stampeded south, running away from the wolves. We're going to follow the tracks in the morning," Steve said.

"Okay," Adrian said. "I estimate we are about twenty acres away from the Northside herd. We were going to rally them in the morning."

"All right," Steve said. "Be careful."

"You, too, over and out," Adrian said and put the walkie-talkie back on his belt.

"Boss, if we're dealing with wolves, especially a crossbreed sort, this is a whole new ball game," Isaiah said.

"I know," Adrian breathed. Coyotes were easier to deal with. They don't attack humans, and they were easy to scare off. Wolves were more aggressive and territorial. Sometimes they didn't attack for food, they attacked for dominance. They weren't tolerant of humans either. Plus, wolves were fifty to hundred pounds bigger than coyotes.

The traps might get a few of them still," Joey said. "They can hold up to a hundred pounds."

Adrian nodded. "Maybe," he mumbled.

"It's a good thing I brought my shotgun," Duke said.

Chapter 14

It was Faith's second day at the dentist office. It looked like it was going to be a good job. Dr. Brent was a sweetheart. These days, dentists had hygienists to do regular cleanings. Not Dr. Brent. He did all the work on his patients, so it was only Faith and Dr. Brent in the office. He was in his mid-forties and married with two kids. Her hourly rate was a dollar lower than what she was making at the hotel, but she got full-time health benefits and free dental work. Dr. Brent's last secretary fell in love with a drifter. She quit the dentist office and went on the road with the man she loved.

Drew, the owner of the local bar, waddled in. "Well, hello," he said with a big smile. "I heard you were working here now. Glad you decided to stay."

Faith smiled at him. "Yeah, for now. It seems like a decent town."

"It is," Drew said. "How are the Matthews brothers?"

"Good, as far as I know," Faith said. "I haven't seen them in two days. They went out on the range to gather the cattle. We got coyotes."

Drew's head rocked back. "Honey, they're not dealing with coyotes. They're dealing with some sort of super wolves."

"What?"

"Last night, my neighbor's dog got attacked. I heard the dog whining, too. By the time I got out there, my neighbor had shot one wolf, and the others were running off," Drew said. "Wolves are extinct around these parts, but I guess they're not anymore. We called the game warden. It was the size of a wolf, but had traits of a coyote. I've lived here all my life, and I've never seen an animal like that. The game warden told us that there have been sightings in the county, but this is the first time he had gotten proof of it. He thought the people who called it in were mistaking a coyote for a wolf. Here I got a picture of it." Drew pulled out his cell phone and started pushing the buttons. He turned his phone to Faith so she could see the picture.

It looked like a large dog with thick brown and reddish fur. It looked intimidating, that was for sure. "Goodness," Faith said with a bewildered look. "In Florida, all I had to worry about were gators and fire ants."

"There are a lot of large predators in Texas, but the one thing we didn't have to worry about was wolves. Well, you know what they say, all good things….," he trailed off, leaving Faith to fill in the old saying.

"Adrian and the guys think they are dealing with coyotes," Faith said. "Someone should warn them. I don't know much about wild animals, but wolves sound more dangerous than coyotes."

Ten minutes later, Faith was on the phone with Aunt

Bea. Faith told Aunt Bea what she had learned about the wolves. Aunt Bea got on the walkie-talkie to contact the boys. Then, she got back on the phone with Faith. Aunt Bea told Faith that she was on the walkie-talkie with Steve and they had already figured out what they were dealing with. Faith was somewhat relieved, but not completely. Adrian and the guys were out there in the middle of the night with two trucks and tents. That wasn't a good defense.

A young man came into the office. He looked to be in his early twenties. He must be Dr. Brent's next appointment.

"Mr. Antonio Rodriguez?" she asked tentatively.

"Yes," he said. "I'm here for a cleaning."

"I'll check you," Faith said. She asked him a few billing questions.

He answered them, straight and to the point.

"Thank you, Dr. Brent is still with a patient, but he should be finished in a few minutes. If I may ask, are you related to Jose Rodriguez? The one who owns the ranch a few miles away from the Lone Wolf Ranch," she said.

"I am. He's my dad," he answered with a smile.

"Oh, I met him a few days ago. He warned Adrian and Steve about the coyotes, I mean wolves," Faith said.

"You must be Faith. I didn't know you worked here," he said. "Yeah, at the time we thought they were coyotes. I mean that was the only logical thought at the time because wolves hadn't been seen in these parts for ages." Antonio scoffed. "Last night, we heard howling – a lot of it."

Faith frowned. She was worried. Yes, Adrian had a

lifetime's worth of experience being a rancher, but danger was danger.

"Are you all right?" he asked seriously.

"I'm worried about Adrian – and the rest of the guys of course," Faith said.

Antonio smiled. "I've known those guys almost all my life. If anyone can beat a pack of wolves, it's the Matthews family; especially Adrian. If he survived my cousin's treachery, he can handle some wild dogs."

"Your cousin?" Faith inquired.

"Me and my big mouth. You don't know about Rosita," Antonio said.

No, but I would love to. "No, I don't. Will you fill me in?"

"I don't want to blabber about….what I will tell you is that Rosita and Adrian were supposed to be married. Circumstances beyond Adrian's control happened, therefore, the marriage didn't happen. Before the….circumstances, my family and Adrian's family were good friends. We still are on good terms, but the dark cloud of Rosita's treachery affected the closeness we had with the Matthews."

"I see," Faith said in a low tone. *Married? Adrian was going to get married?* "I take it that this happened about four years ago, right?"

"Yeah," Antonio said. "How did you know?"

"Let's say I'm good at putting pieces together," Faith said.

Dr. Brent and Drew walked from the hallway to the lobby.

"Thanks, Doc," Drew said. "Hey, Antonio."

"Hey, Drew," Antonio said.

"Faith, Drew needs to make another appointment," Dr. Brent said and handed her the chart. Faith glanced at it. Drew needed to come back to have a cavity filled.

"Yes, sir," Faith said.

"Come on back, Antonio," Dr. Brent said.

"See you later, Faith," Antonio said and followed the doctor to the back room.

"What days are good for you to come back, Drew?" Faith asked.

"Mondays and Tuesdays," Drew answered.

Faith looked at the schedule. "We have an opening next Tuesday at two o'clock. How 's that?"

"That's great, honey," Drew said.

Faith scheduled the appointment and gave Drew an appointment card.

Drew put the card in his wallet.

"I'll bill your insurance," Faith said. "And…Drew," she stuttered.

"Yes."

"Do you know…I mean if you feel comfortable telling me…I," she stuttered. Faith was nervous. A part of her was desperate to know what happened with Adrian and the woman he was supposed to marry. The other half of her didn't want to pry.

"Whatever it is, honey, just spit it out. Straight and to the point is usually best around these parts," Drew said.

Faith took a deep breath. "Do you know what happened between Adrian and a woman named Rosita?" she whispered.

Drew's eyebrows shot up. He stared at Faith for what seemed like five minutes. To Faith's relief, he finally spoke. “What time do you get off today, honey?”

“Four. Why?” she asked innocently.

“I'll tell you what you want to know, but not here. It’s a long and nasty story. Most people don’t bring it up anymore out of respect for Adrian,” Drew said as he put his wallet back in his pocket. “Meet me at the bar when you get off. We don’t open until 5:30 today. Come around the back entrance. Ring the bell. Either the cook or I will answer. Okay?”

Faith shook her head. “Okay.”

Chapter 15

The Matthews brothers and the ranch hands had gathered three hundred head of cattle and were herding them back home. Steve and his team had found the Westside herd almost dead center of the property. Adrian and his team had found the Northside herd where they were supposed to be.

The teams came together in the middle of the property. Adrian and Steve along with two ranch hands managed the back of the large herd. Four ranch hands were controlling the center, and Joey and the rest of the hands were leading in the front with a couple of horses and the trucks.

"Adrian, we should stop for an hour," Steve yelled over the mooing herd.

"If we keep going, we can make it back before dark," Adrian yelled.

"An hour isn't going to hurt," Steve said. "We've been at this for five hours straight. The creek is a few feet west. The horses should rest and get water. We should eat, too."

Adrian knew Steve was talking sense, but the

quicker they got the herd back home and in the corals and barns, the better off they were.

Steve could see that Adrian was struggling with the decision. "One hour," Steve shouted. "An hour and a half, at the most. We're only forty acres away. We can make it back home by dusk."

"All right, radio Joey," Adrian yelled over the noisy herd.

Thirty minutes later, the men were eating freeze-dried food, and the horses were grazing next to the creek.

"Thanks for the break," Tony said. "We needed it."

"Yeah, my ass was definitely getting chapped," Jake said with a chuckle.

Some of the guys chuckled at Jake's comment.

"Hey guys, I gutted the wolf I shot the other night," Tony said. "It's on the back of Steve's truck. You wanna see it?"

"Yeah," Adrian said.

Adrian, Steve, Ray, Joey, Isaiah, and Duke followed Tony to the truck. Tony unwrapped the clear bag so they could get a good look at the animal. "I think something was wrong with this one. It was alone. When I gutted it, it looked like worms were forming in its organs."

"Shit," Duke said as he stared at the dead animal.

The wolf had brownish-reddish fur. It was thick. It had ears like a coyote, but the mouth of a wolf.

"Look at its feet, Adrian," Steve said. "Feet like a coyote. That's why Jose thought it was a pack of coyotes that attacked his bull calf."

"Yeah," Adrian said as he examined the animal. "Ain't this the damnedest thing you've ever seen?"

"Sure is," Ray said. He was in his late forties and the oldest hand on the ranch. "I've been a ranch hand since I was fifteen years old and I've never seen no shit like this."

Adrian cleared his throat. "We'll take another thirty minutes, then we gotta get back at it. I want to get back as soon as possible."

The ranch hands nodded. Tony covered the dead wolf back up. The ranch hands walked to the creek to check on the horses. Joey, Adrian, and Steve leaned against Steve's truck.

"Are you using our current problem to hurry back to Faith?" Steve teased.

"No," Adrian answered quickly. "This is a serious situation. Until the wolves are dealt with or they move on, our stock is in danger."

"Yeah," Joey said. "But, he wants to get back to her, too. Don't let him fool you."

"I'm not trying to fool anybody," Adrian said defensively.

"Bull," Joey said. "If you can't admit you like her to us, at least admit it to yourself. Don't give us some BS excuse that you might die out here and kissed the woman as a last hoorah."

Steve turned to look at his brothers. "He kissed her again?"

"Yep," Joey confirmed.

"Joe!" Adrian said. "When did you become a blabbermouth?"

"When?" Steve asked, ignoring Adrian.

"Night we left. Flossed her tonsils good. I thought she was going to get the vapors as we pulled off. I saw her through the side mirror," Joey said.

Steve burst out laughing. "Let me guess. You kissed the hell out of the poor woman, and then hopped in the truck and sped off."

"Yep," Joey said.

"Ugh," Adrian groaned.

"You didn't even look back?" Steve asked with a smirk.

Adrian shrugged and looked down at his boots. "I might have glanced in the rearview mirror," he mumbled.

Joey snickered.

Steve smiled. "Adrian, all three of us here know that life is too short. Swallow your pride and fear and tell the woman you like her. Ask her out on a date."

Adrian's ego kicked in. "I'm not afraid of anything," he said darkly.

"Oh yeah? Prove it," Steve said with a grin.

Chapter 16

Faith called Aunt Bea and told her she would be late coming home so she wouldn't hold dinner for her. Aunt Bea had asked what her plans were. Faith had said that she wanted to hang out in town for a few hours. She felt like a sneak lying to Aunt Bea, but she couldn't tell her the truth. Luckily, she was driving Joey's jeep while he was out on the range. She didn't want to drive Aunt Bea's car while the guys were gone just in case she needed transportation.

Faith rang the doorbell at the back door of Drew's Bar. A few moments passed before someone opened the door. It was Drew.

"Hey, honey, come on in," Drew said.

Faith smiled and crossed the threshold. Drew walked her through the kitchen. A tall and slim black man was dumping a bag of wing dings into a bowl filled with herbs and spices. They stopped in front of the steel table the man was working at.

"Faith, this is Mark," Drew said. "The best cook I've ever had."

Mark smiled, showing his gold tooth. "Hi, Faith.

Nice to meet you."

"Nice to meet you, too. How long have you worked here?" she asked.

"Oh, I say about two years," Mark said. "Drew's a good guy. Gave me a chance to do what I love."

Faith smiled.

"Are you hungry?" Drew said. "Mark can burn. We get all our beef from the Lone Wolf Ranch."

Faith chuckled. "I know it's good beef, but I've been bombarded with beef since I arrived in town. I guess that can happen when you live on a cattle ranch."

"How about a club sandwich?" Mark asked. "The bacon we use is thick and tasty."

"That sounds great," Faith said. "I'll have that."

"Good, I'll bring it out to you in fifteen minutes," Mark said with a smile.

"Thanks," Faith said.

"Let's go out to the bar," Drew said.

They walked to the front of the bar. Faith stopped short when she saw Sheriff Langford sitting at the bar eating a cheeseburger and fries.

Drew swung open the swinging door for her. "Grab a stool, honey," Drew said.

Faith walked out on the floor.

"How ya doin', Faith? Drew said you were coming by," the sheriff said with his mouth full.

"Fine. Any leads on the driver who hit me?" she asked as she approached him.

Sheriff Langford swallowed his food. "Afraid not," he answered. "I'm still on it, but it's going to take some time. I only got two deputies. Adrian told us what he could. He only got the first three letters of the license plates. It's going to take some more time."

"I understand," Faith said.

"Have a seat next to me," Sheriff Langford said. "Drew said that you came here for answers about another matter. The least I can do is help fill in the blanks for you."

Faith's eyebrows shot up. "You…told him...why I'm here?" she asked Drew.

"Yeah," Drew said as he approached them from the other side of the bar. "Willie and I share things like brothers. We're cousins really, but close enough. You want a beer?"

Faith liked beer, but she was getting tired of that, too. "I like to switch it up. You got any wine?"

"Not the kind you would want to drink," Sheriff Langford scoffed.

"Shut up. My wine ain't cheap," Drew said.

Sheriff Langford laughed his head off.

Faith chuckled. "All right, what about a Tom Collins. Do you know how to make that?"

"I sure do," Drew said proudly. "I'll make it good and strong. You might need it strong during this story."

Faith waited patiently as Drew made her drink. He sat it down in front of her. He put a straw it in. "Thank you," she said and took a sip. Damn, it was strong.

"Now, I decided to tell you this story because I suspect you are sweet on Adrian. You wouldn't be the first girl, but you are the first girl that Adrian might be interested in since Rosita. I saw how he looked at you last week before the fight broke out. He's interested," Drew said.

"How much do you know?" Sheriff Langford asked

and ate a fry.

"Not much," Faith answered. "I just know that Adrian was engaged to a girl named Rosita who is related to the Rodriguez family who owns the ranch twelve miles away."

"The Matthews and Rodríguezes were close back in the day. Jose Rodriguez and Arn Matthews used to come in here every Saturday for a beer or two. Jose's son, Antonio, is two years younger than Joey. Antonio used to hang out with Joey and Steve at the pool hall. It's closed now. Anyway, Rosita Rodriguez, the cousin, moved here from Mexico six years ago. Of course, her family took her in. She was trying to become a legal citizen. She came here on a temporary citizenship," Drew explained.

"Okay," Faith said.

"I was at the Matthews Ranch the day Antonio brought Rosita over to meet the neighbors. I was canvassing the area because two guys had robbed the bank two towns over. My men and I were keeping an eye out for them. Adrian took one look at Rosita on that thoroughbred stallion she was riding and fell head over heels. What Arn Matthews and I saw was a conniving slut," Sheriff Langford sneered.

Faith eyes widened at the sheriff's last sentence. "How could you tell?"

"Grown men like us know an easy lay when we see one, honey," Drew said. "Adrian started pursuing the girl. It wasn't long until they started dating on the regular. A year later, a man from L.A., who owned a food company, was looking for a beef vendor for his frozen foods division had contacted Arn. Shit, what was his name?"

"Maurice Lewis," Sheriff Langford answered.

"That's right," Drew said and continued. "Arn gave Maurice a tour of the ranch and showed them how they raised the cattle. Maurice was impressed and wanted to deal with Arn. They made a deal one month later."

"After that, Rosita started showing the town her true colors. She had slept with one of my deputies, the bag boy at the grocery store, and a couple of tourists all behind Adrian's back," Sheriff Langford said with disgust.

"Adrian found out," Faith guessed.

"Not at that point," the sheriff said. "Everybody in town was afraid to tell Adrian. He was wild about the girl. No one thought he would believe it. Then, Rosita hit on someone that had no choice, but to tell Adrian."

"Who?" Faith asked with intense interest.

Drew took a deep breath. "Steve."

Faith's head jerked back. "You mean she was so brazen that she tried to sleep with Adrian's brother? Are you sure?"

"Hell, I'm positive because it happened right here in the bar," Drew said flatly. "Rosita was already here boozing it up with some of the local girls. The girls didn't want anything to do with her because of her duplicities nature, but they didn't want to be rude either. She wasn't drunk, but she was tipsy. She knew exactly what she was doing. Rosita took her shirt off and started dancing on top of the tables. Normally, my customers would enjoy something like that, but everyone knew she was Adrian's girl. We had some roughnecks in here that night and let's say those guys....well, the nickname fits them. They started throwing money at her. I was about to call Jose to come get the girl before she got herself into a situation that she couldn't get out of. That's when Steve walked in. He snatched her off the table and shoved her shirt at her. Told her to put it on."

Mark came out of the kitchen and sat Faith's club sandwich in front of her. He put chips and a pickle on the side, too.

"Thanks," she whispered.

"What are you guys talking about?" Mark asked.

"Rosita Rodriguez," the sheriff answered.

Mark rolled his eyes. "I wasn't living in Elliot at the time, but my sister told me about her. She sounded like a piece of work."

"You have a sister?" Faith asked.

"Yeah, Linda, she owns and runs the clothing store in town," Mark answered.

Faith didn't know Linda had a brother. "I've been in there. Nice woman. What happened after Steve told Rosita to put her shirt on?"

Drew shook his head. "The little….lady and I use the word loosely, grabbed Steve's cock in front of everyone and planted a kiss on him."

Faith's eyes widened with shock. "Geez," she breathed.

"That was everyone else's reaction. Women gasped. The men were shocked shitless. Steve pushed her off of him. I've seen Steve mad before, but not like that. That was the first time I thought he was going to hit a woman. He wiped Rosita's lipstick away and grabbed her arm…presumably to take her home," Drew said. "That's when the real hell broke loose. The roughnecks took exception to Steve dragging the night's fun time girl away. One of them punched Steve in the face. They started ganging up on him, but luckily, there were guys in the bar that were friends of his and helped him get the upper hand. Steve and his friends dragged the roughnecks out back and proceeded to beat the tar out of them."

"I had to look into it," the sheriff said. "They beat the roughnecks up pretty bad. One of them had a broken nose, and another one had a broken arm. The other four had scrapes and bruises. Steve ended up at the medical center, too. Before his friends got to him to help, the roughnecks had cracked one of his ribs."

"My God," Faith said and sipped her drink. *Drew was right. I needed something strong for this story.*

"I questioned Rosita, too," the sheriff said. "I found her at the motel across the street in one of the rooms making out with a tourist only two hours after the fight."

"Now this part is straight from the mouth of Arn Matthews himself. He came here a night later and told me about it over a beer. Steve left the medical center the same night - after Dr. Green wrapped him up. He headed straight home. His family asked him what happened, but he didn't tell anyone until he spoke to Adrian in private first," Drew said. "According to Arn, Adrian turned on Steve. Adrian called him a liar and a sneak and accused him of trying to sleep with Rosita himself. A fight broke out between the brothers. Joey and Arn had to break it up. Adrian threatened to kill Steve. Poor Ms. Dana. She watched with teary eyes as her sons went at it over a girl that wasn't worth a quarter," Drew said and shook his head. "Long story short, Adrian told his father that either

Steve goes or he does. Arn said he couldn't choose between them and that they were a family. Adrian chose for Arn. He packed up some clothes and moved out. He moved in with the Rodríguezes…to be with Rosita."

"Arn was sad about Adrian working someone else's ranch, but what could he do? Adrian was a grown man. He made his own choices. Ms. Dana was sick about the rift in the family," the sheriff said. "A few months later, Rosita was pregnant. Adrian asked her to marry him. She accepted. The entire town was mortified because everyone liked Adrian. He deserved better, but no one interfered."

"This part came from Jose Rodriguez. He came in and shared it over a beer. Rosita was about six months pregnant when she told Adrian that she didn't want to marry him anymore. Rosita had the nerve to tell him that he was good in bed and he was handsome, but she never loved him. She agreed to marry him because she didn't think she had a better option in her current condition. She confessed that the baby wasn't Adrian's and it was Maurice Lewis's. The man was old enough to be her father," Drew said as his upper lip turned up.

"Shit," Mark whispered. "Linda told me some of this stuff, but I never heard every detail before. Adrian is a good dude. He didn't deserve that."

Faith was flabbergasted.

"Rosita said that Maurice had contacted her again and that's when she told him about the baby. He was excited. He wanted her and their child. The old fart agreed to marry her. Rosita said goodbye to Adrian and her family and checked into the hotel on the outskirts of town to wait for the father of her child to pick her up,"

Drew said. "Rosita had an eye for money, too. The Matthews are well off, but not like Maurice Lewis. Rumor was that he's worth five hundred million."

Faith took a long draw from her straw.

"Your food is getting cold," Mark said.

Faith shook her head. "I know, but I…I've lost my appetite, I think." She sipped through her straw again.

"Honey, do you need another drink?" Drew asked.

She shook her head.

Drew started preparing another Tom Collins.

"Get me another beer, too, Drew," the sheriff said as he wiped his hands on a napkin. "While Drew gets us a refill, I'll take it from here. When Lewis showed up at the hotel to pick Rosita up, someone else was waiting for him. Adrian. He pulled Lewis out of his limousine as soon as it pulled up outside of the hotel. The driver tried to stop Adrian from beating the holy hell out of the man; however, he got two of his teeth knocked out for his troubles. The hotel clerk saw what was going on through the windows. She called the station. One of my deputies and I headed out there. We had to pull Adrian off the guy. He damn near beat that man to death."

Faith gasped. She's never seen Adrian that mad before and she didn't think she wanted to see it. Not that she blamed Adrian.

"I had no choice, but to arrest him," the sheriff said with regret. "He was up for assault and battery. Because of the severity of the beating, he was looking at ten years."

"Oh no," Faith groaned.

Drew sat the drinks down. "Nasty business. For a guy in his early sixties, Maurice was in good shape –

lucky for him. If he wasn't, he never would have survived that beatdown. From what Arn told me, Adrian blackened Maurice's eye, broke his nose, broke two of his ribs, and gave him a severe concussion."

"How did Adrian get out of going to prison?" Faith asked and sipped her refill.

"I'll tell you what I know. What I don't know I never want to know," the sheriff said seriously. "The hotel clerk changed her statement. She said that Adrian tried to talk to Lewis and Lewis swung on him; despite the fact that Adrian didn't have a mark on him. Rosita was going to testify, but then she had refused. The paperwork had disappeared from the station, and to this day I still don't know how that happened. Adrian's arrest was even erased from the computer. I suspected one of the deputies, but I was never sure. It looked like an outside party hacked the system. Maurice tried to pull rich man rank, but he had pull in California, not here. Texas is different than all the states in this country. We look out for our own. The governor got involved, from what I understand. He called the Wichita County Courthouse. I don't know what was said during that phone call, but I do know the district attorney dropped the entire matter and Adrian's record is cleaner than a baby's bottom."

"Arn also canceled the contract he had with Maurice Lewis," Drew added as he sat down their fresh drinks. "His boy was made to look like a fool. That was Arn's way of being loyal to Adrian."

"Wow," Faith murmured. "Poor Adrian. And after all that, a month or two later, his mother got cancer?"

"That's right," Drew said. "I take it you know how

Arn died, too?"

Faith breathed in. "Yes, I do."

"Don't let this affect your affections for Adrian," the sheriff said. "He's a good guy. He just got really angry once and couldn't control himself. Truth be told, I'm glad the boy didn't get sent up the river for it." The sheriff took a swing from his beer bottle.

"Like I said before," Drew began. "I told you because I can tell you fancy Adrian. If it doesn't work out, you'll know it wasn't you. Imagine falling in love with a woman, you think she's pregnant with your child, you get engaged, and then she tells you it belongs to a guy that's old enough to be her father…anybody would snap. A few weeks later, your momma gets sick and dies, and then your father commits suicide shortly after. An ordeal like that would scar any man, no matter how tough he is."

"Damn, all that drama over a ho," Mark said as he shook his head. "So, whatever happened to Rosita and the old man?"

"According to Jose, Maurice recovered. He and Rosita got married, and she had the baby. Rosita had the nerve to call Jose to come to the wedding to give her away. Jose had refused and told her that she had disgraced the family and to never contact them again," Drew said.

Faith sipped her Tom Collins as her wheels turned. This was what she was up against. She wasn't a counselor. Faith doubted she could heal Adrian's scars. Perhaps the best thing was to forget about him.

"Honey, you better eat something," Drew said as he watched her sip. "You don't want to drink on an empty stomach."

Chapter 17

The sun was setting by the time Sheriff Langford drove Faith to the ranch. She had eaten at Drew's and gotten drunk. She left Joey's jeep in Drew's parking lot. Drew had said it would be fine there until morning. Faith figured she would get Aunt Bea to drive her into town tomorrow to pick it up, and then go to work.

"Thanks for the ride," Faith slurred as she struggled to get out of the cruiser.

"Are you sure you don't need any help?" he asked.

"Sure," she said loudly. "My door is right here."

The sheriff had driven around the main house to the guest house in the back. Aunt Bea came out of the patio doors.

"Thanks again," Faith slurred and drunkenly closed the cruiser door.

"Hey, Aunt Bea," Sheriff Langford said from the driver's side window.

"Hi," Aunt Bea replied as she watched Faith with wide eyes.

Faith knew she was walking in a funny way. At the moment, she didn't care. "The sheriff was nice enough to drive me home," she slurred as she waved her hand in the air.

Aunt Bea smirked. "I'm glad he did. Where's the jeep?"

"It's in Drew's parking lot," the sheriff answered.

"I see," Aunt Bea said. "Thanks for driving her home, Willie."

The sheriff tipped his cowboy hat at her. "No problem at all. You ladies have a good night." The sheriff backed the cruiser up and pulled off.

"Looks like I'm going to have to fix you something to eat," Aunt Bea said.

"I already ate…thank you," Faith slurred.

"Looks like you might have to eat again," Aunt Bea said with a smile. "Looks like you had fun."

Fun? I had spent an hour learning why the man I am attracted to had women issues. Then, I spent the last hour trying to drink away what I had learned. "Yes," she slurred out.

"Honey, let me fix you something so you won't have a hangover in the morning," Aunt Bea said sweetly.

"Okay," Faith said too loudly as she waved her hand in the air again. "But, nothing heavy. I like to have a sandwich, please."

Aunt Bea chuckled. "All right, I got some turkey meat in the fridge."

Thirty minutes later, Faith was tipsy, but not staggering around drunk like she was when she had arrived home.

"How are you feeling?" Aunt Bea asked.

"Great," Faith chirped. "I want to take a shower. In that outside shower. I've never taken a shower in the great outdoors before."

Aunt Bea chuckled. "It's a nice night for it. I'll get you some linen and some soap." She stood up from the kitchen table.

"Yep. I'm going to experience the nakedness of Texas," she bragged with a goofy grin.

Aunt Bea laughed as she walked to the linen closet. "Oh dear, maybe I should fix you another sandwich."

"Nope, I got the perfect effect," Faith said proudly. "Matter of fact, I might get that bottle of gin in the cabin and take a shot before I go to sleep."

"I'm not sure if that's a good idea, but I'm not your mother," Aunt Bea said as she carried the items that Faith would need. She stopped and opened the bottom cabinet under the sink. She pulled out a fifth of gin. "I enjoy gin myself from time to time. Mind you, I just take a sip here and there. I have to be careful at my age."

Faith lazily drew a cross over her heart with her finger. "No one will learn it from me."

Despite the fact that this family has way too many secrets, she thought.

The ladies shared two shots of gin and went out the patio doors. They giggled like school girls. Faith adjusted her hair tie to turn her ponytail into a bun. She didn't want to get her hair wet. Faith started unbuttoning her blouse.

Aunt Bea sat down a large sky blue towel with a matching washcloth along with a white bar of soap. "I'll leave you for a bit, but I'll be back to check on you."

"Okay," Faith said as she removed her shirt.

Aunt Bea went inside and closed the patio door.

Faith continued to undress. The air was warm and

muggy, but her nipples budded nonetheless. They were sensitive. Faith turned on the shower. Once she had adjusted the knob to her liking, she stepped in it. She looked up at the starry sky as the water beat on her breasts. This was cool. She washed herself as she enjoyed the freedom of being naked outside. Now she knew why Adrian liked showering out here. She would have never gotten to do this in Florida.

She could stay in the shower for hours, but she knew she couldn't. After ten minutes, she turned the shower off with regret and stepped out. Faith sat the washcloth and soap on the cement bench and then grabbed the towel. She quickly dabbed the excess moisture off her body and wrapped herself in the towel. She still felt the effects of the alcohol, which felt good. Faith took a deep breath. She wished Adrian was there – rubbing lotion on her skin.

A growl came from the gravel path that led to the front of the house. Faith turned quickly. She was facing two large wolves that weren't happy to see her no more than she was happy to see them. They looked like the one in the picture Drew had shown her. Faith froze. She was half drunk and in nothing but a towel with two wolves growling, grinding their teeth, and staring daggers at her. She knew she couldn't make any sudden movements or call out for help because they would attack. Yet, they might attack anyway. One wolf took a step towards Faith, showing its sharp teeth. Faith wouldn't be able to make it to the cabin. She knew they were too fast. The house was closer, but would she make it? Faith glanced at the patio doors. She saw Aunt Bea with a grave expression through the clear glass doors.

She wasn't sure what to do either. Her eyes were tearing up.

Faith realized that this could be it. Her luck had finally run out, and she was about to die in a small town in Texas by a freak wolf attack.

The two wolves and Faith jolted at the clicking sounds that echoed in the night. The wolves quickly turned, and then snarled; ready to fight whatever the noise was.

Faith was about to make a break for the patio doors when a gunshot went off. She squealed with shock and grabbed the knot on her towel. Then, another shot went off right after the other one. The two wolves were dead.

Adrian and Joey emerged from the darkness, jogging to her as they held their shotguns.

Aunt Bea swung the doors open and rushed outside. She grabbed Faith and cradled her in her arms like she was a child. "Oh, sweetheart," she cried.

Faith was trembling in the woman's thick arms. Her eyes were tearing up. She didn't want to cry. She blinked rapidly, trying to fight it. She was strong. She wasn't a baby.

"Are you all right?" Adrian asked as he rushed to them.

Faith tried to speak, but she couldn't. All she could do was shake in Aunt Bea's arms. She was looking over Aunt Bea's shoulder, facing the house. Faith heard Isaiah and Steve's voices.

"Adrian!" Steve shouted in the distance.

Faith could hear running feet on the gravel.

"We heard gunshots!" Isaiah shouted.

"Shit," Steve hissed. Faith assumed Steve got a look

at the wolves or maybe her wobbly body in a towel, she didn't know which.

"They sure are brazen," Isaiah said. "They came right to the house."

"I think she's in shock," Aunt Bea whispered.

Adrian's face appeared in front of Faith. "It's all right now, Angel. I'm not going to let anything happen to you," he whispered.

Her shaking eased a little, but she still trembled. She was able to raise her head and look around. Steve and Isaiah had worried looks on their faces. They were holding guns. Faith didn't remember Joey going into the house, but he walked over the threshold of the patio doors with a blanket.

Adrian took the blanket from Joey and held it out for Faith.

"Come on, honey," Aunt Bea said as she helped Adrian wrap Faith in the blanket.

"Let's get her into the house," Adrian said.

"I'll gather a couple of the boys and make sure that the pack is gone," Steve said.

"All right. I'll be along in a minute," Adrian said.

"I'll wait for you, Adrian," Joey said.

Aunt Bea and Adrian walked Faith to the guest house.

Chapter 18

Adrian and Aunt Bea guided Faith to the sofa and sat her down. Aunt Bea sat down next to her.

"Thank God you boys came back when you did," Aunt Bea said as she wrapped her arm around Faith's shoulders.

"Tell me about," Adrian said as took off his Stetson and whipped his brow with the back of his hand. Faith was almost dinner to that inbred pack. "Faith, are you okay?"

"Yes," she whispered as she clutched the blanket. She wouldn't look at him or Aunt Bea. "Thank you."

"Yeah," Adrian said. "We just got back. As we were approaching, the wolf pack was congregating about an acre away from the house, sniffing around, while some were resting. The two horses we keep in the barn were going crazy. Duke and Tony went to see if they could calm the horses down. The headlights from the trucks spooked the pack. They ran off, but Joey and I wanted to make sure they hadn't approached the house. Luckily, the stock we were herding was another acre away. Joey spotted separate tracks in the grass leading to the back of the house."

"How many did you see?" Aunt Bea asked.

"About twelve not counting the two outside," Adrian said. "Those two must have gotten thirsty. Smelled or heard the water in the shower."

"Did you boys set traps?" Aunt Bea asked.

"Yeah, but we only set them on the West and Northside," Adrian said. "We got a few left. We were planning to set them on the South and Eastside tomorrow morning."

"Good," Aunt Bea said as she rubbed Faith's shoulder. "I'll sit with her for a while. You go do what you need to do."

Faith was so quiet, so shaken up. Not that Adrian blamed her. "I'll be back to check on you, I promise." Adrian went to the door.

Joey was putting his walkie-talkie in his pocket. "I just radioed the guys. Once they get the herd secured, Duke and Jake are going to bring the truck up to take off these carcasses."

Adrian looked at the dead wolves. Set traps his ass. He wanted to hunt every single one of them down and shoot their asses off.

For the next two hours, the Matthews brothers and the ranch hands secured the herd and put up temporary barbed wire fencing around the coral as a precaution. The pack was gone for now, but Steve left a message for the game warden to come up in the morning to take a look at the two Joey and Adrian shot.

The guys went home, and the Matthews brothers cleaned up. Joey and Steve were in the kitchen making sandwiches. "Hey, Adrian, you want a tuna sandwich?"

Steve asked.

"I'll fix one later. I want to check on Faith," Adrian said.

"Give us a holler if you need us," Steve said.

"All right," Adrian said. He grabbed his shotgun that was leaning against the wall and headed out the patio doors. He wasn't going to take any chances tonight. The pack could come back looking for their two missing members.

He knocked on the door of the guest house. He didn't wait for an answer. He cracked the door open.

"Come in, Adrian," Aunt Bea said.

Adrian walked in and closed the door. "How is she?"

"She seems to be okay, now. She's gathered her faculties. I poured her a stiff drink, and now she's getting ready for bed. I offered to spend the night here with her, but she said no that she would be fine."

Adrian nodded. "I can stay for a little bit to make sure."

"I think a visit with you would do her some good," Aunt Bea said. "Faith, I'm heading back to the house. Call if you need me. Adrian is here. He's going to hang around for a few minutes."

"Okay. Goodnight, Aunt Bea. Thanks for staying with me," Faith said from the bedroom.

Aunt Bea walked to the door. Adrian followed behind her with the shotgun. He watched from the door until Aunt Bea was safely inside.

"Adrian," Faith called out.

"I'm still here," he said as he closed the door. Adrian's boots clunked on the hardwood floor as he walked back to the bedroom. The door was open, but he didn't want to intrude if she was changing clothes. "Is it all right if I come back?"

"Yes."

Adrian stepped into the room to see Faith turning down the covers. He smiled at the sight of her. "I see you're still wearing my shirt."

She turned around. "If you need it back-"

"No, I don't. I got more than one white dress shirt. Keep it. You like it," he said with an easy smile.

She smiled bashfully. "I do, actually," she whispered. "Are you hungry? I can fix you something to eat."

"You're about to go to bed," he said. "I'm not hungry, anyway."

"I'm not exactly sleepy. It's ten o'clock, but I'm a little wired," she said.

Adrian smiled to restrain the urge of saying that he would rock her to sleep if she wanted it. *Damn, she looks sexy in my shirt*. "Well, maybe if we talked for a while it will relax you."

"Okay," she said with a sweet grin.

"Now, hop in bed," he said as he leaned the shotgun against the door jam.

Faith sunk between the rose-colored sheets and under the thick handmade quilt. Adrian approached the bed and sat down next to her.

"I'm glad you and the guys made it back safely," she said.

"And I'm glad I got here in time," Adrian said seriously. "Until we get this problem under control, I don't want you going out after dark alone. If you need to be out, let me or one of the guys know so we can come with you, okay?"

She shook her head. "Okay," she whispered.

"Other than this evening, how was your day?"

"Good," she said.

"Do you like your new job?"

"Yes, actually," she said with brightness in her tone. "I think it will work out."

He smiled. "Good."

"That brings up something that Aunt Bea said that I should take up with you. I would like to stay here in this charming little cottage, but I should pay some sort of rent," she said.

He was surprised. Adrian hadn't thought about charging her for staying here. However, it did warm his heart that she wanted to stay on the ranch – with him – with his family. "You don't have to pay rent. You can stay here as long as you want."

"Adrian, I use your water and electricity. I eat most of my meals in the main house. I should pay something."

Adrian shrugged. Then, he got a naughty idea. But, would he dare speak it? "First of all, we got five wells on the property, so there is no water bill. The little bit of food you eat and the electricity you use isn't going to break us. Besides, I feel uncomfortable taking money from a woman I like," he said with a grin.

She smiled. "Really? You like me?"

"I do," he admitted. "I…I want to get to know you better, and I want you to get to know me. One thing I have learned in the past few days is that I can't keep living my life the way I have been. That wasn't living. I was existing. I…we should have a talk about that, but some other time. It's a heavy topic for tonight, but if you want to feel like you're repaying me for letting you stay here rent free…how about two kisses a day."

She giggled and bashfully turned away.

He chuckled.

"Okay," she said with a big smile. "When do you want to start?"

Adrian leaned in and grazed her lips with his. He wrapped his arms around her as he deepened the kiss. He laid her down in the bed. She opened her mouth. The tip of their tongues brushed together. Faith pulled her tongue back, letting Adrian's tongue taste her warm sweetness and – gin. The swell of her breasts were pressed against his chest. Adrian's hands itched to travel down her body, but he couldn't allow it. It was too soon. He hadn't even taken her out on a date. Adrian slowly pulled out of the kiss, but he kept her in his arms.

She let out a soft moan when their lips parted.

"I should go," he said in a graveled tone.

"Wait," she said softly. "Can't you stay for a little while longer? Just until I fall asleep. We can…we can hold each other."

He gave her a big smile. "I would love nothing more than to stay here all night with you, but I don't trust myself to just…hold you," he said in a deep tone.

"Oh, Adrian," she blushed. "I'm not that irresistible."

He laughed. "I don't think you realize the potency of your charms, Ms. Roberts." Adrian lapped at her full luscious lips. He lifted his lips from hers. "I better go now while I can still control myself."

"You can sleep on the couch," she suggested.

He thought for a moment. *No, all I have to do is*

walk a few feet and strip off my pants and slip between the sheets next to her. He shook his head. "Still too tempting. You'll just be inches away with only my shirt to protect you."

"I don't need protection from you. I'm safe with you," she whispered.

He smiled. Adrian wanted her safe, and he was glad that she felt safe with him. Adrian took his finger and traced the exposed skin of her neck between the open slit in the shirt. He glided his finger to her chest. "Hmmm," he groaned. "I won't let anything happen to you. But, I would probably ravish you before I should." He reluctantly released her and got off the bed because his cock was getting hard.

"If you feel that it's best. I want to take things slow, too," Faith said as she sat up.

He smiled. "I would kiss you goodbye, but I definitely wouldn't leave then. Goodnight, Faith. Sweet dreams."

"Goodnight," she whispered.

Adrian grabbed his shotgun and left the cabin. He carefully walked across the patio to the kitchen doors.

Joey and Steve were still sitting in the kitchen.

"Hey, we didn't expect to see you…back in the house," Steve said. "Go back. We'll cover for you with Aunt Bea in the morning."

"Yeah," Joey said.

Adrian gave them a little smile. "I just went over to check on her. Make sure she was settled in for the night."

Steve raised one golden eyebrow. Then, realization registered on his face. "Oh, I get it. You couldn't get it up," he said with a straight face

Joey burst out laughing. He laughed so hard that he doubled over on the kitchen table.

"No!" Adrian exclaimed over Joey's laughter. "I…that is not an issue."

Joey started sucking in air. His face was red with amusement.

"Don't pay any attention to Joey," Steve said nonchalantly. "You're tired. You've been on the range for days with little sleep. It has happened to all of us at least once."

Joey cracked up again. "Not me."

"That's because you haven't been with a woman in years. You probably walk around with permanent blue balls," Steve shot out.

The insult didn't faze Joey. He chuckled.

"That is not the problem," Adrian said sternly. "We're taking things slow."

Steve frowned. "Why? You like her. She likes you."

Joey shook his head.

Adrian rolled his eyes. "Steve, the woman has been through a lot tonight. The last thing she needs right now is me pawing at her. Faith needs her rest."

"All right," Steve said in defeat.

Chapter 19

A week later, the wolves had been killed, but not before causing more havoc. The pack had gone back to the Rodriguez Ranch, but Jose and his men were ready for them. They shot three of the wolves, sending the rest running for their lives. The Matthews brothers had caught two in the traps that they had set. The ones that were left tore up the locals' trash cans and scratched up their cars. The game warden set up traps in town that caught the rest. They were euthanized. They were too dangerous to keep alive.

It was ten days before the Lone Wolf Ranch's annual BBQ. Aunt Bea was excited. Faith was starting to look forward to it as well.

Faith and Adrian were in the stables. He was teaching her more about horses and how to take care of them. She found the lesson interesting. He had asked her if she wanted to go for a ride before dinner. She had happily accepted and asked if she could ride Lily again.

Adrian saddled the horses up, and they were off. Adrian was riding an Arabian stallion named Blaze. He got the horse when he was young, and broke him himself. Blaze was Adrian's favorite horse on the ranch.

They stopped to look at the horizon.

"I was wondering," Adrian said as he sat on his horse. "How would you like our first date to be at a cattle auction?"

Faith laughed before she could think. "Are you serious?"

"Yeah," he said. "I mean, we won't be alone on the trip, but we'll be able to have a nice private dinner."

"The trip?"

"Every year, a few of the ranch hands and I drive out to Corsicana Livestock Auction. Sometimes we buy some steers, sometimes we don't. It's about a three-and-a-half-hour drive. We usually ride out on Friday, check into a hotel, and attend the auction on Saturday. We come home on Sunday. So, how about it?"

Faith didn't know what to say. The truth was that she didn't see them spending their first date with a bunch of smelly cows. She had hoped for a nice quiet dinner and a movie. However, this was what Adrian did for a living, and this was his way of showing her what he was all about. "I…I have to say that sounds…unorthodox, but I'm willing to give it a try."

"Good," he said with a big grin.

"What time do you want to leave Friday?" she asked.

"I would love to leave in the morning so we can get settled in and look around. There's also a fair two miles up the road from the auction. We'll stop there, too."

Faith liked the idea about going to a fair. "There's only one problem. I have to work on Friday."

"Can't you get the day off?"

"I just started that job. I mean Dr. Brent is a nice man, but I think it would be presumptuous to ask for a day off with only two days' notice. Not even two days, today is Wednesday."

"Just ask him," Adrian said simply. "It's just one day and doesn't the dentist office close at one on Fridays?"

"Yeah," she said softly. "I'll ask."

"Good. Dr. Brent is a good guy," Adrian said. "We better get back before it gets dark. You wanna race?" he asked with a grin.

Faith smiled. "I don't feel comfortable enough to race just yet. Can I have a rain check?"

"Absolutely," he said with a grin.

****

Dr. Brent had been happy to let Faith have Friday off. He had told her to enjoy the fair and the auction. Faith rode in Adrian's truck to Corsicana. Steve followed in his truck. Isaiah and Ray trailed behind in the stock trailer.

They got to Corsicana at eleven o'clock. Since Faith decided to go last minute, they couldn't get a room for her. Isaiah and Ray told Adrian that they would share a room so she could have one to herself. The hotel room had all the basics; a bed, a TV, a bathroom, and a mini-fridge. All Faith cared about was that it was neat and clean.

They all had lunch at a local diner filled with out-of-town ranchers and farmers. Faith thought the food was subpar, but she didn't say anything. The men seemed not to notice. Then, they went down to the auction. The auction allowed potential buyers to survey the stock that was up for sale. It was a little crowded, but not bad.

Adrian left Faith with Ray for a few minutes to go with Isaiah to check out some bull calves. Ray and Faith stood in front of a medium-sized steer. Ray was explaining to Faith what to look for in a good steer.

"This one has a strong coat, but it's a little scrawny for its age," Ray said as he made a note on the auction list.

"Whatever he is telling you little lady don't you believe a word of it," a man said with a smile that was nothing but teeth.

Ray laughed. "Wes Johnson, how the hell are ya?"

The men gave each other a hearty handshake as they laughed.

"Great," Wes said enthusiastically. "Ray, is this your girlfriend?" he asked as he leered at Faith. The man was tall and slim. He wore a cowboy hat bigger than Sheriff Langford's. His mustache was dark with sprinkles of white. He had on a black dress shirt and dark blue jeans.

"No. She's a friend. Wes, this is Faith Roberts," Ray said. "Faith, Wes Johnson owns a large spread outside of Dallas."

"The biggest spread within two hundred miles actually," Wes bragged. "Over four thousand acres and seven hundred head of cattle. It's nice to meet you, sweetheart. My goodness, you are a pretty little filly. I like your hat."

Faith was speechless for a moment. She wasn't sure how to take what he said. Did he just compare her to a horse? Was that supposed to be a compliment? "Um, thank you, Mr. Johnson."

"Call me, Wes, sweetheart," he said as he leered at Faith. It was like he was trying to undress her with his beady eyes.

"All right, Wes," she said, trying not to sound nervous.

"If you want to learn about cattle, honey, you should sit with me tomorrow," he oozed. "I can teach you everything you need to know."

"Easy, Wes," Ray said in a teasing, yet, serious sounding tone. "The lady has already been claimed – by one of the Matthews boys."

"Oh no," Wes said with a mischievous grin. "Sweetie, don't tell me you're one of Steve Matthews's chickadees."

"I'm not," Faith answered quickly with a hint of surprise. She knew Steve had a reputation with the ladies, but she didn't know it spanned over a hundred miles outside of Elliot.

"Good," he said with a hint of relief. "Ray, you still work for that no good SOB, Steve?"

Ray let out a scoffed laugh. "I do, and he's a great guy."

"I'm telling you, man," Wes began. "Come back our way. I'll make you the foreman. More pay and more freedom. I'm looking for someone I can trust to run the place while I attend to other things and," Wes stopped to give Faith the once-over, "enjoy the finer things in life," he completed as he looked at her. Wes looked at Ray again. "Ray, you're the only one I could trust with my place. You're the most experienced hand in the business."

"I can't do it, Wes," Ray said. "I appreciate the offer, though."

"You'll make double what you make now, guaranteed," Wes said. "You'll have your own cabin on the property."

"I thought I smelled cheap cologne," Steve said as he, Adrian, and Isaiah approached them.

Wes laughed. "Steve, how are ya?"

"I was doing fine until I saw you," Steve said with a smirk.

They both laughed as they shook hands.

Wes turned his attention to Adrian and Isaiah. "Adrian, Isaiah, how ya doin'?"

"Good," Isaiah said as he shook Wes's hand.

Adrian and Wes shook hands. "Wes, you wouldn't be trying to pouch Ray from us again, would you?" Adrian asked.

Wes laughed. "Come on, Adrian. You can't blame a man for trying."

"I guess not," Adrian said.

"I heard you boys had trouble with some wolf-hybrid type of animals," Wes said.

"More like a cross-breed," Steve said. "A mix of coyote and wolf."

"You heard about it your way?" Isaiah asked.

"Yeah. You know how word travels fast in ranching," Wes said. "Anything to do with cattle I hear about it. Heard you got them all."

"Well, the neighboring ranch got a couple, and the game warden got the rest," Adrian said.

Wes chuckled. "You've always been modest,

Adrian. It was nice seeing you boys, but I have to check out a bull calf I got my eye on."

"It wouldn't be number 204, would it?" Adrian asked.

"Yes, it is," Wes answered.

"He's ours," Steve said with a smirk.

Wes laughed. "We'll see. Faith, it was very nice meeting you. I hope to see you tomorrow."

Adrian immediately put his arm around Faith's shoulders. "Later, Wes," Adrian said.

Wes chuckled as he walked away.

Chapter 20

Adrian took Faith to a country-western bar for a dinner date. This bar was different than Drew's Bar in Elliot. The floors were hardwood; they looked like they had been spit-shined. The atmosphere wasn't as friendly as Drew's place, but people were polite. Country music played on the jukebox.

A waitress brought Adrian a T-Bone, a baked potato, and mixed vegetables. Faith had ordered a fried chicken sandwich and a side salad. The waitress told them to holler if they needed anything else and left them.

"So, what did you think about today?" Adrian asked.

"I enjoyed the drive here. Beautiful scenery. I was a little confused about the cattle, though. Ray tried to teach me how to look for a good steer. I understood what he was saying, but I don't think I'll ever be a good cattle buyer," she said softly. Faith sipped her soda. "Truth is, they all look the same to me."

Adrian smiled as he cut into his steak. "Trust me, they're not. It takes time to notice differences in steers. Don't be discouraged. If I work with you – you'll be a rancher who can buy, herd, and brand cattle in no time."

Faith chuckled. She couldn't see herself doing any of that. She was just a woman trying to survive and hoping that the man across the table could be the one.

"There's something I've been wanting to ask you," Adrian said.

"What is it?"

"How did you get the name 'Faith?'" Adrian asked. "I like it, but it is a name that has meaning."

She smiled. "When my mom was in labor with me, the umbilical cord was wrapped around my neck. My parents were afraid I was going to die. My grandmother was in the room, and she had told them that they had to have faith that I would make it. Since I'm sitting in front of you, I made it. My mother remembered what my grandma said, and she named me Faith."

"So," he began, "the hit and run incident wasn't the first possible life-ending experience you've had, right?"

"No," she said quietly. "When I was eighteen, I was a clerk in a convenient store. A guy walked in and stuck up the place. I gave him the money from the register, but he put the gun in my face anyway and pulled the trigger. The gun jammed. Once that was discovered, the two customers that were in there with me tackled him to the ground."

"Jesus," Adrian mumbled. "I take it he went prison."

"Yeah," Faith said. "He got five years. When I was twenty-one, I was working at a bar as a bartender. Three guys walked in and started shooting the place up. The manager, three waitresses, and thirteen customers were killed. I survived." Faith looked up at Adrian.

Shock and awe was written all over his face. "How did you survive?"

"I ducked behind the bar. They shot up the bar, of course. I got a few cuts on my arm from the glass, but other than that, I came out unscathed. I don't know if they didn't know I was back there or they didn't think it was worth the effort to shoot me."

"Why did they do it?" Adrian asked with furrowed brows.

"The owner of the bar ratted out a friend of theirs for selling drugs in his neighborhood to kids," Faith said. "The attack on the bar was a message. An intimidation tactic the cops called it. They were trying to get the owner to change his statement."

Adrian blew out. "Did they catch the guys who shot up the bar?"

"Yes. Since they killed all those people, they were sentenced to life in prison," Faith said.

"Any other life and death stories I need to know about?" he asked with concern.

"Well, you know about the car accident and the wolves," Faith said. "That's about it."

"You have been through a lot in one lifetime," Adrian said and took a bite of his steak.

"Yeah, but I've survived. I guess someone out there likes me," Faith said with a weak smile. She wanted to change the subject. She didn't want to think about her uncanny luck right now. "Did you see anything you like at the auction to buy tomorrow?"

Adrian shook his head as he swallowed his food. "Absolutely, they got a good stock this year. It's a good thing because we slaughtered about seventy head of cattle this week. Half of the meat is going to be used for the annual BBQ. However, the amount I would like to buy, I'll have to get delivered. The stock trailer can't carry them all."

"Is getting them delivered a bad thing?"

"Not really. It's just an extra expense," he said. "What I really want is that bull calf Isaiah showed Steve and me. One of the bulls we got now is getting old. I suspect we will have to put it out to pasture in about two years maybe three. By that time, the bull calf will be…up for the job."

Faith couldn't help but smile. "I see. When do you guys…let the cattle mate?"

"Between April and June," Adrian said. "It's a cycle. The heifers who are expecting in June will drop the calf by March or April. Rinse and repeat."

"I see. How many do you have now? Three hundred?" Faith asked.

"Three hundred and twenty to be exact," Adrian said. "We want to get it back up to three-fifty. Joey, Steve, and I would love to expand the herd, but we don't have the land to do it." He shrugged. "One of these days, I hope."

"I'm sure something will happen so you can do it," Faith said with an easy smile.

An hour later, Adrian took Faith to the county fair. They rode rides and ate cotton candy. They were having a wonderful time. Faith felt like a kid again. Adrian wanted to go to the stalls and barns to look at this year's livestock.

Adrian was talking to a guy who was selling chickens. Faith walked over to a guy in the corner who had puppies. The pups were black and white. They walked, ran, jumped, and played with each other in the wood bordered pen.

"Border collie pups, ma'am," the man said proudly. "Purebred. I got the papers. Their momma is a sturdy one. Second liter."

"They're beautiful," Faith said with a smile as she watched the puppies play.

"You like dogs, little lady?"

"I love dogs. We had a Cocker Spaniel when my brother and I were little. When we were teenagers, my dad bought us two Labs. They weren't purebreds, but they were good dogs. It drove my mom crazy because they shed all over the house, but that's what dogs do. Before I came to Texas, I was living with my brother. He had a German Shepard. I miss that dog," she said the last sentence in a low tone.

"You don't have a dog, now?"

"No, I only moved to Texas a few weeks ago. I just got settled," Faith said.

"Well, step on in the pen. Have a good look at them."

Faith lifted her leg over the wood barricade and got in. Three dogs immediately came to her and started sniffing her feet. She knelt down and petted them. One rolled over on his back so Faith could rub it. It was male. Faith obliged it. The other puppy started licking her boots, and then licked its lips and smacked its mouth. The third one was jumping up at her. The temporary floor was clean in the pen, so she sat down. She started playing with the puppies.

"If you don't mind me askin', what kind of place do you live in? Do you have land?"

"Yes, but it's not mine," Faith said as she picked up

one of the puppies. "I live in a one-bedroom home on a ranch."

"Cattle ranch?"

"Yes."

"You know, border collies are working dogs, herders," he said. "Sounds like you live in a place where one of these pups would be happy at."

Could she get a dog, right now? There weren't any other dogs on the ranch. How would Aunt Bea and Adrian feel about it? She thought.

"I don't know how my landlords would feel about it," Faith said quietly.

One of the puppies barked twice and climbed on her leg.

"Hell, if they're ranchers, they'll probably love it. Help them on the land. How many cattle?"

"A little over three hundred," she said.

"Then you should get two or three," a man said as he approached them. It was Wes Johnson. "Hey, Al. How are ya?"

"Fine, Wes, fine," Al said.

"Are you trying to sell my friend a dog?" Wes asked with his big teeth filled grin.

"I am. She's thinking about it. I can tell."

Faith smiled at Al. "For the sake of argument, how much are these dogs?" Faith reached down, and scratched a pup next to her behind its ear.

"I usually sell them for eight-hundred a piece," Al said as he looked down at her. "They are purebreds after all."

Faith's eyes widened at the price.

"But, you seem like a nice girl, and I want you to

have a pup. Seems like you miss having a dog. I'll let you have one for $600," Al said.

That was still too much. Faith looked down at the puppy that was cradled in her arms. "I still can't afford it. I'm trying to save up for a car."

Wes smiled. "I'll be happy to buy one for you."

Faith was taken aback by his offer. "I appreciate it, but I can't."

"Why?" Wes asked innocently.

"We….we just met today. I just….I'm grateful, but I can't take you up on your offer, Wes."

"Sweetheart, it's just money," Wes said. "It's no good if you don't use it. Six hundred dollars isn't going to break me and I like to see a pretty lady smile."

Faith was about to refuse again when Adrian approached the pen.

Chapter 21

Adrian had noticed that Faith went over to Al Perkins, the dog breeder. He had finished his chat with the chicken breeder and headed over. That damn Wes Johnson had sniffed Faith out.

"Jesus, Wes," Adrian said as he approached them. "Every time I turn around, you are trying to chat up my lady," Adrian said in a teasing tone, but he was serious. Wes Johnson loved chasing women.

Wes chuckled. "Not at all, Adrian. I just offered to buy the lady a pup."

Adrian was surprised to see Faith in the pen with the little nippers. He remembered that she had told him that she had dogs growing up, and her brother had one, but he had no idea she loved them this much. "You want a dog?"

"I….I don't know," she stuttered. "I just got settled and I just started a new job. And I'm technically renting."

Adrian smiled at the last reference. They haven't had a dog on the ranch since his father died. She was a Border Collie, too. Janie was his father's favorite dog, but after his father died the Matthews brothers couldn't stand having her around anymore. They had ended up giving the dog to Larry St. John who lived in town. His son wanted a dog, but Larry couldn't afford to buy one at the time. Joey had given the dog to the boy. Adrian took a deep breath. "If you want a dog, no one will have a problem with it. Hell, Collies are good at herding. When it gets a little bigger, it will help the boys out a lot."

"I can't afford it," Faith said.

"That's why I offered to buy her one," Wes said. "Looks like she has a way with 'em."

Adrian looked at the pup that was licking Faith's cheek. He didn't agree with Wes most of the time, but this time he did. Faith did have a way with them. The corners of Adrian's mouth turned up. "How much, Al?"

An hour later, Adrian and Faith were leaving the livestock area. Adrian paid $1400 for two purebred pups. Faith swore up and down that she would pay him back, but Adrian had refused. Seeing the light in Faith's beautiful brown eyes was all the payback he needed. Faith was only going to get one, but she had trouble deciding between two of them. Adrian had told her to go ahead and get both. Since Adrian decided to buy two, Al gave him a discount. The one puppy that looked a little chunky and licked his lips all the time, Faith had named Chop. The other one had one green eye and one blue eye and seemed pretty active, Faith named him Hagar. They were going to pick the pups up on Sunday afternoon on their way back to Elliot.

"Did I thank you?" Faith asked as she walked beside Adrian.

"Yes, Angel, you did," Adrian said in a deep tone.

Faith encircled her arm under Adrian's. He looked at her. She was beaming. Adrian's heart warmed. She was looking at him like he was her hero.

"Hey, young man," a man yelled to Adrian from a shooting booth. "How about you win the lady a prize?"

Fair games were a racket, he knew that. But, he looked down in Faith's wide eyes and fell in. Before Adrian could stop himself, he started walking to the booth.

"Step on up, son," the man said. "We got bears of all sizes."

Faith came alongside Adrian.

Adrian watched the targets rapidly spin on three wheels. The wheel at the bottom had bigger bullseyes than the one in the middle. The one up top had the smallest bullseyes, and it was spinning almost as fast as a truck wheel. It would take an expert marksman to hit that.

"If you hit three bullseyes on the bottom wheel, the pretty lady will have her pick of the smaller animals on the bottom shelf. The middle wheel, hit three, and she can pick out what's on the middle shelf. The top wheel, hit four bullseyes, and she can pick a cute teddy bear," the man said happily.

"How much?" Adrian asked.

"Ten dollars a try," the man said.

Adrian pulled out his billfold and took out ten dollars.

The man handed him the BB gun. "You'll get six pellets, my boy."

Adrian shook his head. He aimed for the wheel in

the middle. He fired off a shot. The BB gun trembled in his hands. The gun was rigged. He should have known. He missed. Adrian took a deep breath and fired again. He missed. His eyes zeroed on the target that came around. Adrian pressed the gun tight against his shoulder to ease the shaking. He shot. He got it. He zeroed again. He got it. Just one more. Adrian took a deep breath and pulled the trigger. He got it.

"Whoa!" the man exclaimed. "Nice shooting! Which prize do you want, little lady?" the man asked.

Faith smiled. "The duck," she said as she pointed to the stuffed duck on the middle shelf.

The man grabbed it and gave it to her.

"Thank you," she said with a bashful smile and cuddled the duck.

Adrian got the urge to get her a teddy bear. He knew how to handle the gun now; he might be able to get her one. Adrian pulled out his billfold again. He pulled out another ten dollars. "I want to give it another go."

The booth runner looked elated. "All right." He took the money and reloaded the gun.

Adrian aimed for the top wheel. If he didn't know any better, it seemed like it was spinning faster than before. Then, he realized that the booth runner probably had a button under the table he could flip to speed the wheels up.

Adrian relaxed the tension in his shoulders, and let his eyes do the driving. He pulled the trigger. He hit the bullseye. The trembling of the gun made him have to re-adjust his aim. He pulled the trigger again. He hit it.

"Just two more," the man chirped, but Adrian knew he was hoping he'd miss the rest.

Adrian took a deep breath and pulled the trigger. He missed. Adrian blinked his eyes and readjusted his aim. He counted in his head, one, two, three, then he fired. He got it. Just one more. You had to hit four targets for the top wheel. Adrian rolled his shoulders and blinked a few times. He aimed. His eyes were blurry, but he could still see. He pulled the trigger. He hit the fourth bullseye.

Faith squealed, and then leaped in his arms. Her arms swung around his neck. Adrian caught her waist with one arm. He laughed.

"That was fantastic!" she said with glee. She gave him a big kiss on the cheek.

She really had a way of making him feel like a man.

"Where the hell did you learn how to shoot like that, boy?" the man asked with less cheer in his tone than he was previously using.

Adrian handed the man the BB gun. "I grew up on a ranch."

"Half the men walking the grounds grew up on a ranch. They can't shoot like you," the man said. "Okay, little lady, which bear do you want?"

Faith lifted one arm off of Adrian's shoulder and pointed to a brown bear wrapped in plastic. "The brown one with the red bow tie."

The man pulled out a short ladder and climbed it. He pulled down the bear Faith wanted. "Here you are, miss," he said as he handed Faith the large bear. "Enjoy."

"Thank you," she said with a big smile.

"Step on up. Step on up!" the man yelled. "Win a prize, like this young man."

Three guys walking with ladies on their arms looked

over at them. They started walking over to the booth.

Adrian laughed. "Come on, Angel. It's getting late. We should go." *While I still have money in my pocket.*

As they walked to the parking lot, Adrian couldn't help but be goaded by other booth vendors. He got the best of them, too. He won a medium-sized stuffed polar bear, an oversized blue bear dressed like a cowboy, and six dozen roses for Faith.

It was 11:30 by the time they made it back to the hotel. Adrian walked Faith to her door.

"I had a wonderful time," Faith said with a big smile.

"I did, too," Adrian said as he looked at the stuff animals and flowers in her arms. "You want me to get the door for you?"

Faith giggled. "Yes, please. My room key is in my pocket." She turned her hip towards him.

Adrian gently reached into her pocket with two fingers and pulled out the key card. He unlocked the door and held it open for her.

"Thanks," she said and walked in the room.

Adrian walked in and closed the door.

Faith placed the items on the bed. "Do you want a soda?"

"No, thanks. I should get going. We got to get up early in the morning for the auction," Adrian said as he adjusted his Stetson on his head. "I'll come by at eight, okay?"

"Okay," Faith said as she approached him. She wrapped her arms around his neck.

Adrian smiled as he went in for a kiss. He made it quick and short. It was getting harder and harder to resist Faith. It was still too soon for them to make love.

Chapter 22

Today, the Corsicana Livestock Auction was more crowded than it was the previous day. It was a sea of people with cowboy hats. They had arrived at the auction at 8:30, and the parking lot was full of pickup trucks – not one car was in the lot.

The dirt, dust, and sand that were being kicked up by all the people made Faith's throat dryer than a desert. This much dust didn't get kicked up at the Daytona Speedway.

"The auction starts at nine," Adrian said. "Let's get something to drink."

Thank God, I'm about to die of the dehydration, she thought.

Faith got the biggest fountain drink the concession stand had and went into the building that the auction was being held in with Adrian.

Steve, Ray, and Isaiah saved them a seat. Adrian sat down next to her. On the other side of Faith was an older man that looked to be in his seventies.

"Mornin'," he said to her and tipped his brown Stetson at her.

"Good morning," she replied.

Ten minutes later, the auction started. An hour went by, and then two. Faith was bored senseless. Everyone in the place was stone-faced and practically still. She couldn't understand a word the auctioneer was saying over the microphone. It sounded like fast hick gibberish to her. She had to fight not to groan and roll her eyes.

Steve bid on three heifers and got them. Isaiah bid on one, but let it go. Faith assumed that the price got too high. The old man next to her bid on two and got those.

The gate opened for what seemed like the hundredth time, and a small bull was let into the little arena. Adrian sat up. It must be the one he wanted.

The man on the microphone said – something. Faith figured it was stats on the bull calf. Adrian raised his hand. Several men in the large arena-type building raised their hands. It seemed like the auctioneer was talking faster.

Adrian grunted like he was annoyed. He raised his hand again.

"Don't let that ass get our bull calf, Adrian," Steve said.

Faith followed Steve's gaze across the way. It was Wes Johnson.

Wes pulled his ear. Then, Adrian raised his hand. Another guy two rows over raised his hand. The back and forth was interesting.

Faith raised her arm and scratched her head.

The auctioneer said something.

Adrian, Steve, Isaiah, and Ray looked at her like she was crazy.

"What the hell are you doin', woman?" Adrian

whispered.

"Nothing," she said defensively.

"You just bet on the bull calf," Ray said.

"No, I didn't," she said with astonishment."

"What did you raise your hand for?" Adrian asked.

"My head was itching," Faith said with wide eyes.

Steve smirked. "It's too late, now. You're in it."

She didn't want a damn cow. What was she going to do?

The old man next to her started snickering. "It's happened to everyone at least once," he mumbled through his chuckles.

She looked over at Wes Johnson. He was grinning from ear to ear.

"He's not going to bid against a woman," Steve said. "He'll let her have it."

A man, one row behind Wes, raised his hand up high.

"Shit," Adrian said. "Raise your arm again, Faith."

She raised her arm like she was going to scratch her head again.

The man on the other side raised his hand again.

"Raise your hand, Faith," Adrian said.

She did.

The man didn't move.

The auctioneer spoke and hit his gavel.

"Congrats, honey," the old man next to her said. "Nice lookin' bull calf you bought."

Faith and Adrian blew out.

"How much was it?" Faith asked.

"A little more than I wanted to pay for it, but we got it," Adrian said. "About nine hundred and some change."

"God," Faith whispered. Nine-hundred dollars for a baby bull was crazy to her, but she didn't know anything about cattle.

Another thirty minutes went by. Steve bought two more steers.

A small heifer was brought out. It looked skinnier than the others.

The auctioneer spoke again, and again Faith didn't understand a word he said. She reached over and scratched her arm.

The auctioneer spoke.

Isaiah, Steve, Adrian, and Ray looked at her.

"Why the hell did you bet on that scrawny thing?" Adrian asked with surprise.

"I didn't," she said with raised eyebrows.

"Um, yes, you did," Ray said.

"Shit," Faith hissed with irritation. "You can't scratch your own ass in this place without buying a cow."

The old man next to her snickered loudly.

Luckily, another man raised his hand.

"Stay still," Adrian chopped out.

She froze like a mannequin until the auctioneer banged his gavel.

"Let's go before you accidentally buy something else," Adrian said with a smirk.

"There are four more I want to try and get," Steve said. "We'll meet you at the hotel in two hours."

Chapter 23

It was Friday night, and Faith was at Drew's Bar. She was sitting at the bar bragging to Drew about Adrian's prowess at fair games. Drew happily listened as Faith chatted and enjoyed her beer. She had spent half the afternoon and evening helping Aunt Bea prepare food for the Lone Wolf Ranch BBQ tomorrow. Faith wanted to stretch her legs and enjoy a quiet drink out. Aunt Bea let her borrow her car and told her not to get soused since they still had more work to do in the morning.

Jose and Antonio Rodriguez walked into the bar. They approached Faith and Drew.

"Hola," Jose greeted in his Mexican accent.

"Hola," Faith said with a smile. "Can I get you boys a drink?"

Antonio chuckled. "I know you're an independent woman, Faith, but in Texas, we are still gentlemen."

"We buy you a drink," Jose said and placed a twenty on the table. "Two beers on tap and a refill for the senorita."

"You got it," Drew said and started getting their

drinks.

"Are you guys coming to the BBQ tomorrow afternoon?" Faith asked them.

"Wouldn't miss it," Jose said. "We've gone every year for fifteen years."

Faith smiled. "I'm glad you're coming." Perhaps this rift between the families can be healed.

Drew sat down their frosted beer mugs.

"You're coming to the BBQ, too, right?" Faith asked Drew. "When Aunt Bea told me how many people were coming, I almost fainted. You may as well come, too."

"Absolutely," Drew said. "I wouldn't miss a chance to get a bowl of Aunt Bea's chili. Have you tasted it yet?"

"I did, tonight," Faith said. "It's the best chili I've ever had. If you want some, you better get to the ranch early tomorrow. She made three big pots of it, but I don't think it's going to last with a guest list of three hundred plus."

"Thanks for the tip," Drew said with a smile.

Low whistles echoed throughout the bar.

"Sounds like a good-looking woman just walked in," Drew said as he looked over Jose and Antonio's heads.

Jose hissed something in Spanish. He sounded angry.

Faith looked over his shoulder to the doorway.

A tall, curvy light-skinned woman sashayed towards them. Long dark hair flowed down her back. She had dark brown eyes. She wore a long black form-fitting dress with a slit on the side.

"You got a hell of a lot of nerve coming back here," Drew retorted.

"What happened to Texas' hospitality? Things have changed for the worst in this town," the woman oozed with a mischievous smirk.

Jose said something to her in Spanish.

"I went to the ranch," the woman began. "Aunt Maria wouldn't let me pass the threshold. She told me to get out of there before you came home from the bar. I left. Then, I came here to find you, Uncle Jose," she hissed. "Surely, you aren't still holding this ridiculous grudge."

A chill went up Faith's spine. *My God, is she Rosita Rodriguez?*

"Ridiculous?" Jose hissed. "You embarrassed us. Disgraced our family reputation around here, Rosita."

"What sins I have committed are mine and mine alone," Rosita said. "Surely, people around here aren't that short-sighted – still."

"We never were," Drew said.

"I didn't come here for all this nastiness," Rosita huffed. "I came here to see my family."

"You have another family," Jose said. "A child and a husband. Go spend time with them."

"You have a three-year-old great nephew that you've never seen," Rosita said. "I've tried calling, you hang up. I assume you threw my letters away, too."

"You assume correctly," Jose said.

Rosita took a deep breath. "I had no choice, but to come. Uncle Jose, we are family. I want you, Aunt Maria, and Antonio to meet little Carlos. He's with the nanny now at the hotel outside of town. I brought him all this way so you could meet him. See him. He's your sister's grandson."

"No," Jose said bitterly.

"Papi," Antonio began. "The child is innocent."

"I know that," Jose said quickly as he turned to look at his son. "It is unfortunate that he has to pay for his mother's sins, but life isn't fair, as you know."

"I see," Rosita said with a frown.

If this woman hadn't broken Adrian's heart and driven him to beat a man nearly to death, Faith would have felt sorry for her.

"Take your child and go back to California," Jose said to Rosita.

"The least you could do is allow Antonio to introduce me to his lady friend," Rosita said and looked at Faith.

"Faith, this is Rosita, my cousin," Antonio said and placed his hand on Faith's shoulder. He whispered in Faith's ear, "Follow my lead, if she learns that Adrian has moved on, she will stay and cause trouble." Antonio smoothed his hand around Faith's shoulders.

Faith didn't react to Antonio's touch.

Rosita quickly whirled around Jose. She stood in front of Faith and offered her hand.

Faith took it, playing along.

"It's nice to meet you, Faith," Rosita said and let go of Faith's hand. "How long have you and Antonio been seeing each other?"

"Um, a few weeks," Faith answered.

Rosita gave her a little smile. "You're pretty. Please treat my cousin right. He's a good guy."

She has a hell of a lot of nerve telling me that.

"Yes, a very good guy," Faith said with a tight smile. Faith wanted to kick her ass.

"It's time you left," Jose sneered.

"I'll walk you to your car, Rosita," Antonio said.

"She found her way in. She can find her way out," Jose said.

"It's the gentlemanly thing to do, Papi," Antonio said and took his hand from around Faith's shoulders. "I'll be back," he said to her, playing the role of boyfriend.

"Gracias, Antonio," Rosita said. She looked at Faith. "I hope we'll see each other again under more pleasant circumstances."

Faith just nodded at her.

"Come on, Rosita," Antonio said.

Faith watched them walk out of the bar.

Jose snatched his beer mug off the bar with aggression. He spurted in Spanish and took a big gulp from his mug.

Faith exhaled and turned on the bar stool to look at Drew.

"She's gone, Jose," Drew said. "No reason to dwell on it."

Jose swallowed. "I'm afraid she might show up at the BBQ tomorrow."

Faith's eyes widened. "She wouldn't dare."

"She would," Jose said. "If it was something in it for her. But, I think she is happy with her rich husband. She probably hasn't given Adrian a second thought in years, but you never know with that chica. How in the world did my sainted sister give birth to such a banshee?"

Antonio came back into the bar. "She's gone. She had a rental car. Thanks for going with the flow, Faith. I know Rosita. If she gets wind of Adrian seeing someone, she will throw a monkey wrench in it just for sport."

"I understand and thank you for…protecting Adrian and me, I guess. I mean, I don't know what we are to each other, but we do like each other," Faith said.

"Good," Jose said. "You're a decent woman. Not like my horrible niece."

"Did she say how long she was staying in town?" Faith asked.

"She had hoped to stay for a week, but since Papi made it clear that we still want nothing to do with her, she's planning to go home tomorrow. Her husband owns a plane. She can come and go as she pleases," Antonio said.

"Good," Jose said.

"Yes," Faith said. "But, should one of us tell Adrian she's in town?"

"No!" Jose, Antonio, and Drew exclaimed at the same time.

"Okay, okay," Faith said. "But, I'm already keeping it a secret that I know what went on between Adrian and Rosita from Adrian and the rest of the family."

"One more isn't going to hurt," Jose said and patted her hand. "I know you don't owe my family or me anything, but please, senorita, don't open old wounds. My family and the Matthews are slowly becoming close again."

"I don't think they ever blamed your family for what Rosita did," Faith said.

"I know, but after it all happened, there was a chill in the air. Then, after Arn and Dana died, the chill became a gap. Antonio and Joey used to be good friends. They used to hang out all the time," Jose said. "That stopped."

"It's okay, Papi," Antonio said. "I don't think Joey and I havc that much in common, anymore. People grow. People change."

Chapter 24

Faith was full of worry and trepidation. She should just get out now while the going was good? She adored Adrian, but this was more drama than she wanted to deal with. She wasn't the type of woman to fight and claw for a man. If a guy liked her, and she liked him, great. If a man didn't want her, she moved on. One thing her mom taught her was that there wasn't a man on earth that was worth a woman going through constant hell for.

Yet, Adrian and the Matthews family have been good to Faith. If anything, she had a nice place to live and it was cheap. Aunt Bea had helped Faith secure a job with benefits. She couldn't cut and run. Not yet. Maybe she was worried over nothing. Adrian wasn't carrying a torch for Rosita, right?

As Faith drove Aunt Bea's station wagon into the garage, she made a decision. She wasn't going to tell Adrian that Rosita was in town, but she was going to tell somebody. She needed an ally; someone who could advise her and knew the situation better than anybody. Faith needed several somebodies to collaborate with.

Faith got out of the car and closed the garage door.

She walked to the front door of the house.

"Hey Faith," Steve said as he jogged to her. "How was Drew's?"

"Interesting," Faith said. "Where's Adrian?"

"Ray's truck broke down out in the county," Steve said. "Adrian went to go get him. He'll be back in an hour."

"Good. I need to talk to you, Joey, and Aunt Bea – without Adrian around," Faith said seriously.

"Why am I getting the feeling that you are going to tell us something we aren't gonna like?" Steve asked with worry in his tone.

"Probably, because it is something that you guys aren't going to like," Faith said solemnly.

Twenty-minutes later, Faith, Aunt Bea, Joey, and Steve were in the den. Faith had just finished telling them that she knew what happened with Adrian and Rosita and it wasn't Adrian that told her. She also told them that she knew Adrian almost went to prison for beating Maurice Lewis up for sleeping with Rosita, and then stealing her from him.

"Why are you telling us this?" Joey asked seriously. "You know. Okay?"

"I'm telling you because Rosita is in town," Faith announced.

Aunt Bea went pale.

"Shit!" Steve shouted and shot up from his seat.

Joey groaned loudly.

"How do you know?" Steve asked darkly.

"She waltzed into Drew's tonight. She tracked Jose and Antonio there. She wanted to make peace with her family. Jose had refused and sent her on her way," Faith said.

"Good for him," Joey said.

Steve went to the bar. "I need a glass of bourbon. Anyone else want a drink?"

"Nope," Joey said.

"I'll take a half of one," Aunt Bea groaned.

"Rosita told Antonio that she was leaving tomorrow since Jose made it clear that he still didn't want anything to do with her or her child," Faith said.

Steve walked from behind the bar and gave a quarter glass of bourbon to Aunt Bea. "Well, there's nothing wrong in making sure that she leaves tomorrow," he said darkly, and then took a long draw from his glass.

"What are you going to do? Run her out of town on a rail?" Joey asked.

"She'll be lucky that's all I'll do," Steve said.

"Don't," Aunt Bea said. "If you go to her like a bat out of hell, it will just tweak her nose to show up here. I don't want that girl ruining the BBQ."

"I just thought I should let you guys know," Faith said. "I don't know if….Adrian should know or not."

"He definitely shouldn't," Steve said. "He hasn't been this content in years. That will change if he knew that whore was loitering around town."

"I agree," Joey said. "We just have to hope that she was telling the truth about leaving tomorrow."

"I agree with that as well," Aunt Bea said and took a swallow of her drink. "It's getting late. I need to be up by eight tomorrow. The vendors will be here to set up tables and chairs for the BBQ. I also have to warm up the chili and brief the cooks that will be running the grills and smokers."

Faith wasn't sure if this was the best course of action, but she was outnumbered. Besides, it's not like she was a part of the Matthews family. Faith didn't have a vote. She was an outsider they had adopted. Nothing more.

Chapter 25

Balloons of different colors hovered in the yard. Cars and trucks were parked along the dirt road leading to the Lone Wolf Ranch. A dunking tank was set up on the far side of the land along with a bouncing gym and outdoor games for the kids. Hired cooks filled the air with meats that were in smokers and on grills. A live band played county music over the sound of chirping birds. Two outside bars were set up. The bartenders filled drinks and popped caps off of beer bottles. The wait staff carried trays of bourbon and branch. Women in skirts, jeans, and sundresses twirled around on the dance floor with their partners. Texan men wearing cowboy hats covered the lush green land of Lone Wolf Ranch as far as the eye could see.

The BBQ started at one o'clock, but people began arriving at 12:30 in hopes to get a taste of Aunt Bea's chili. Faith had made cornbread to go with it. The guests loved it as well.

Aunt Bea's chili and Faith's cornbread was gone within an hour. It was hot out, so Faith decided to change into a white sundress. It came above her knee.

She wore white heeled sandals. Faith walked out among the sea of guests.

"Yummy," Steve said as he approached her.

She laughed. "Thanks."

"Why did you change?" Steve asked.

"I got a little too hot in blue jeans and boots," she said.

"You look delicious," Steve said and put his empty glass on a passing waiter's tray. "You want to dance?"

Faith took the music into consideration.

Like he was reading her mind, "It's a slow song, not the two-step."

She smiled. "All right."

Steve escorted Faith to the dance floor.

****

Adrian and Joey were enjoying a glass of bourbon and branch with some good ole boys from the next town. It was a beautiful day for a BBQ.

Luke Warrington approached them. "Hey, fellas."

The men greeted him.

"Great BBQ as usual," Luke said to Joey and Adrian. "Aunt Bea's chili gets better every year and the cornbread – did she try something different with that?"

Adrian smiled. "My little lady made the cornbread."

"And the potato salad," Noah, a black man from the next town, said. "I haven't been able to stay away from that stuff."

"Take my advice, Adrian," Mr. Doyle, a farmer from the next town, said. "Marry that girl."

The men chuckled.

During the past few weeks, Adrian had grown to care for Faith – a lot. It excited him and scared him all at the same time. Her sweet smile, her easy personality, and her honesty struck him to his core. Being married to a woman like her would be a dream.

"I'll take it under consideration," Adrian said with a smile.

"You better do more than that," Daryl, the black guy who owned the barber shop in the next town, said. "Women, these days, can't cook anymore or even know how to let a man be a man. I talked to Faith earlier. You won't have any problems with her."

"Didn't she make the dessert, too?" Noah asked.

"She made the strawberry cake and two chocolate cakes," Joey answered.

"Excuse me, fellas," Mr. Doyle said and headed for the dessert table.

"I'm with Mr. Doyle," Daryl said. "I'll catch up with you boys later."

The men laughed.

"I'm going to follow the guys' lead," Noah said. "Oh, and Adrian, you better secure that woman for yourself before another man wises up and snatches her from up under you."

"Advice noted," Adrian said as he raised his glass to Noah.

Noah walked to the dessert table.

"I'm glad to have a moment alone with you two," Luke said.

"Oh yeah," Joey said.

"I've decided to sell the ranch," Luke said. "Before I

get a realtor involved, I was wondering if the Matthews boys would be interested in buying it."

Adrian and Joey's eyes widened. They looked at each other with shock on their faces.

Adrian adjusted the Stetson on his head. "Hell, Luke, that ranch has been in your family for three generations. Are you sure you want to sell it?"

"Absolutely," Luke said with conviction. "The only reason I kept it after my father died was because it was what he wanted. I like oil. My oil company in Dallas is doing better than expected, and I want to devote my time to that. I already have a place outside of Dallas that is about fifty acres. That's more than enough for me. Running the Warrington Ranch has become a burden. I would like to sell it to someone who would preserve the land and raise cattle on it like my ancestors did. I figured the Matthews family would do that."

It made sense. The only thing that separated the Warrington Ranch and the Lone Wolf Ranch was the property line.

"How many acres is your place? Two thousand?" Joey asked.

"Two thousand five hundred and fifty-two precisely," Luke answered. "It could all be yours for three million dollars."

Joey's eyebrows rose at the prize. "Three million dollars is a lot."

"We're talking about a lot of acres, Joey," Luke said. "Plus, I'm throwing in the cattle, the helicopter, the equipment, and the ranch house."

"How many heads of cattle?" Adrian asked.

"Two hundred and thirty. All young and fertile. Plus,

three bulls in their prime," Luke answered. "The helicopter is only three years old. The house needs some work, but all three of the barns and corals are in great shape. The stables are in good condition, too. I also have three contracts with food companies to supply them with beef; those are worth one million dollars all together," Luke said. "If you buy the ranch, it will pay for itself in a couple of years. The contracts won't end for five years. I just renewed all three of them."

If what Luke said was true, it was a decent deal. "I would like to take a look at the property before we agree to anything," Adrian said.

"All three of us should take a look," Joey said.

"Not a problem," Luke said. "I'll be there tomorrow at one. Is that a good time?"

"It is, for me," Adrian said.

"Me too," Joey said. "I think Steve is free, too."

Luke grinned. "Excellent. If you like what you see, and I'm sure you will, we can make a deal by the end of the month."

Expanding the ranch has always been Adrian's dream. If they can secure the Warrington Ranch, they could triple their stock and service more vendors.

Luke swallowed the rest of his beer. "I'll see you boys tomorrow. Now, if you will excuse me, I'm going to see if I can get some of that potato salad that Noah was raving about." Luke left them.

"It sounds good," Joey said. "But, chopper or not, three million dollars is still a little steep."

"That's because you're cheap," Adrian said with a grin. "Nevertheless, we might get him down a couple of hundred thousand. We're not hurting for money. We can pay for it."

"What about the house on the property?" Joey asked. "Luke admitted it wasn't in good shape."

"Go talk to Lance," Adrian said and nodded in the contractor's way. "See if he will meet us at the Warrington Ranch tomorrow. He'll be able to tell us if the house is sound."

"All right," Joey said and walked off to speak with Lance.

Adrian looked out on the dance floor. Faith was dancing with Steve.

Chapter 26

Faith and Steve swayed to the music and chatted. Faith spotted Adrian walking towards them. He looked like a stud in his black Stetson, tight blue jeans, black boots, and white dress shirt.

"May I cut in?" Adrian asked as he approached them.

"Sure," Steve said. He let go of Faith and tried to dance with Adrian.

"Get the hell out of here, Steve," Adrian said with annoyance and stepped to the side.

Faith and Steve laughed.

"It's been a pleasure as always, Faith," Steve said and walked away.

Adrian placed his hands on Faith's waist. He shook his head. "My brother, the joker."

Faith wrapped her arms around Adrian's neck. "How ya doin', cowboy?" she said in a flirtatious tone.

He smiled. "Great now that I'm with you. Are you having a good time?"

"I am," she said. "Are you?"

"Absolutely. I just got offered an opportunity of a

lifetime. Luke Warrington wants to sell his ranch."

"That's good?"

"Yes. That's the property on the other side of us," Adrian said with a smile. "If we can make a deal, the Lone Wolf Ranch will be over three thousand acres."

"Would that make you happy?"

"It would, but what makes me happier is dancing with you," Adrian said.

For the next two hours, Adrian and Faith danced, socialized with guests, and ate. Faith had excused herself to go to the bathroom. Adrian and Steve talked while she was away.

"The Warrington Ranch would be a great coo," Steve said. "We can afford it. I was talking to Josiah Phillips. He told me that two restaurants in Dallas were looking for meat suppliers. I think I can get the contracts."

"That's good," Adrian said. "The more business, the better."

A waiter walked up to Adrian. "A pretty woman asked me to give this to you, Mr. Matthews," he said.

"Thank you," Adrian said and took the note.

The waiter walked away.

Adrian opened the note. *Meet me in the barn.* He smiled. Faith had a naughty side. He felt like a teenage boy who was excited about a make-out session with his girlfriend.

"I take it that it's good news – judging from the smirk on your face," Steve said and sipped his bourbon.

Adrian chuckled. "Faith is so cute. She wants me to meet her in the barn."

"Go, man," Steve said with excitement. "If anyone

asks where you are, I'll cover for ya." Steve took the drink out of Adrian's hand.

Adrian grinned. "Thanks. You're a good brother."

Steve's face brightened. "It's about damn time you realized that."

Adrian gave Steve a hard pat on his shoulder and headed for the barn.

****

Faith went to the bathroom and freshened up. She walked around the guests, looking for Adrian. She asked a couple of folks if they had seen him. They said no. Faith had hoped to spend more time with him today.

Steve approached her. "What in the hell are you doing out here?" he whispered.

"Um, I'm looking for Adrian," Faith said.

"You were meeting him in the barn. What happened?" Steve asked with confusion.

Faith was confused, too. "What in the world are you talking about?"

"The note, Faith," Steve whispered. "You gave a waiter a note telling Adrian to meet you in the barn."

"No, I didn't," Faith said.

****

Adrian entered the barn. The daylight shined between the cracks in the wood. He saw a figure in the shadows. Adrian closed the barn door.

"Hey, Angel," Adrian said as he took a few steps

towards her.

She stepped out of the shadows. Adrian's heart dropped. An ocean of emotions swept through him; rage, disbelief, disgust, bewilderment, outrage, shock. "Rosita," he said.

"Hola, Adrian," Rosita said as she walked to him.

"Stay back," he said sternly.

She stopped in her tracks. "I had to see you. To make sure you were doing well."

"How the hell did you get on the ranch without anyone seeing you?" Adrian asked.

She gave him a small smile. "There are hundreds of people here. I stuffed my hair under a cowboy hat, put on some blue jeans, and blended in. I saw you dancing with my cousin's girlfriend, who I now suspect is really your girlfriend."

"What do you want, Rosita?" he asked darkly.

"I told you. I wanted to see you. To make sure you were all right."

"When have you ever cared about my well-being?" he asked darkly.

"I've always cared about your well-being," she said and took a step towards him. "I know now. I know how I hurt you. I know I made the biggest mistake in my life when I betrayed you. Oh, Adrian."

"Stay away," he said and took a step back. "You're poison."

"No," she said loudly. "Not anymore. I've learned the error of my ways. I've paid for them – in spades. I'm stuck in a loveless marriage with a man who doesn't want me…or his child. I came back to make peace with my family, but Uncle Jose and Aunt Maria have refused my efforts. My husband...he has kidney failure. It's made him a crude man. So much so, I have to go through extra efforts to stay away from…to protect my child from him."

Adrian wasn't sure if she was telling the truth or not. Rosita was an excellent actress. That's how she was able to hurt him the way she had. "How is this my problem?"

Rosita was stunned by the question, but she recovered quickly. "I…I'm not here to make it your problem. I came here to see you. To make amends."

"It's been four years," Adrian said with astonishment. "I've moved on."

"Yes," Rosita said, and walked towards him. "Faith is an attractive and sweet woman, but does she have my fire?"

"No, and I'm glad," Adrian said sharply.

Rosita kept approaching him. She pulled her hat off her head, letting her long dark hair fall down her back and shoulders. She tossed the hat to the side. Her blouse was unbuttoned, showing off her blue lacey bra that hugged her DDs. "Adrian, I know that I hurt you. I know that I caused you and your family trouble, but I'm here now. I'm here to make it right. You're a good man. I see that now. I see what I destroyed." She unbuttoned the last two buttons on her blouse, and shrugged it off her shoulders, letting the cloth fall to the ground. "Adrian, I was young and foolish. I'm not foolish anymore. I've grown. I've changed. If you can find it in your heart to forgive me, we can start over. We-"

"No," he shot at her. "Even if you are telling the truth, it's too late. I don't love you anymore."

The words stung her. Adrian could tell. He just

wanted her gone. "Get off of my ranch," he said darkly.

She blinked, but she kept coming. "You don't mean that. You had a passion for me. I can make it right again. We can be happy. You'll love my little Carlos. He's the sweetest little thing."

Adrian felt bad for the kid, but he couldn't get involved. "You made me think he was mine."

"No, you assumed that he was. I just didn't correct you until later," Rosita said.

Adrian scoffed with disgust. "Changed, my ass. You haven't changed. If anything, you've become worse, playing word games with me now. You knew what you were doing back then. If that rich fat cat hadn't come for you, you would have let me give that boy my name and lied for a lifetime about me being his father!"

Her lips trembled.

"Oh no," he said as he pointed at her. "That 'pouty lips, I'm about to cry' routine doesn't work on me anymore."

She leaped like a cat into his arms. "Kiss me, *mi amor*," she whined. "Then, you will know that I am true." Her lips pressed against his as she rubbed her breasts against his chest.

He wanted to vomit in his mouth. If he didn't know any better, he would have sworn he could taste the venom in her. Adrian placed his hands on her upper arms, pushing her away.

"Holy shit!" Steve shouted.

Adrian turned his head, breaking the kiss. He opened his eyes to see Steve and Faith slack-jawed with shock.

"What the fuck are you doin'?" Steve asked with astonishment.

Faith turned and quickly walked away.

"Faith!" Adrian yelled.

"Leave her alone," Steve snarled. "Now, answer my question. What are you doing in here with this...this…bitch?"

"She kissed me," Adrian said defensively

"*Si*, but he wanted me, too," Rosita said with malice. "We belong together whether you like it or not."

"Steve," Adrian said. "Rosita ambushed me."

"Really? How did her shirt disappear?" Steve asked with twisted lips.

"Damn it, Steve!" Adrian yelled. "You knew that I thought Faith was in here. I said it to you. Remember?"

Steve's head cocked up. He looked at Adrian, and then he glared at Rosita. "You are the most treacherous leach of a woman I have ever seen in my life," he said to Rosita. "Get out before I break your neck."

"Are you going to let him talk to me like that, Adrian?" she whined defensively.

"You heard him," Adrian said darkly. "Put your fuckin' shirt on and get the hell out of here. Unless you want me to tell your Uncle Jose that you're here. Something tells me he is lying in wait to tear into you."

"You'll pay for treating me like this," Rosita shrieked like a banshee. "Hypocrites. All the people in this town are hypocrites, and you are not better than me! I make one mistake, and I am branded with an A on my chest for the rest of my days!"

"Yeah yeah yeah, get the fuck out!" Steve yelled.

Chapter 27

After seeing Adrian and Rosita together in the barn, Faith went to the stables where the horses were kept. She went in and was surprised to see Ray making out with a blonde.

Ray's shirt was unbuttoned. "Shit, Faith, uh," he stuttered.

The blonde's mouth dropped open.

Is everyone making out on the ranch today? Faith thought with annoyance.

"Easy, Ray, I'm not your mother. I just came down here to get Lily. I'm in the mood for a ride," she said.

"I'll saddle her up for ya," Ray said.

"I know how to saddle a horse now," Faith said as she walked to the saddles and harnesses.

"I know, but let me do it," Ray said as he quickly buttoned his shirt. "You look like you're mad about something, and horses pick up on emotions. You might spook her."

"Fine, fine," Faith said and crossed her arms.

As Ray was saddling up Lily, Faith looked at the blonde. "I'm sorry for interrupting. I didn't know you were in here. I'll be gone for a while. You two can get back to…what you were doing."

"It's fine, honey," the blonde said. "I'm Mary."

"Faith," she said.

"I know we don't know each other, but are you all right?" Mary asked. "It seems something is really bothering you."

"I'll be okay," Faith said. "Truth is, I have no one but myself to blame."

Faith should have known it was too good to be true. Nice good-looking men didn't fall for Faith. She attracted losers, bums, and trifling asses. She should have known that a man like Adrian wouldn't move on that easy. Deep down, he still loved Rosita. He started settling for her because he thought Rosita was lost to him forever. Faith wanted to get away from everyone for a while so she could think.

"All right, Faith, she's ready for ya," Ray said as he led the all-white beauty out the stable doors.

Faith followed.

"Odd riding outfit," Ray teased with a smile.

The corner of Faith's mouth weakly kicked up. "Yeah, but it's not going to hurt. That's why they invented washing machines."

"I put a bottle of water and a walkie-talkie in the side satchel. You know where ya going?"

"Yeah," Faith said as she got on the saddle. "Adrian gave me a mini-tour of the ranch a week or two ago. I have a good sense of direction."

"All right, but if you get in trouble or lost, use the walkie-talkie. Someone will hear ya," Ray said.

"Thanks," Faith said and gave the horse a swift kick.

"Yah."

The horse started off in a gallop.

****

Adrian had been looking for Faith for an hour through the crowd of guests. Steve and Joey were keeping an eye out, too.

Adrian and Steve approached Aunt Bea. "Any sign of her?"

"No," Aunt Bea said. "I asked a couple of folks, but they hadn't seen her."

"She'll turn up," Steve said.

Adrian had no doubt that she would, eventually, but he needed to talk to her now. Who knows what she's thinking right now. "Do you think she left the ranch?"

"I don't think so," Aunt Bea said. "She wouldn't take my car without telling me, no matter how upset she is." Aunt Bea looked up in the sky. "It's a good thing I ordered tents this year. It looks like we might get a shower."

Adrian and Steve glanced up to see dark clouds rolling in from the horizon.

Ray and Mary approached them.

"Hey, why the long faces?" Ray asked merrily. "I know it looks like it's going to rain, but it won't ruin the BBQ. We'll get under the tents."

"It's not that. Faith is missing," Adrian said.

"No, she isn't," Ray said. "We saw her an hour ago."

"Where?" Adrian asked.

"The stables," Ray said. "She wanted to go for a

ride. I saddled Lily up for her, and she took off."

"How did she seem?" Adrian asked. "I mean....did she say anything?"

"Not much," Mary said. "She seemed mad about something. I tried askin' her about it. All she said was that she had no one but herself to blame.

Adrian's gut churned. "Which way did she ride off to, Ray?"

"She rode towards the east end," Ray said.

"Thanks," Adrian said and started walking away.

"What are you going to do?" Steve asked.

"I'm getting Blaze and going after her."

"Want me to come with you?" Steve asked.

"No. I need to handle this," Adrian said.

"Don't worry," Ray said. "She has the walkie-talkie."

Adrian nodded and started striding to the stables.

Chapter 28

The sky opened up to a downpour. Faith was too far away to make it back to the ranch before it started. She didn't really care, though. It would let up or stop altogether soon enough. As long as thunder and lightning didn't come along to spook her horse, she would be fine. Lily didn't seem to mind the rain. The wet skirt of Faith's dress clung to her thighs.

Faith couldn't get over how stupid and naïve she had been for the past four weeks. She should have known that this thing with Adrian would fall apart. She was thirty-one years old, and she hadn't had one relationship work out. She and her high school boyfriend broke up three months before graduation. The guys she dated in community college turned out to be a self-serving jerk. The guy she dated when she first got the job at the hotel turned out to be married. When it came to men, it never worked out for her. She had thought she was destined to be alone for the rest of her life, and then Adrian came along. During the past few weeks, she actually started thinking Adrian could be the one. He was a kind man who loved his family and had a strong character, or so she thought. No. Adrian couldn't help how he felt about Rosita. If he wants her, so be it. She was alone before she came to Texas. She can be again.

She wiped the excess water from her face with her hand. A barn came into view. She had seen it before. It was a spare barn the ranch hands used to store hay and the horses if they were working at this side of the ranch. Faith guided Lily to it. She was a foot away from the overhang outside of the barn. There was a trough and dry hay. Faith dismounted. She was going to walk Lily to the overhang. Then, she was going to go inside the barn and wait out the rest of the shower.

"Faith!" a man shouted in the distance.

Faith turned around abruptly at the sound of her name.

Adrian was riding hard towards her on Blaze. He pulled the reins up when he got closer to her. The stallion's front hooves rose off the ground an inch as he came to a stop six inches away from her.

Adrian was just as drenched as she was. His shirt clung to his upper body.

"What are you doing out here?" Faith asked.

"Me?" he asked an octave above his normal voice as he dismounted. He grabbed Blaze's harness and started walking toward her. "What are you doing out here?"

"I got caught in the rain," Faith said. "I was going to wait it out here."

His eyes traveled over her body.

She felt exposed. Her dress was clinging to her body. Since it was white, she figured it didn't leave much to the imagination. She wasn't even wearing a bra.

"Let's get the horses in the overhang. Then, we'll go

in the barn and talk," he said.

"No," she said as she started to guide Lily to the overhang. "There's no need. I get it. You want to be with her. That's fine," she said over her shoulder. She guided Lilly to the entryway. The horse walked in on her own.

"No, I don't," Adrian said as he guided Blaze to follow Lily.

"You could have fooled me," Faith shouted as rain fell on her face. "Do you normally kiss women in their bras when you don't like them?"

"She came on to me," Adrian said.

Faith blew out and wiped the water away from her face again. "You don't have to sugarcoat it. I get it, okay?" She started walking away from him. It was hard to walk in her heels in the wet grass. She took her shoes off and carried them in her hand.

"Look at me," he said desperately as he came up behind her.

Faith turned around. She lifted her head up to look at him.

Adrian's eyes were vulnerable and full of worry. "I got a note asking me to meet you in the barn. Well, I thought it was from you. When I got there, it turned out to be Rosita. I told her to leave. I told her to go back to wherever the hell she came from. She kept coming. She took off her blouse and kissed me. I was trying to push her off me when you and Steve came in."

Faith thought about what he said. It could be true or was she hoping it was true?

"I think you know me pretty well by now. If I wanted her and not you, I would have told you straight up. Not hide it in the barn like some teenage boy. If I wanted Rosita and not you, I wouldn't be out here in this damn downpour looking for you. I would be with her," Adrian said seriously.

That was true. She knew that. If he cared for Rosita more than her, he wouldn't be there. She placed her hand on her forehead. "Oh Adrian, I'm sorry, I saw you with her and - of course, you would have told me if you wanted her instead of me. You're an honest man. I'm sorry I doubted you. I'm so used to people changing on me on a dime. Every time I had thought a guy was decent, it turned out he was a snake all along."

Adrian's wet hands cupped her soaked face. "I'm not a fool like the others. I know how special you are." He laid his lips on hers.

She moaned against his mouth. Adrian's tongue slipped between her lips. His tongue grazed her parted lips from side to side before it dipped into her mouth.

Faith grabbed his wet dress shirt, holding on as he stole her breath. A low groan echoed from Adrian's throat. He tore his mouth away. Adrian continued to hold her face in his hands. They stared into each other's eyes as the rain beat down on them.

"Let me show you," he said in a hungry tone. "Will you let me show you how much I want you?"

"Yes," she whispered as she shook her head.

Adrian took her mouth again, lapping at her lips like a starving man. His hands grabbed the skirt of her sundress. He worked the wet garment up her body. He broke the kiss long enough to pull the drenched cloth over her head. He tossed the sundress aside.

Faith stood bare-chested in front of him. The rain beat on her C cup breasts. Her brown nipples were knotted, hard, and tight.

After taking in her form, Adrian captured her in his arms and laid her down in the grass. He hovered above her. Faith's fingers worked the buttons of his shirt as Adrian braced one hand on the ground next to her. Adrian started undoing his belt buckle.

Faith struggled with slipping the buttons through the slits in the wet fabric. Adrian grabbed her hands and put them down at her sides. He reached up and ripped his shirt open, exposing his light muscled chest that was sprinkled with brown hair. Faith sat up. She placed her hands on Adrian's chest as he put his wrist behind his back, pulling the shirt off his shoulders

Faith had dreamed about rubbing her hands over Adrian's tan chest. It wasn't a dream anymore. Her manicured hands rubbed his wet pecks. She glided her hands down his chest. Her fingers danced over his toned abdomen. He had already loosened his belt and unbuttoned his pants. She unzipped his jeans and dipped her hand under the waistband of his Hanes. She took his hard staff in hand, and started stroking it.

Adrian desperately grabbed her upper arms. She looked up at him as the rain continued to beat down on them.

"I'll let you do that another time," he said hoarsely. He came down on her, making her lie back down in the grass.

Adrian tugged down her white thongs. Faith pushed her feet down, making the middle of her body rise up so Adrian could pull her panties over the curve of her hips. Faith lifted her legs in the air, letting Adrian dispose of the annoying barrier. She opened her legs. Adrian wasted no time pushing his jeans down to his knees and snuggling his hips between her valley.

Adrian reached between them, taking himself in hand and guiding his tip around in her moistness.

Faith gasped with want and excitement. "Yes," she moaned. "Take me, Adrian, please."

Adrian found her center, and with one swift thrust, he entered her.

They both groaned at the sensation of becoming one. Adrian slowly grinded in her as he lay on top of her.

"Ah," Faith cried as her walls adjusted to his manhood.

Adrian's hands gripped her wet hair as he quickened his pumping.

Faith's mouth opened; rain from the sky entered her mouth.

"Oh God," he groaned as he buried his face in her neck.

Faith wrapped her legs around Adrian's waist as he quickened the pace. Rain beat on Adrian's back. She nicked at his earlobe as he groaned against her wet skin. He let out a low growl. She felt his lips turn into a smile against her neck. She nicked him again.

"Ah," he groaned. Adrian planted himself in her and swirled his hips, making his staff grind in her, teasing her.

She whimpered his name.

Adrian pumped in her again, and then stopped. He swirled and grinded his hips like before, making her pant with want.

"Adrian!" she cried with a hint of a desperate whine.

He gathered her in his arms and rolled them over,

then he thrust his hips upward.

Faith hissed with pleasure. "Oh yeah! Ah!" she moaned as she sat up. She planted her palms on his glorious chest and started bouncing on his staff, meeting his thrusts.

He groaned as his head flung back on the ground.

The downpour continued as they made love.

Faith's breath caught as a shiver went up her spine. Her fingers dug into his pecks. Adrian squeezed her hips as he quickened his thrusting.

Her nipples tingled and throbbed as she flung her face to the heavens. "Oh, Adrian!"

As Faith's body trembled and her valley became soaked in-between them, Adrian let out a long groan. As she was coming back to earth, she could feel hot cream making her wetter than she already was.

"Faith," he groaned as he held her hips down and stilled his movements.

The rain eased into sprinkles as Faith lay on top of Adrian. He tangled his fingers in her wet auburn hair, bringing her down for a kiss to seal their erotic experience.

Chapter 29

The rain had stopped, and the sun had set. Half of the guests were still on the Lone Wolf Ranch. White lights and lanterns were lit, which surrounded the dance floor.

Faith and Adrian had circled around and entered the back of the house without anyone seeing them. Adrian went upstairs to change, while Faith went to her cottage to change. Faith took a quick shower. The air had become cool, so she put on the blouse and jeans she had on earlier. She dried her hair and put styling oil in it. She ran a hot straightening comb through her hair to work out the kinks that formed from the rain.

She walked into the living room of the main house. Adrian had asked her to meet him in there before they returned to the BBQ.

He was already in there. He was nursing what looked like bourbon in his glass. "Hey, beautiful," he said with an easy smile.

She grinned. "Hey."

"Come over and sit with me for a minute," he said and padded the open spot next to him on the sofa.

Faith walked over to him and sat down.

He put his arm around her shoulders. “It’s time I told you what happened four years ago…between Rosita and me.”

“Before you do,” Faith said, “I have a confession to make.”

Adrian’s eyebrow cocked up. “Oh?”

“Yes,” Faith said and swallowed. She prayed he wouldn’t be angry with her. “I kinda know already.”

“Know what exactly?”

Faith cleared her throat. “A couple of weeks ago at work, Antonio Rodriguez came into the office for an appointment. He asked how you were. I answered, and then he let something slip about a woman in your past that caused you trouble.”

Adrian nodded. “Antonio told you,” he said solemnly.

“No,” Faith said. “He didn’t feel comfortable telling me the whole story. I let it go at the time, but I couldn’t help wondering what the secret was that was keeping us apart. An hour later, Drew came in for an appointment. I…I asked him who Rosita was to you. He asked me to meet him at the bar after I got off of work. He said he would tell me what he knew.”

Adrian blinked. “Drew knows a lot,” he said in a low tone. “Hell, he knows a lot about most people who live here. People go to the bar and lay their problems down over a beer.”

“He wasn’t the only one I talked to,” Faith confessed. “When I got there, Sheriff Langford was there, too. Both of them told me the story. They had told me that you and Rosita were dating; that you were in love with her. Drew had told me what happened in the bar that night Rosita kissed Steve and…groped him in front of everyone. There was a rift between you two because of her."

Adrian nodded. "That's about right. I accused Steve of wanting her for himself; for going after her behind my back. I didn't believe what happened that night and I didn't believe all the rumors he told me about her either; which turned out to be more facts than rumors. I moved off the ranch and moved to the Rodriguez Ranch."

"Drew and Sheriff Langford said you got engaged to Rosita after she got pregnant. That you thought the baby was yours. Then, the rich man, Maurice, came for Rosita and the truth came out; and then you beat the hell out of the guy for it."

Adrian blew out. He leaned back on the sofa. "That was the first time in my life I went looking for a fight. I almost paid a high price for it, too. I almost ruined my life because of her."

"How did you….not go to prison, Adrian?" she asked tentatively.

"All I know is that my father pulled a lot of favors," Adrian said and sipped his drink. "I never knew the details. When it was all over, my father sat me down in the office in the stables. He told me to never let anyone come between the family and me again because he might not forgive me if there was a second time. He understood that time because I was young and never been in love before. He also told me to watch my temper because if there was a next time, he might not be there to help me." Adrian blew out. "At the time, I had no idea that….when he died, I felt responsible. I wasn't here. If I was here, maybe…he wouldn't have died."

"You had your own life to live. Parents understand that. You're not doing yourself any favors by blaming yourself," she said.

Adrian looked at her. She could tell he was wondering how much she knew about his father.

She decided to change the subject back to the trouble Rosita instigated. "How…how did you and Steve make up?" Faith asked.

"The standup man that my brother is," Steve began as he walked into the living room. Joey followed behind him. "He came to me and apologized. It takes a helluva man to admit when he's wrong."

Adrian gave Steve a small smile. "And it takes a helluva man to forgive when he was the one that was wronged." Adrian turned to Faith. "Do you have any other questions?"

"No, but I have another confession to make," Faith said sheepishly.

Adrian stilled. "How bad is it?" he asked.

"Not bad, exactly," Faith said. "It depends on how you look at it. You see, I knew Rosita was in town. She was at the bar last night. She came in looking for Jose. They argued, Antonio introduced me as his girlfriend, and then she left."

Adrian's eyes widened. "Go back to the part where Antonio introduced you as his girlfriend."

"Antonio thought if Rosita knew I was….in your life she would stay in town and cause trouble," Faith said. "Unfortunately, she did that anyway."

"I see," Adrian said.

"I didn't know whether to tell you if she was here or

not, so I told-" Faith stopped talking and nodded in Steve and Joey's direction.

"We thought it best not to tell you. We thought Rosita would tuck her tail between her legs and leave town on her own since Jose ran her out of the bar," Joey said.

"We didn't know how you would react," Steve said.

"They know you better than me, so I went with the decision," Faith said.

Adrian was quiet for a moment. "It's okay. You guys didn't know how I would react if I knew she was back in Elliot. If the situation was turned around, I would have decided the same thing."

Faith relaxed. She was so glad that Adrian wasn't upset with her for keeping secrets from him.

"However, you, Miss Faith," Adrian said and leaned towards her, "don't keep any more secrets from me. The only way this works between us if we are upfront with each other. Kapeesh?"

She smiled. "Kapeesh. With that being said-"

"You're kidding?" Adrian said. "You're holding onto more information?"

"Just that....I wanted to let you know that Aunt Bea told me a few weeks ago....how...your parents died," she said carefully. "I wanted to let you know that I knew." Faith looked at Steve and Joey. "I wanted you guys to know that Aunt Bea told me, too. I didn't ask. She....she told me on her own. I think she needed to talk about it with someone."

You could hear a pin drop in the room.

She didn't mean to knock the wind out of them.

Steve broke the silence. "Well, if Bea needed to talk

about it for whatever reason, she wouldn't have come to us. We hadn't mentioned it since the day after Daddy's memorial service."

"I understand why Aunt Bea told you," Joey said. A small smile spread across his lips. "You're family, now."

Faith looked down bashfully.

"He's right," Adrian said. "You're family." He kissed Faith on the cheek.

"Now that we've gotten all that depressing shit out of the way, we need to get to the real matter at hand," Steve said and rubbed his palms together.

"And what's that?" Adrian asked with curiosity.

"Why are you two in different clothes and why is your hair wet, Adrian?" Steve asked with a smirk.

Faith buried her face in Adrian's shoulder.

"Yeehaw!" Steve shouted. "This calls for a drink. Adrian got some!"

"Oh God!" Faith exclaimed against Adrian's shoulder with embarrassment.

The men laughed.

Chapter 30

Joey drove his jeep with Steve in the passenger seat to the Warrington Ranch. Ray and Lance, a builder who owned a sawmill in Elliot, rode in a separate truck. Adrian and Faith followed in Adrian's truck. Adrian wanted Faith to come along to look at the property

The grass was as green on the Warrington land as it was on the Lone Wolf Ranch. Luke came out of the house as they pulled up. The house wasn't as big as the Matthews', but it was cute. It was only one story.

Everyone got out of the vehicles.

"Hey, boys," Luke said. "Faith." Luke tipped his cowboy hat to her.

"Hi," she said.

"I hope you don't mind us bringing Lance and Ray along," Adrian said. "I thought Lance could look at the house to see what kind of work it needs. Ray is here to help us assess the land for the cattle."

"I don't mind at all," Luke said cheerfully. "I thought we could get in the chopper so you guys can get a grade A tour of the land."

"That sounds great. Plus we can see how the chopper

handles since it's being thrown in with the package," Steve said.

"You know how to fly a helicopter?" Faith asked.

"Sure do," Steve said. "When I turned eighteen, I left home for two years. I moved to Oklahoma, got my pilot's license, and worked as a crop duster."

"Impressive," Faith said.

"I got a pilot's license too, Angel," Adrian said. "I didn't get mine in Oklahoma though. I took classes in Dallas. Daddy was going to buy a chopper for the ranch, but Momma kept groaning about how dangerous they were. He gave in and didn't buy one."

"What about you, Joey?" Faith asked.

"Pssh," he said and turned his nose up. "I like to keep my feet on the ground – where they're meant to be."

Everyone chuckled.

"I take it that you're not going on the chopper tour," Luke said.

"Thanks, but no thanks," Joey said. "I'll stay on the ground and look around that way."

"The chopper only fits four, anyway," Luke said.

"I'll stay here with Joey," Faith said. "Maybe next time."

"I came here to look at the buildings," Lance said.

"All right, Ray, Adrian, Steve, let's do it," Luke said with excitement.

Adrian put his hand on Faith's shoulder. "We should be back within an hour and a half. Look around with Joey and Lance. Take a look at the house. See if you like it, okay?"

Faith tilted her head to the side. Why did it matter if

she liked the house or not? She didn't ask. She just went with it. "Okay," she whispered.

Adrian lapped at her lips as he rubbed her shoulder.

"Hell, Adrian, she'll be here when we get back," Steve joked.

Adrian lifted his lips from hers. "Shut up," he said with a chuckle.

"The helipad is five acres out," Luke said. "Let's ride down there. It's quicker."

Two hours later, Faith, Lance, and Joey were in the main barn. The barn was twice the size of the main barn on the Lone Wolf Ranch. They had toured the house, the log cabin by the creek, and the stables which were twice the size of the Lone Wolf stable.

Adrian and the rest of the guys had landed on the helipad. Adrian called Steve's cell to see where they were at. They were going to meet at the barn.

Faith climbed up in the hayloft. She looked at the big piles of hay. "How in the world do you get hay up here?"

"A tractor with a lift that scopes hay does that," Joey answered.

"Oh," Faith said.

The floor in the loft was covered with strands of hay. There was a big window. It looked like it could open, but Faith didn't open it.

Adrian, Ray, Steve, and Luke walked into the barn. Faith watched and listened to the men from the hayloft.

"How was the ride?" Joey asked.

"Great," Steve said. "Adrian and I got to take it for a spin. The chopper handles great."

"Glad you like it," Luke said.

"The three horses in the stable," Joey began. "Are they included in the deal?"

"No," Luke answered. "I'm going to have them moved to Dallas as soon as the place is sold."

Joey nodded.

"We got a look at the cattle," Adrian said. "Great herd."

"When do you need an answer?" Steve asked.

"I'll like to hear back from you boys in a week," Luke said. "I want to have the place sold within the next sixty days. I need the cash for a pending deal."

"We can let you know in a week," Adrian said. "Where's Faith?"

"Up here," she said.

Adrian, Ray, Steve, and Luke looked up.

Adrian smiled and adjusted his Stetson. "Having fun, Angel?"

She giggled. "I am. I feel like a kid up here."

"Keep enjoying yourself," Luke said. "Listen, I got to go meet…well, a very pretty lady in fifteen minutes for an early dinner. You guys can stay as long as you need to. Just make sure to lock the gate up when you leave."

"Sure thing," Ray said.

"Enjoy your date," Steve said with a smile.

"Bye, boys. Goodbye, Faith," Luke said.

"Bye," Faith said as she waved.

They waited for Luke to get in his truck before they spoke candidly.

"I love the place," Steve said. "Let's buy it."

Adrian chuckled. "It's three million dollars. Don't you think we should discuss it first?"

"Yeah," Joey said. "The horses aren't even included."

"Three horses isn't a big deal," Adrian said. "Lance, how did the house, the stables, and the barns look?"

"The two barns further out are sound, and in great shape like the one we are in. Nothing needs to be done to them. The fishing cabin next to the creek is still in good shape. My guys and I built it ten years ago. Luke has kept it up well. The stables are twice the size of the one at the Lone Wolf, and it is in excellent condition too, but the ranch house-" Lance stopped and shook his head. "It's structurally sound from what I can tell, but there's water damage on the ceiling, the wallpaper is peeling off the walls in all three bedrooms, the kitchen appliances are at least forty years old, but they still work, which is a miracle. The tile on the kitchen floor is chipped and loose. Every step you take the floor creeks. The boiler is so old that you can't get parts for it if it breaks down. Oh, and one side of the house is lower than the other side."

"So it needs to be gutted throughout," Adrian said as he adjusted the hat on his head.

"Yep, but it might be better if you knock the whole thing down and build a house," Lance said. "If you want a house here, that is."

"Hmmm," Adrian mumbled as he mulled over what Lance had said.

"We can use that to bring the price down a little," Joey said.

"Not that much," Lance said. "The house is probably worth eighty thousand. That's my guess, anyway. I'm a contractor, not an appraiser."

"I'm getting hungry," Steve said. "But, my vote is yes. We've wanted to expand for years. If we buy this place, that dream will come true. The creek runs through our property and this one."

"Ray, what did you think of the land?" Adrian said.

"It's terrific," Ray said. "It's been well cared for, and we can increase our hay production, too."

"Joey?" Adrian said.

"It's the ideal location, I'll say that. I just wish we can get the price down about five to seven hundred grand or so," Joey said.

"Did you boys see everything you needed to see?" Adrian said.

The men mumbled that they did.

Faith went to the ladder to climb down.

"Stay up there," Adrian said as he looked up. "I expect you to give me the grand tour of the loft."

Faith smiled. "All right."

"Thanks for coming out on a Sunday, Lance," Adrian said and shook Lance's hand.

"No problem," Lance said. "The bill will be in the mail."

The men chuckled.

Chapter 31

Faith watched Adrian climb the ladder to the hayloft. His easy cowboy smile made her tingle all over.

"What do you think of the ranch, Angel?" Adrian said as he approached her.

"It's nice," Faith said. "Beautiful."

"I like it, too," Adrian said. "I kinda agree with Joey, though. I would like to get the price down a little to have cash reserves to increase the herd. If we buy it, we'll need to hire extra hands and buy a few more horses to work it." Adrian wrapped his arms around Faith's waist. "But, in the meantime, let's take the barn for a test run."

"What do you mean?" Faith asked. "You want to pitch some hay?"

His laughter filled the massive barn.

Faith smiled.

"Well," he said as he tightened his hold around her. "If that's what you want to call it, I'm not going to argue about it." A boyish smirk played on his lips. His eyes sparkled.

Faith figured out what he meant. "Adrian, we can't do that here," she whispered.

"Why?" Adrian said and started kissing her neck.

She giggled. "The place doesn't belong to you yet."

He started laying a trail of kisses down her neck. "We both know we're going to buy it," Adrian said against her chest. "May as well break it in while we're here."

"Mmmm," Faith moaned lightly. "We'll get caught."

"We have a better chance getting caught at home," Adrian said and raised his head to look at her. "Despite how big that place is, there is always someone lingering about. If it isn't that, Aunt Bea is hovering to make sure I don't corrupt you." Adrian started unbuttoning his shirt.

"No," she whispered and placed her hands over his. "What if Luke comes back or one of your brothers come looking for you?"

Adrian chuckled and started walking forward, making her walk backward. "My brothers aren't going to come back. I think they had a feeling as to why I stayed behind. Luke got a date of his own. He probably won't be back for hours." Adrian grabbed her and fell on top of her.

They both laughed as they collapsed on top of a hay pile.

Adrian quickly unbuttoned her yellow blouse, exposing her white bra. He groaned his approval of her chest and started rubbing his hands over her breasts.

Faith gasped at his touch.

Adrian grabbed the bra cups and maneuvered her breasts out of them. He tossed his hat to the side. He started kissing down her chest to one breast.

Faith bit her bottom lip as he kissed his way to one

dark brown nipple that was getting hard. He took her budding nip in his mouth. Adrian's tongue started flickering against the bud.

She cried out at near orgasm pitch as she grabbed his shoulders.

He raised his head. He looked pleasantly surprised.

"I'm sorry," she breathed. "They're…my breasts…are very sensitive. That's why I wear padded bras."

"Oh," he said with intrigue in his tone. "That is a very good thing to know." He covered her nipple again with his mouth. His tongue swirled around her bud like he was licking an ice cream cone. He moved to her other breast, flicking his tongue over the throbbing mound.

Faith was panting now.

Adrian raised his head and used his hands to smash her C cups together. He buried his face between them, laying wet kisses on them. He sucked, licked, and kissed her breasts and nipples, worshipping them. Her pelvis writhed and wiggled against him. Adrian didn't stop until she cried out his name.

His hands moved down to her skirt. He pushed the jean skirt above her thighs, exposing her soaked womanhood. His eyebrows rose as a smirk spread across his lips. "You're not wearing any panties?"

Faith put her fingertip in her mouth. "It's hot out and…I didn't think anyone would notice," she said bashfully.

Adrian chuckled as he unbuckled his belt. "Saves me time from taking them off." He unzipped his jeans and pushed them down past his hips. Adrian placed his hands under Faith's knees, opening her legs wide. He guided his erection into her well. He groaned as he came down on top of her. "You're so wet," he moaned.

"Ah. Yes, well, that's your fault," she teased as her fingers roamed through his light brown hair.

He started pumping. "I'm happy to take responsibility for that, Angel," he said with a smile.

They kissed as Faith matched his movements. She started moaning against his lips. After a few minutes, she tore her mouth away, needing oxygen.

Adrian laid kisses on her cheek. "God, you feel so good," he mumbled against her face.

"Oh, you do, too," Faith moaned.

Adrian started thrusting. His wood was plowing fast and hard.

Her walls tightened around his glory as her back arched. "Yes, Adrian. Ah, that's it. Yes!" she moaned. She raised one leg and started rubbing her calf against his hip. She turned her face towards him.

He captured her mouth, swallowing her cries of pleasure. Then, he stopped kissing her. "Look at me, Angel. Look at me when you come," he said in a deep tone.

She opened her eyes.

Adrian changed his ministrations. He went into a hard deliberate thrust that made Faith's mouth form a perfect O. She grasped the back of his shirt, balling the fabric into her fists. "Oh God, oh!"

She stopped breathing for a second, the hard thrusts shaking her to her core. Faith sucked in a breath, and then let it go as a moan. Her breasts bounced, her nipples throbbed as her shoulders, back, and thighs quaked with the burst of rosy pleasure that surrounded her. A long satisfied moan escaped her throat as a smile curled on her lips. Adrian was the best lover she has ever had.

He kept thrusting until her orgasm subsided. Then, he took her by the waist. "Turn over for me, Angel," he said raggedly and pulled out of her.

She started to turn on her stomach, but she must have been taking too long because Adrian took her waist and flipped her over in the hay.

Faith giggled as she smashed the hay down away from her face.

Adrian chuckled as he lay on top of her.

Faith felt his wet hardness enter her backdoor.

"Oh," she said with surprise as his staff dipped inside.

He growled as he maneuvered back and forth in her.

Faith's skin warmed with tingles. She put her thumb in her mouth and started sucking it as she cooed with delight. She should have been embarrassed, but she wasn't. The hay prickled her exposed chest and the front of her legs.

Adrian kissed her cheek as he started thrusting in her. His heavy sack was slapping against her ass. He groaned and growled against her cheek like a wild animal. He started breathing so heavy that he was practically wheezing. Faith felt his milk, hot and true, shooting in the back of her. He let out a long, loud groan like he had been holding it in for years. Adrian collapsed on top of her. "My little angel," he breathed.

Faith let her thumb slip out of her mouth. They lay in the hay, hot and sweaty, cheek to cheek as they caught their breath.

After a few minutes, Adrian rolled over on his back,

letting his member slip out of her. His shirt was open and his jeans were hugging his hips. He reached out for her. Faith snuggled against him, laying her head and one hand on his chest.

Adrian took a deep breath as he wrapped one arm around her. He placed his other hand behind his head. "After we buy this place, I'm going to have the ranch house demolished. Then, I'm going to hire Lance to build a new house – a home. I want you to work with Lance. I want the place to be a place….well, that you would want to live in."

Faith looked up at him. *What was he thinking?* "Why?" she asked with wide eyes.

"I know we haven't been seeing each other as much as we would have loved to, but when I see something or someone I want, I go for it. No need in pussy footing around," Adrian said thoughtfully.

Was he serious? "Adrian, are you saying that you want to live here…with me? You want us to move in together?"

The corner of his mouth kicked up. "That's one way of putting in. I guess what I'm trying to say is that….I'm in love with you and I want us to build a life together. When the time is right….when you're ready, I want you to become my wife."

Faith's mouth dropped open. She adored Adrian. She was falling in love with him, but she didn't dare say anything like that to him because she thought it was too soon. "I…I am falling in love with you, Adrian, but we've only known each other for six - seven weeks. I mean…I don't know if it happens this fast. Does it?"

"My parents fell in love within a week of meeting

each other. Aunt Bea fell for her husband over a weekend in Houston. It happens," he said and raised his head to kiss her forehead. "Are you not sure about me?"

"Oh, Adrian, I know that what you see is what you get when it comes to you, but I have a bad track record with men," Faith said. "For one reason or another, it doesn't work out."

"That's because you weren't with the right person," Adrian said with conviction. "I'm starting to believe that I was meant to meet you on that road the night you got hit by that Hummer."

"Like it was destiny intervening so we could meet?" she asked with a wry smile.

"Yeah," Adrian said as he rubbed her back. "So, what do you say? Do you want to take a chance?"

Faith took a deep breath. She took a chance quitting her job without having another one to go to, and it worked out. She took a chance using her savings to go on a long road trip, and it worked out. Three times the charm. "Yes," she said with a big smile.

Adrian claimed her with a kiss.

Chapter 32

Three weeks later…

Adrian, Steve, and Joey had purchased the Warrington Ranch for $2.7 million. Luke had vouched for the ranch hands he had on staff, and the Matthews brothers already knew them, so they were comfortable with letting the men stay on.

Adrian, Steve, and Joey were watching Lance's men remove the Warrington Ranch sign from the gate. The Lone Wolf Ranch sign was sitting on top of a flatbed truck, waiting to be hung.

"This is a beautiful sight," Steve said with a big grin.

Joey shook his head up and down in agreement.

The ranch house was demolished yesterday. Lance was at the Lone Wolf Ranch with Faith. They were working on plans for the new home. If they started on the house right away, they could have it finished before January.

Adrian smiled. "It looks like it's going to be sunnier pastures for now on, guys."

The Matthews brothers smiled as they watched the

workmen hook up the Lone Wolf Ranch sign onto a lifter.

****

Faith and Lance were in the den at the Lone Wolf Ranch. They were developing plans for a large Cape Cod style home with a loft and a basement.

"I would like to have it rustic looking, you know, since Adrian is a Texan," Faith said with a smile.

Lance smiled back at her. "It will have all the Texan flare that Adrian likes."

Thirty minutes later, Lance and Faith had finished their meeting and Faith was walking Lance to the door.

"I'll get together with the architect. I should be able to show you formal plans next week," Lance said.

Faith opened the door. "That sounds great. Hopefully, Adrian can be at that meeting to look at the plans. I want to make sure he likes it, too."

Lance and Faith shook hands as Joey approached them.

"Hey," Joey said.

"Hey, Joey," Lance said. "I was just leaving to see how things are going on the other side."

"Going good," Joey said. "The sign is up and the guys from yesterday are back to clean up the debris from the old house."

"Great," Lance said. "I'm going to go check in with them."

"All right," Joey said.

Lance walked away and headed for his white truck

that had “Lance’s Construction” on the side.

“Home for lunch?” Faith asked.

“Yep,” Joey said. “Steve and Adrian are sticking around to wait for Ray and Isaiah to show up with some new equipment. They’ll be along for lunch later.”

Thirty minutes later, Joey, Aunt Bea, and Faith were eating roast beef sandwiches and homemade fries for lunch. They chatted about the new land and the house that would be built on it. Faith couldn’t remember a time when she was this happy. Joey and Aunt Bea seemed happy, too.

The doorbell rang.

“You guys keep eating, I’ll get it,” Faith said with a smile.

“Thanks, honey,” Aunt Bea said.

Faith went to the foyer. She saw two cruisers and three black SUVs through the side windows next to the door. “What the hell?” she mumbled as she opened the door.

Sheriff Langford, a deputy, and a man in a white shirt with a black tie were on the porch. There were at least a dozen men in jackets that had the letters DEA on the back of them in the front yard. They were pulling German shepherds out of the SUVs.

“Sheriff, what is going on?” Faith asked with wide eyes.

“Ma’am, we are with the Drug Enforcement Agency,” the man said. “I’m Agent Carl Witherspoon. Are you one of the legal owners of this property?”

“No,” Faith said in a high-pitched voice.

“I need to speak with one of the owners, ma’am,” Agent Witherspoon said. He was holding a folded piece of paper in his hand.

Faith wasn't so far removed from the ghetto to not know what that was. It was a search warrant. Faith stepped back into the foyer. "Joey! Joey!"

A moment went by before Joey and Aunt Bea came jogging to the foyer.

"What the hell is going on?" Joey asked with wide eyes.

"Joseph Matthews?" Agent Witherspoon asked.

"Yeah," Joey said.

"I'm Agent Carl Witherspoon. This is a search warrant to search your ranch for illegal substances," he said and handed Joey the search warrant.

"What the hell are you talking about?" Joey asked with wild eyes as he took the paper.

"We got three anonymous tips during the past three weeks that drugs were being trafficked from Mexico through this property, sir. We have to investigate."

"That's horse shit!" Joey yelled and opened the search warrant.

"We will be searching the premises for the next few hours including the house, the barns, the stables, and any other structure on this property," the agent said.

Four men whisked by them with a drug dog and went into the house.

"My God," Aunt Bea moaned and placed her hand on her chest.

"If you cooperate, don't interfere, and if the place is clean, we'll be on our way," the agent said. "If not, well, people are going to jail today." The agent entered the house without saying another word.

"Joey, come on back," Tony said with shock over

the walkie-talkie.

Joey snatched the walkie-talkie from his belt. “Yeah, Tony.”

“There are a bunch of agents down here saying that they have a warrant to search the stables and the barns. What the hell is going on?” Tony asked with stress in his voice.

“They got a warrant. Let them do their job,” Joey said. “Cooperate and there won’t be any trouble - or should I say any more trouble.”

“This… this is ridiculous,” Faith stuttered. She was absolutely floored. There was no way Adrian, Steve, and Joey were drug traffickers. Right?

“I gotta go get Steve and Adrian,” Joey said. “They don’t have their walkie-talkies with them.”

“I’m sorry, Joey, but I can’t let you leave my sight,” the sheriff said solemnly.

“Why not?” Joey asked with confusion.

Sheriff Langford sucked in a breath. “I have to place you under arrest, son,” he whispered.

Joey’s eyes widened. He was absolutely shocked.

“For what?” Faith asked with astonishment.

“I’m sorry, Joey,” Sheriff Langford said. “I don’t have a choice. If it wasn’t for the DEA getting involved, I would have just talked to you about it before I would have done this. But, with the trafficking accusations and…I can’t cover for ya. Not this time.”

“Joseph Alexander Matthews, you are under arrest for breaking and entering into the Elliot Sheriff’s Department, obstruction of justice, and launching a cyber-attack of a law enforcement facility and the Wichita County Courthouse,” the deputy announced.

Joey's entire body stiffened. His lips went thin. He closed his eyes.

Faith looked at Joey's body language. *Oh my God, he did all that. He looks guilty.*

"Jesus wept!" Aunt Bea cried out as she lowered herself onto a light brown wicker chair on the porch.

"Place your hands behind your back and turn around," the deputy ordered.

Joey handed Faith the DEA search warrant, and then complied with the deputy's instructions.

Sheriff Langford didn't look at anyone. He acted like he was ashamed to be there.

As the deputy cuffed Joey, he read him his rights.

Faith tried to comfort Aunt Bea as she cried in an embroidered handkerchief.

The deputy and Sheriff Langford were escorting Joey to a cruiser when Adrian's truck barreled into the driveway. Steve and Adrian leaped out of the vehicle. They were awestruck at the scene on their ranch.

"What the hell is going on?" Adrian shouted as he and Steve approached Sheriff Langford. They both looked around.

Faith went out into the yard, and Aunt Bea trailed behind her.

Sheriff Langford handed Adrian a copy of Joey's arrest warrant. "I gotta take him in. With the DEA investigation and this....I have to take him," the sheriff said sadly. He couldn't even look at Adrian.

"DEA investigation!" Adrian exclaimed. For a man that was naturally tan, he turned pale real quick.

"The DEA agent said that they got three anonymous tips that you guys run drugs through the ranch," Faith said. "They have a search warrant." She handed Adrian the search warrant.

Steve was speechless.

Sheriff Langford walked away from them.

Adrian's mouth opened, but nothing came out. It was like he couldn't believe what was happening.

"When will we be able to bail him out?" Faith asked the cops.

"It'll be at least a day," the deputy said. "We have to take him to the Wichita County Jail." The deputy put Joey in the back of the cruiser.

"Shit," Steve mumbled. "It could take two days to get a bail hearing out there."

"Joey, don't say anything until we call our lawyer," Adrian yelled.

Joey nodded, and then the deputy closed the door.

Aunt Bea broke down crying again. Steve went to her and held her.

The agents had made Steve, Aunt Bea, Faith, Adrian, and the ranch hands stay on the front porch as they tore through the ranch. The DEA agents spent four hours searching the Lone Wolf Ranch. They even brought in two veterinarians to do cavity searches on the horses, the Border Collie puppies Adrian bought Faith at the fair, and some of the cattle. In the end, they didn't find a thing.

"Well, we didn't find anything, but that doesn't mean this is over," Agent Witherspoon said to them. "We'll be watching you." He turned and got into one of the SUVs.

"Prick," Steve mumbled under his breath.

"You boys should go back to the stables and check

on the cattle that are close," Adrian said in a low tone. "Make sure they didn't upset the horses."

The ranch hands walked off to carrying out the order without saying a word.

Aunt Bea, Faith, Steve, and Adrian walked into the house.

Adrian and Steve called the family attorney while Aunt Bea and Faith cleaned the place. The agents had rummaged all over the house. They even unmade the beds in all the bedrooms including Adrian's parents' old bedroom. Aunt Bea had said no one has been in there since the week after Arn's funeral – until today. They had gone through every drawer that could be opened. Some of their clothes were thrown in the floor, no doubt for the drug dogs to sniff.

They even went through the guest house. Some of Faith's clothes were on the floor, and her dresser drawers were open.

They all felt violated.

Once Adrian and Steve finished talking to the lawyer, they pitched in to help clean up the house. It took them two hours to put the house back into its former condition. Of course, there was extra laundry to do since the clothes that were on the floor had dog drool on them.

It was 9:30 at night when they all reconvened in the den. Steve quietly and angrily made bourbon and branch for everyone. Faith had never drunk bourbon and branch before. Then again, she's never had her home searched for drugs before. There was a first time for everything.

Steve quietly passed around the drinks. Then, he broke the silence. "I have something to tell ya'll," he said in a low tone.

No one responded. They waited for Steve to say what he had to say.

"A few days ago, I found a bag of coke in the stables. A big bag of coke," Steve announced.

"What?" Adrian said with a furrowed brow.

"I thought it belonged to one of the boys," Steve said. "Hell, I don't care what they do on their personal time, but I didn't want the crap here. I held a meeting, and I showed it to them and said that it wasn't cool to keep their stash here. I told them I didn't know who it belonged to and I didn't care as long as the shit didn't end up here anymore. No one fessed up to it being theirs, but I wasn't expecting them to. I flushed it down the toilet and went on about my day."

"Why didn't you tell us about it?" Adrian asked angrily.

"I didn't think it was a big deal," Steve said. "Besides, I know how you are, Adrian. You would have had us out there all night waiting for someone to fess up that it was theirs. Then, we would have lost a perfectly good ranch hand because he did a little recreation on his own free time."

"If whoever it was is doing it on his own free time, he wouldn't have stashed it here," Adrian sneered. "What if they had found that crap? All of us would have gone to prison forever. Whoever owned it is involved in something, and it damn near took us down."

"Adrian, I didn't think it would lead to our place being raided by the damn DEA," Steve said. "Or that Joey would get arrested for it."

"Drugs was the only thing that they didn't charge

him with," Faith said and sipped her drink. The concoction was a little too strong for her, but it was what the occasion called for.

The Border Collie pups, Hager and Chop, were lying down at Faith's feet.

"Whoever it belonged to, they got the message," Aunt Bea in a soft voice. "If they kept stashing it here, the agents would have found it."

"Maybe one of them kept it here so their wife or girlfriend wouldn't find it," Steve said. "Hell, I don't know."

Faith didn't think it was that simple. All this happened at once. "Call me paranoid, but something isn't right. It is too much of a coincidence that Joey gets arrested on a completely separate matter and the place is raided for drugs on the same day. Do you have enemies that want to see you ruined?"

They were quiet for a moment. "No," Adrian said. "Not unless lover boy over there has pissed off a lady."

Steve gave Adrian a nasty look.

"This isn't the time for you two to start turning on each other," Aunt Bea said. "Faith has a point. All this didn't happen for the heck of it."

"Oh hell," Steve said as realization registered in his eyes. "Rosita Rodriguez. She did this."

"What?" All of them said at once.

"Think about it," Steve said. "She's the only one that hates us enough to pull this. She was furious when we kicked her off the ranch during the BBQ."

"Yeah, but she's back in California, isn't she?" Faith said.

"Well, they do have phones in Cali," Steve said.

"The agent said they got three anonymous calls," Adrian said. "They would know if it was the same person."

"Not necessarily," Steve said. "She could have gotten a friend or two to call."

"For the sake of argument, let's say you're right," Faith said. "What about Joey getting arrested? Obstruction of justice? Cyber-attacks on county facilities? How would Rosita know about that and what is it all about? I didn't know Joey could turn on a computer much less hack one."

"It must be some sort of frame-up," Steve said. "Joey isn't a computer guy. He doesn't even like carrying a cell phone."

"What did the lawyer say?" Aunt Bea asked. "Will we be able to get him out of county tomorrow?"

"Mike hopes so," Adrian said. "It was too late to call a judge tonight, but Mike promised he would call one first thing in the morning."

"It is late," Aunt Bea said. "Let's figure all this out in the morning."

Chapter 33

The next day, Faith, Steve, and Adrian drove to the Wichita County Courthouse. It was an hour drive from Elliot. Mike Scully, the Matthews' family attorney, was able to get Joey a bail hearing at noon.

"Case number 3872," a bailiff announced. "The state versus Joseph A. Matthews."

Mike stepped forward, exchanged a quick handshake with the defense attorney from the last bail hearing, and then stood at the defendants' table.

Another bailiff escorted Joey into the courtroom. He walked Joey to the defendant's table where Mike stood. Joey's light brown hair was combed, but he was in a short-sleeved orange jumpsuit. His ankles and wrists were chained like he was a danger to society.

Thank God Aunt Bea stayed at home. She would have fainted at the sight of Joey dressed like this, Adrian thought.

Steve blew out when he saw Joey.

Joey gave his family a quick nod of acknowledgment.

Steve and Adrian nodded back at them.

The judge opened the folder that the court clerk gave him. He quickly skimmed it and looked at the assistant district attorney. “All right, it says here that the defendant has been arrested for breaking and entering into the Elliot Sheriff's Department to steal files which leads to the obstruction of justice charge. It also says here that the defendant is responsible for hacking the computer system at the Elliot Sheriff's Department and the Wichita County Courthouse. All crimes were committed four years ago,” the judge said.

Adrian’s head rocked back. The hair on the back of his neck stood up. *No. Joey couldn’t have....*

“That’s correct, your honor,” the ADA said as he stood up.

“Bail recommendations?” the judge asked.

“The DA’s office recommends that Mr. Matthews be held until trial,” the ADA said.

Adrian’s eyes bugged out.

Faith’s mouth dropped open.

Mike quickly stood up. “Your honor, what my client is being accused of are non-violent crimes. Holding him without bail is extreme.”

“Mr. Matthews is a flight risk,” the ADA said. “His family has several million dollars at their disposable. Mr. Matthews could disappear overnight.”

“Over crimes that will only carry a two-year sentence altogether? I highly doubt it, your honor,” Mike said. “My client has family ties in Elliot and he helps run the family business in Elliot. He has lived in the town for most of his life. He is not a flight risk.”

“Mr. Matthews is a crafty individual. He launched an attack that broke into this very courthouse’s computer records to erase evidence of a crime that one of his brothers committed four years ago."

Adrian's eyes closed as guilt wretched his gut. *Oh God, what did you do, Joey?*

"Allegedly launched an attack, your honor," Mike corrected. "My client doesn't even own a cell phone. The charges are ridiculous. He's a rancher, not a computer programmer."

"Which leads to the DEA matter," the ADA said quickly. "Just yesterday, Mr. Matthews' ranch, which he co-owns with his brothers, was raided by the DEA for suspicion of drug trafficking."

Adrian scratched the back of his head. He couldn't believe this was happening to his kid brother – to his family.

Faith reached over and placed her hand over Adrian's.

"And the DEA agents didn't find a thing," Mike argued.

"Yes, but they are still investigating. They are certain that Mr. Matthews and his family are dealing drugs. With the current charges and the DEA investigation, the pressure is on the defendant. He is a flight risk."

"My client has no priors and his living family members don't have any priors," Mike said.

Mike was about to say something else, but the ADA interrupted him. "We wouldn't know if they did have priors since Mr. Matthews can go in and out of the law enforcement and court computer systems whenever he wants."

The judge slammed down his gavel. "Mr. Novak,

you know better," the judge said sternly.

"I apologize to the court," the ADA said quickly.

"Continue, Mr. Scully," the judge said.

"As I was saying, my client is not a criminal or a hacker. The charges were brought up by an acquaintance that my client met years ago. An acquaintance that is desperate for money. My theory is that he remembered meeting Mr. Matthews years ago and is trying to cash in," Mike said.

"Your honor, we have the computer disk evidence of the hacking," the ADA said. "The so-called acquaintance turned it over to us. We have a signed statement. If you let Mr. Matthews out on bail, he could tamper with evidence or intimidate the witness."

"That is an outrageous accusation," Mike said. "My client-"

"All right," the judge said. "I've heard all I need to hear. Mr. Scully, does your client have a passport?"

"No, your honor," Mike answered.

"Taking into consideration the nature of the crimes and the DEA investigation, I'm setting bail at $100,000. The defendant must wear an ankle monitor that won't allow him to leave his property. Court is adjourned for one hour for lunch," the judge said and banged his gavel. He stood up.

Everyone in the courtroom stood up. No one moved until the judge left the courtroom. The bailiff came for Joey.

Adrian and Steve rushed to the front of the courtroom. They didn't get to talk to Joey before the bail hearing. Faith trailed behind them.

"Wait, please," Steve said in a half-pleading tone.

"Can you give us a minute before you take him?"

The bailiff nodded. "Just a few minutes," the bailiff said and walked away from the defense table.

"Are you all right?" Adrian asked.

"Yeah," Joey said flatly.

"Adrian, do you have the-" Mike began to ask.

Adrian knew what he was going to ask. "I got the cash. As long as they'll take a check, he can be back home today."

"Good," Mike said. "I'll walk with you to start the process. Then, you guys can go back home. Since Joey has to wear an ankle monitor, law enforcement isn't going to let him out of their sight whether the bail is paid or not. They'll drive him back to the ranch and put the monitor on him there. I'll be with him every step of the way."

"You won't be the only one," Adrian said.

"Yeah, we're not leaving this place until Joey does," Steve said with conviction. "I don't care who's driving him."

"It will take at least two hours to process him and then the hour drive back to Elliot, Steve," Mike said. "Ya'll go home, we'll meet you there."

"We're not leaving this town without him," Adrian said.

"All right," Mike said.

Joey looked at Adrian. "Everything is going to be all right."

Adrian scoffed. "I'm supposed to be the one that tells you that."

Joey gave him a half smile.

Adrian hugged Joey. His brother couldn't hug him

back because of the damn cuffs. Adrian released him.

Faith gave Joey a little hug and a kiss on the cheek.

Joey smiled at her. "You keep taking care of him," he said to her as he nodded at Adrian.

"I will," Faith whispered and rubbed Joey's shoulder.

Unbelievable. Joey was the one in hot water, and he was worried about Adrian.

Steve practically pulled Joey in his muscled arms. He gave Joey two hard pants on the back as he hugged him. "Keep being strong, hard ass," Steve said.

Chapter 34

After Adrian had paid Joey's bail, Steve, Adrian, and Faith grabbed lunch at a fast food joint. Adrian had called Aunt Bea on his cell phone to let her know that Joey had been granted bail, but he had to wear an ankle monitor. Aunt Bea didn't care as long as Joey got back home.

Three hours after the bail hearing, Adrian pulled his truck into the ranch with Steve and Faith in the front with him. The cruiser, with Joey in it, followed Adrian. Mike Scully followed in his Cadillac behind the cop car.

They all got out of the vehicles. Aunt Bea came jogging out the front door. She opened her arms wide to Joey as she jogged off the porch. They hugged.

"Oh baby boy," she moaned over his shoulder. "Are you all right?"

"I'm fine," he said like he had only been gone for an hour.

They all went inside.

The two police officers set up the base to the ankle monitor in the den and secured the monitor on Joey's ankle.

"All right, Mr. Matthews, you're all set," one of the officers said. "You can go to the end of the driveway, but that's it. If you stray too far from the base, an alarm will go off. If you keep going while the alarm is going off, the Elliot Sheriff's Department will be notified electronically through the device. It will be considered a violation of your bail, and you'll be back in county. Do you understand?"

"I do," Joey said.

"All right, you folks have a good evening," the officer said.

The two cops left.

"I would kill for a drink right now," Joey said.

"What would you like?" Aunt Bea asked.

"Bourbon, beer, vodka, anything as long as it is alcohol," Joey said and ran his hand through his thin brown hair.

"Let's all have bourbon," Steve said as he walked to the bar.

Aunt Bea joined Steve at the bar to help him fix the drinks.

"Mike, you want one, too?" Aunt Bea asked.

"Yes, please," Mike said. "We need to discuss your case, Joey. Since you can't come down to the office, we'll just meet here when we need to."

"All right, fine," Joey said.

"I need to know everything that happened four years ago. Every detail," Mike said and sat down in an armchair.

Joey blew out. "Mike, it's not that easy. This was supposed to go with me to the grave."

"Well, you getting arrested shot that plan all to hell,"

Mike said bluntly. “I can’t help you unless I know everything.”

Aunt Bea walked over to everyone with a tray filled with glasses full of bourbon. She sat the tray on the wood coffee table. “Joey, I don’t know what’s going on, but something tells me it has something to do with your father.”

“And me,” Adrian said as he sat up on the sofa and took two glasses off the tray. He gave one drink to Faith who was sitting next to him on the couch.

“May as well tell us the story, Joey,” Steve said. “You know we aren’t going to let it go now.”

Aunt Bea handed Joey a glass.

“Start from the beginning,” Mike said.

“Four years ago, after Adrian got arrested for beating up the guy that got Rosita pregnant, Daddy scrambled to get Adrian out of trouble. He was able to bribe the girl who worked at the hotel to change her story. Daddy gave her enough money to get out of town and to stay out of town. The governor of Texas – at that time - was an old school friend of Daddy’s. He called him up and called in a favor. The governor owed Daddy for saving his life twenty years ago. I don’t know that story. All Daddy would tell me was that he saved the governor’s life twenty years ago and that’s all I needed to know,” Joey said and took a gulp of his bourbon. He swallowed hard.

“So, Daddy brought you in from the beginning,” Adrian said.

“No, I found out what he was doing by accident. He told me all this after the deeds were done,” Joey said. “You see, I was in the stables one day, and Daddy didn’t know I was there. He had left his office door open. He was talking to the governor over speakerphone. The governor could get the charges dropped against Adrian, but he didn't know how to cover it up. He had said no one was willing to risk getting caught erasing computer files and destroying evidence in the courthouse or the police station in Elliot. That's when I made my presences known," Joey said, and then took another sip of his bourbon. "Daddy told the governor he would call him back and quickly hung up on him. Daddy was pissed. We went at it for I don't know how long, but in the end, I convinced him that I could help and wanted to help."

Steve said what Adrian was thinking. "I can't believe you convinced him to let you get involved," Steve said and sipped his bourbon.

"I think he was stuck on how to….erase the rest of the evidence," Joey said. "Do ya'll remember when I went to that community college in the city for a year to take some classes?"

"Yeah," Adrian said.

"Well, I met a lot of folks there. One guy was going there to save money on general ed. classes. He was going to transfer to a four-year college in a year. He was into computers. Real good with them. It was rumored that he hacked into the school's database once and changed some grades for a couple of students. He never got caught. Hell, I paid him to type my papers for me. I wrote them longhand, but he would type them up. His name was Andy. Anyway, I told Daddy about him and I was sure he would help us out for a fee. Daddy agreed to let me talk to the guy about it. Reluctantly, but he agreed," Joey said.

Mike stood up. "I see. Go on." Mike took a sip of his bourbon as he started to pace.

"I called Andy up and met him a few miles outside of town. I told him what we needed done. Andy had said he had to study the courthouse and sheriff station's computer system before he agreed to anything. A few days later, he called me back and said he could pull it off, but it was going to costs us fifteen hundred and he had to be in the courthouse or the sheriff's station to hack into the county system's router – whatever that is. Well, the courthouse was too hard to break into," Joey said with a shrug.

"So you broke into the sheriff's office," Adrian said flatly.

"Yep. I know how to pick a lock, but it would have been obvious," Joey said. "Daddy came up with an idea. He invited the sheriff and both his deputies to Drew's one night to buy them a beer. I came along. Of course, I wasn't old enough to drink at the time, but Drew still let me in. Daddy bought them a round of drinks, and then another, then another, and another until one of the deputies was good and drunk. I offered to drive him home. He agreed. I drove him home, and when I got him home, I swiped his keys. I met Andy a block away from the station, snuck in the station with him, and he hacked the system with his laptop. While Andy was doing that, I found Adrian's case file in the file cabinet and took it. We left the station. I left the window open at the deputy's house, so all I had to do was reach in and put his keys on the nightstand in his bedroom. He was still passed out. Andy and I met Daddy back on the ranch in the stables. I gave Daddy the hard copy file, and he paid Andy. Later on, I learned that Daddy burned Adrian's hard copy file in the barrel behind the barn."

"Shit," Steve mumbled and shook his head. "I knew Daddy was smart, but I didn't know he could plan an operation like Napoleon."

"Yep," Joey said. "After Andy left, Daddy opened the desk drawer and pulled out two glasses and a bottle of top-shelf bourbon. When he was pouring it, he had said I earned a drink. That was the first time I drank bourbon. As we were drinking, Daddy told me the stuff he did before I got involved. Then, he had said that we couldn't tell anybody what we did, not even you, Adrian," Joey said and looked at his brother. "Daddy thought you wouldn't be able to handle the load because of how honest and straightforward you are."

Adrian's father was right. If Adrian hadn't gotten involved with Rosita, – hell, if he hadn't lost his temper so badly, none of this would have happened. Joey wouldn't be facing prison time and Adrian, Steve, and Joey wouldn't be under investigation by the DEA. Adrian felt terrible. He took a long draw from his glass of bourbon.

"This secret stayed between Daddy and me for four years. The governor that got the charges dropped against Adrian died last year. We never heard from the girl who worked at the hotel ever again. Sheriff Langford had no idea what the hell happened. The DA at the courthouse at the time didn't ask questions. Andy had transferred to a college in Cali and gotten a job in Silicon Valley. Daddy is dead, now. I'm the only living soul that knew exactly what was done to save Adrian's ass."

"Not anymore," Adrian said flatly. "If I hadn't-"

"Don't," Joey said in a deep tone. His brown eyes were like steel. "You made a mistake. Everyone has in their life. You didn't deserve to face ten years in prison for it, especially over a tramp like Rosita. I wanted to help you, Adrian. And if I had to do it all over again, I would, no matter what I am facing now."

"I don't understand," Adrian said. "If the authorities knew that my records were erased and destroyed, why didn't they arrest me along with Joey?"

"The statute of limitations has run out on your assault and battery charges, Adrian," Mike said. "Another reason is that the DA's office doesn't have any proof that you were involved in the cover-up. Unfortunately, hacking and cyber-attack crimes can be charged five years after the crime in Texas."

"Goodness," Aunt Bea whispered and sipped her bourbon. "What do we do, now?"

Mike stopped pacing. "Perhaps we should figure out how they figured out how and who hacked the system," Mike said.

"Andy is the only living person for the exception of myself that knew," Joey said. "He had to have turned me in. I don't know why he decided to turn on me, now."

"I'm telling you it's Rosita. She had to find out about him," Steve said.

"How?" Faith asked.

"I don't know," Steve said. "Maybe her husband was trying to find out why the case fell flat. Maybe he found out about Andy and told Rosita about him a while back."

"It's not that farfetched," Aunt Bea said. "That girl

is a viper."

"Do you think she called the DEA about you guys running drugs on your property, too?" Mike asked.

"Absolutely," Steve said. "The more I think about it, the more I am convinced that she got someone to plant those drugs I found a few days ago in the stables. However, who? I don't know."

"What do you think, Adrian?" Faith asked.

Adrian's head was spinning. Could Rosita really be behind all their troubles? God knows, she hated them enough, and she's vengeful enough to do it. Either way, he was too busy feeling the weight of guilt for what his family was going through right now. "I…I don't know. At this point, anything is possible."

"Well, it's no secret that Andy Balsam is their witness," Mike said. "I suspect he exchanged what he knew for immunity. Someone got to him. He isn't getting anything out of this."

"Yeah," Joey said.

"I know a P.I. in Dallas. He's the best. I can have him do a check on this Andy Balsam and Rosita…um," Mike said.

"Rodriguez," Steve said.

"Right, I'll get him to find out where the girl from the hotel is," Mike said. "I'm not planning to approach her, but it would make me feel better that she is far from here and don't want to revisit this part of her past."

"Her name was Betty Scott," Joey said. "She told Daddy she was heading east. Of course, that was four years ago."

"All right," Mike said and took a sip of his bourbon. "In the meantime, perhaps we should think about coping a plea."

"What?" Steve said with wide eyes.

"I don't like it either, but Joey just told the whole story," Mike said. "They got a computer disk of exactly what was done, and Joey was at the helm."

"Hell, Mike, we keep you on retainer to help us not to send one of us to prison," Steve snapped.

If Joey went to prison because of Adrian's actions, he would never forgive himself.

"Steve, I said we should consider it. Not do it. Not yet, anyway," Mike said. "The fact of the matter is that Joey didn't hack the system. I might be able to get that thrown out if Joey pleads guilty to the obstruction of justice and the breaking and entering charges. I might be able to get him probation."

"What if you can't do that?" Faith asked.

"Joey is looking at a maximum of five years," Mike answered.

"Jesus," Adrian whispered and drank his bourbon. Adrian finished it in two large gulps.

"Let's see what the P.I. turns up first," Joey said. "If worse comes to worst, we'll try a plea bargain. Now, I'm going upstairs to wash some of this jail dirt off. I haven't taken a shower since yesterday." Joey stood up and put his glass back on the tray. He had only drunk half of his bourbon.

"We're having ribs for dinner," Aunt Bea said solemnly. "I better go check on them. Mike, you're welcome to stay for dinner."

"Thanks, Bea, but I better get going," Mike said. "The sooner I start on this thing, the better."

Chapter 35

Adrian skipped dinner. He had said he wasn't hungry and he needed time alone. Faith was worried about all of them. This had really taken a toll. The food was excellent at dinner, but the mood was low. They barely spoke. Faith wished she could do something to help, but she didn't know what to do.

Faith called her brother, Cliff. He was a mechanic, but he was a chop shop guy before he went legit. She hoped he had some suggestions.

"What I suggest is for you to wash your hands of this and get your ass back to Miami," Cliff said bluntly.

"That's not what I meant," Faith said with annoyance.

"I know," Cliff said. "You like this cowboy a lot, huh?"

"I more than like him. I love him, Cliff," she said with conviction.

"Baby, what I'm about to say, I'm saying it because I love you," Cliff began. "This isn't the first time you felt this way about a guy. Are you sure he is who you think he is?"

Faith knew what he meant. "I have been wrong about men in the past, but I'm not wrong this time. Adrian is a good man. His family are good people. They've been nothing but nice to me since I got here. They didn't have to take me in when I was hit by that hit-and-run driver." Faith had told her brother about the accident two weeks ago. He was angry that she didn't tell him sooner, but she had said she didn't want him to worry.

"True," Cliff said as he breathed out. "All right, if they really are good people, then they've definitely been greenlit. The hacker was probably paid to turn on the youngest bro. It would have to be big money because the hacker hadn't snitched in four years, and then all of a sudden he gave the popo a blueprint of the hacking and rats out who hired him and got him in the station. Then, the rat copped a deal for himself. I bet twenty dollars on it."

"Big money. Rosita is married to a guy who has hundreds of millions of dollars. Steve could be right. She could have done all of this," Faith said as she paced around the guest house with her cell phone to her ear.

"Big money wills power, little sis," Cliff said. "And judging from what you've told me about this chick, she is a bitch and a half. I wouldn't put it past a woman like her."

"So, what do you suggest?" Faith said. "You're good at getting out of sticky situations. You know how to think outside of the box."

"Hell, I'm not that good, and I've never been in trouble with the drug police," Cliff said. "Wait. It's radical, and I don't know how you would pull it off, but it's worth a try."

"What is it?"

"Get someone to talk to this Rosita chick," Cliff said. "Get her on tape. If anything, you can get her to admit that she sic the DEA on the cowboys. She'll get busted for that, right? If you get her on tape admitting that at least, the DEA will leave those guys alone."

It's not bad, but who would I get to speak to her that she would admit all that, too? "Okay," Faith said. "What about Joey?"

"Pssh, he might be up shit's creek," Cliff said. "Tampering with evidence? Breaking into a police station? I know a guy that got sent up for seven years over some obstruction of justice bullshit. Then again, that involved drugs. I don't know what you can do about that. Baby boy was involved."

Faith had a thought that she couldn't believe she had. It was sneaky, and it was a page out of Arn Matthews' book. "What if the P.I. can find the hacker? Maybe we can offer him a better deal to…drop the matter?"

"I don't know," Cliff drawled out. "It would have to be pretty sweet, or maybe he can get busted on something worse that would make his word discreditable."

"Hmm," Faith said. "I guess it depends on what the P.I. comes up with."

"Yeah," Cliff said. "Either way, don't get caught in the crossfire. Just give ideas to these guys. I don't want to get a phone call from you saying you're in lockup or from someone else that you're in the morgue."

Faith rolled her eyes. "You won't. It's getting late,

so I'm going to get ready for bed."

"All right. Take care," Cliff said.

"You, too, Cliff," Faith said.

****

Adrian had been drinking in the stables for what he thinks was for three hours. He wasn't sure. All he knew was that it was dark when he stumbled back to the house. The air was cool.

Adrian ended up at the front door of the guest house. He turned the knob and walked in. It was dark. He closed the door and pulled out his key ring and turned on his penlight.

He stumbled to Faith's bedroom. He smiled as he shined the light on her sleeping face. He walked as quietly as he could to the nightstand. He sat down his bottle of booze and his keychain with the penlight on the nightstand. Adrian slowly sat down on the edge of the bed. As he raised his foot to remove his boot, he drunkenly leaned backward at the same time. He accidentally lay down on Faith.

She jerked awake. "What the - Adrian?" she asked with groggy confusion.

"Sorry," he slurred and slowly sat back up. "Didn't mean to wake you. I was trying to get my boots off."

"Why?" she asked and sat up.

"So I can sleep here with you," he slurred.

"You can't sleep in here with me," she whispered sweetly. "Aunt Bea would have a fit. You know how she is."

"Hell," he slurred and raised his hand up and batted the air. "We're both grown. What is she going to do? Damn us to hell for sleeping in the same bed when we're not married? Pssh."

"All right," she said sweetly. "But, you are outta here in the morning." She crawled around him on the bed. "Let me help you." Faith started unbuttoning his shirt. Then, she unbuttoned the cuffs on his sleeves.

Adrian slowly shrugged out of his shirt as Faith unbuckled his belt.

She kissed him on the cheek before he slumped backward on his back. Faith chuckled as she stood up, and then she got in the floor to slip his black cowboy boots off. Adrian could feel her pulling off his socks. He heard the zipper come down on his black slacks. He groaned and lifted his hips so she could slide his pants off. Adrian started pushing at the waistband of his boxers.

"You want those off, too?"

"Mmmm, yeah," he slurred.

She yanked his boxers down.

Adrian gazed at the ceiling as Faith pulled his clothes from his ankles.

"Now, get under the covers," she whispered.

Adrian slowly repositioned himself and climbed under the sheet and comforter. Faith grabbed his discarded shirt off the bed and folded it with the rest of his clothes on a chair. She put his boots under the chair as well. She turned off the penlight and climbed in next to him.

He groaned as he wrapped his arms around her waist and laid his head in-between her breasts. At least Adrian still had Faith. He let his eyes drift close.

Chapter 36

Adrian woke up to the soft tone of Faith's voice. He opened his eyes to her light brown face and gentle smile.

"Hey," she whispered and placed her hand on his chest. "Steve snuck over some fresh clothes for you. He said if you're careful you could sneak out and go straight to the stables."

Adrian groaned. "Hell, woman, we're adults not kids sneaking around to make sure our parents won't catch us," he said hoarsely.

"Well, you should tell that to your aunt," she said. "Do you have a hangover?"

Adrian cleared his throat. "No." He felt groggy, but no worse for the wear.

"I should have checked on you last night," Faith said solemnly. "But, I thought you needed your space."

Adrian gave her a small, weak smile. He put his hand over the one she had on his chest. "I did need my space. Thanks for giving it to me, Angel."

It looked like it was still dark outside.

"What time is it?" Adrian asked.

"Four a.m.," she said.

He rotated his shoulders. The whole house usually got up at six. “Oh Faith, what have I done?”

“Adrian,” she began softly. “What happened isn’t your fault.”

He squeezed her hand. “How can you say that knowing what you know? Of course, it is. First, I got involved with Rosita, and I was too stupid to see what she was. When Steve tried to tell me what she was about…” He trailed off and shook his head with shame at the memory of him turning against his own brother. “Then, when I hear it from the horse’s mouth I lose my mind and beat the holy shit out of a man who was probably as blind as I was when it came to her. It all resulted in my father and my baby brother breaking the law to cover my sins and has put my grandfather’s ranch in danger of being seized by the government.”

“So, you believe Rosita is behind all of this?” Faith said.

“I had plenty of time to think last night. No one else would do this to us. You didn’t see Rosita when Steve yanked her out of the barn and kicked her off the ranch on the day of the BBQ. She was livid, sneering like a wildcat promising revenge. It’s her, no doubt in my mind,” he said solemnly.

Faith slowly shook her head. “Well, we just have to find a way to clean this up and stop her. I spoke to my brother, and he-”

Adrian sat up like a shot went off. “No, Faith. I don’t want you or your family getting involved in this.”

“I want to help,” Faith said.

“I don’t want you or your brother anywhere near this,” Adrian said strongly. “I don’t want the witch getting a whiff of you. All right?"

Faith's shoulders slumped. She looked down.

"All right?" he repeated.

"All right," she conceded sadly. "But, whatever you do, don't blame yourself. You were young, and love makes people blind to the truth sometimes. Rosita is the villain in this. Not you."

Adrian smiled. He loved her understanding nature. "Whatever you say, Angel."

Faith leaned down and placed several kisses on his chest. "Now, get up and get in the shower. You got work to do today."

"Yes, ma'am," he said with a light smile.

A few minutes later, Adrian had hopped in Faith's shower. As he let the water wet his body, Faith entered the bathroom.

"You don't mind if I brush my teeth real quick, do you?" she asked.

"Not at all," Adrian said over the running shower head. He peeked behind the curtain.

She was quietly brushing her teeth. He smiled at the sight of her in his white dress shirt. Faith looked so sexy in it. He should bring her more of his shirts to wear at night.

Faith finished brushing her teeth and was wiping her mouth with a hand towel when she spotted him watching her.

They looked at each other for a few moments. Adrian wondered what she was thinking.

She smiled. "You're wasting water."

"Yeah," he said without worry.

She giggled. "Do I have to come in there and wash

you myself so you can be out of here before everyone wakes up?"

Adrian chuckled. It would be a better alternative than drinking himself silly to take his mind off his troubles. "Maybe I could use some help. I'm not used to getting up this early. I'm moving pretty slow this morning."

Faith tilted her head to the side. "Well, all right," she said with the cutest smile Adrian had ever seen on her perfect lips.

He watched her slowly unbutton her shirt. Adrian's staff started rising at the sight of her breasts and the dark hair that covered the bliss between her legs. She let the shirt slide off her shoulders to the tiled floor.

Adrian widened the curtain to let her step into the tub with him.

Faith stood behind him and grabbed the soap from the soap dish on the side. "Let me wash your back," she whispered.

Adrian turned around.

Faith wetted the soap under the stream of water and started smoothing the bar on his back. Her hands were so soft and gentle. Adrian let the water beat on his chest as her hands roamed down to his buttocks.

Adrian's head fell forward, his hair getting wet under the stream of water.

Faith's soapy hands worked their magic.

He let out a long relaxed groan.

"Turn around," she whispered in his ear.

Adrian did what she asked.

Faith smoothed the soap over his chest and arms as the water washed away the soap on his back. She eased the bar down to his erection. “Oh my, it looks like you need special attention down here,” she said with a naughty smile and got on her knees in the tub.

Adrian wasn’t going to argue with her. He licked his lips as he enjoyed Faith’s slippery, soapy hands massaging his throbbing staff and weighty sack.

“Let’s rinse,” she said as she looked at his member with lust in her eyes.

Adrian took a step back to let the water from the shower head beat down his chest. The water ran down his chest to his organ below. Faith expertly worked her hands and fingers to rinse away the suds.

Adrian leaned his head back and closed his eyes. He let out a long exhale. Then, his breath caught at the sensation of his cock being wrapped in the warm, soft wetness of Faith’s mouth. He felt the vibration of her moans as she sucked and worked her cheeks around the most intimate part of him. Then, she took one hand and fisted his cock, working it back and forth as she sucked and licked his tip.

“Ohhh,” he groaned deeply. “Oh God. Oh, shiii."

The room filled with steam. Water beat on his upper back, relaxing his shoulders.

Faith flicked her tongue over his tip as she worked her hand and lightly fingered his sack.

Adrian grabbed her shoulders, holding on as he squeezed his eyes tightly closed. “Oh, Angel. Oh, that feels good.” No, he wanted to look at her when he was ready, and he wanted her to have pleasure. He opened his eyes and looked down at her. “I want to watch you,” he growled.

Faith lifted her head, but her hand kept stroking his

shaft. “What?”

“I want to watch you....wash your breasts. Show me how you bathe yourself.”

She looked surprised by the request, but she stopped stroking him. Faith stayed on her knees and grabbed the soap.

Adrian stepped to the side so the water could hit her skin, too. He took himself in hand and started stroking as he watched her smooth the bar between her suckable breasts.

She shyly soaped her breasts as she breathed heavily.

That’s when he remembered that her breasts were sensitive.

Her hand trembled as she put the bar of soap off to the side. She massaged and squeezed her generous mounds. She swallowed hard, and then opened her mouth.

Adrian quickened his stroking as he admired the pleasure on her face as she started to flick her nipples between her first two fingers.

She started letting out high-pitched moans.

“That’s it, sweetheart,” Adrian groaned raggedly.

Faith placed her hands on the side of her breasts and pushed them together as she squeezed them.

With his hand working overtime, heat rushed over Adrian’s body as his breathing became raspy. He reached down with his free hand and grabbed the nape of Faith’s hair. By instinct, he pulled her head back, and pointed his tip at her wet breasts and rock-hard nipples. He roared as the considerable load shot out thick and quick over her lovely pressed-together tits.

Chapter 37

Five days later...

Faith took an early lunch to go to Elliot Medical Center for a follow-up appointment with Dr. Green. She had called her primary physician in Miami to request that a copy of her medical records get forwarded to Dr. Green. She went to see him three days earlier to get birth control pills.

Faith had wondered what was wrong with her when she had realized last week that she was having unprotected sex with Adrian. Dr. Green had given her a physical and taken her blood. He wouldn't write her a prescription until her blood test came back from the lab. He had called her this morning and said they were back and for her to come in for a consultation.

Faith had told him at her first appointment that she had been on the pill a few years ago and everything was fine. Dr. Green had said that the blood tests were just a precaution since she hadn't had a physical in two years.

Faith patiently waited for Dr. Green in his office at the medical center. Doctors were always late no matter how small the town they practiced in was.

Dr. Green walked in holding a medical chart. He closed the door. “Good afternoon, Faith.” He walked over to the ivory painted desk and sat down in the white leather chair behind it.

“Good afternoon,” Faith said. She discretely glanced down at her watch. She had to get back to the dentist’s office by one. They had a patient with a one fifteen appointment coming in. Faith had called the patient and asked him to arrive a few minutes early so she could get his updated billing and insurance information.

“Well, I got your blood test back from the lab,” Dr. Green began. “We should talk. Have you been feeling…sick recently?”

“No,” Faith said. “Oh wait, I did get a little lightheaded yesterday at work, but it only lasted a few minutes. I thought it was stress…you know, with everything going on with Adrian and his family.”

“I see,” Dr. Green said. “Was that the only time you’ve felt lightheaded in the past few weeks?”

“Yes. Why?” she asked.

“Well, your blood test revealed something….interesting,” he said.

Faith blew out. She knew there was nothing wrong with her. What was he getting at? “Dr. Green, I don’t mean to be rude, but I have to get back to the office by one o’clock. Are you trying to say that you can’t prescribe me birth control because of one little dizzy spell I had yesterday?”

“Yes,” Dr. Green said.

“Is there something wrong with me? Did the blood test reveal I got some sort of illness?” she asked frantically. She felt fine. She was just worried about the Matthews. That's all.

"Well, that depends on how you look at the situation," Dr. Green said. "Faith, have you ever heard the expression, 'Closing the barn door after the horse has gotten out?'"

"Yeah," Faith said. "What does that have to do with prescribing me the pill?"

Dr. Green intertwined his fingers and placed his hands on the desk. He leaned forward and looked her right in the eyes. "A lot," he said coolly.

Faith stared into the old man's gray serious eyes. Goosebumps formed on her arms at the realization of what she was afraid might happen just might have happened already. "Are you saying that…I'm-" She stopped talking, gripped the arms of the chair, and took a deep breath before the words left her lips. "Already pregnant?" she asked in a high-pitched voice.

"That is exactly what I'm saying," he said.

Her mouth dropped open as her eyes felt like they were going to pop out of her sockets.

"I was afraid you might be floored. That's why I wanted to break it to you easy. I figured this was an unplanned pregnancy," Dr. Green said and took his hands off the desk. He leaned back in the chair.

"You're damn right; it's an unplanned pregnancy!" she yelled, and then covered her mouth with her hand. She didn't mean to get loud and ghetto with him.

Dr. Green coughed. *Was he trying not to laugh? There wasn't a damn thing funny about this.* "I know it wasn't the news you were expecting, but here we are."

Faith's hand dropped from her mouth. "What…what

the…what the fuck am I going to do? I can't afford a kid right now. I don't even own a car. I got two puppies to take care of."

"Not meaning to get too personal, but I'm sure Adrian will make sure you and the baby are taken care of," Dr. Green said soothingly.

Faith slumped in the chair. This couldn't be happening.

Dr. Green studied her demeanor. "It is his, isn't it?"

Faith's head snapped up. "Of course, it is," she said defensively.

"I'm sorry," Dr. Green said. "Just…the way you're acting-"

"I'm sorry if I'm acting a little erratic, but this was the last thing I expected to hear. I just had my period three weeks ago. Are you sure I'm pregnant?"

"I'm positive," Dr. Green said with conviction. "I'm just a general M.D. Now that you are expecting, I need to refer you to Dr. Jessica Clinton. She's an OBGYN. I already called her for you, and she can see you today."

Faith looked at Dr. Green like he had lost his mind. "I have to get back to work," she said in a high-pitched voice.

"I know when the dentist office closes, Faith," Dr. Green said with an easy smile. "Your appointment is at 4:15."

Faith just stared at Dr. Green.

****

Faith desperately kept herself busy to take her mind off of her current condition. She even dusted the shelves in the office. Dr. Brent had told her she didn't have to do that because the cleaning lady did that over the weekend. She had told him that she wanted to help the cleaning lady out.

The phone rang.

"Dr. Brent's office," she answered.

"Faith, it's Sheriff Langford," he said. "Can you meet me at the station after you get off today?"

"I have a…doctor's appointment after I get off." Faith rolled her eyes. She still couldn't believe she was pregnant. This was not a good time for her to be pregnant.

"After your doctor's appointment then?" he asked. "It's really important. I…got some information that could be helpful to you."

Faith noticed that he was speaking dicey. "Well, all right. Hopefully, my appointment won't be any longer than an hour."

"Whenever you can come by, but it must be today. I can't…hold the information longer than today," Sheriff Langford said carefully. "See ya when you get here." He hung up.

Faith slowly hung up the phone. What in the world could the sheriff have to tell her that she would be interested in?

Chapter 38

Dr. Jessica Clinton's office was two miles outside of the town limits. Faith had been driving Joey's jeep since he was under house arrest. She walked into the office's lobby, and almost had a heart attack when she saw one of the waitresses from Drew's Bar coming out of the door that led to the back of the office.

The ladies stared at each other for a moment in shocked mortification. Faith gathered up her courage and spoke. "If you don't tell anyone that you saw me here, I won't tell anyone I saw you here, okay?"

"Deal," the waitress said quickly, and then walked out of the office.

"May I help you?" the receptionist asked. Faith had never seen her before.

"Yes, um, I'm sorry, what's your name?" Faith asked.

"Amanda Green," she said sweetly. "I'm Dr. Green's granddaughter."

Oh great, Faith thought. *One more person that knows.*

"I'm Faith Roberts. Your grandfather made an

appointment for me today."

"Oh yes, Ms. Roberts," Amanda said and reached over to the side. "I need you to fill out this form. Dr. Clinton will be with you in a moment."

"All right. Do you live in town?" Faith asked. "I've never seen you before."

"Not really," Amanda said. "Other than coming to work, I mostly stay on the farm. My parents own a farm five miles outside of Elliot."

Faith shook her head. *Good, she won't run into Adrian and spill the beans.*

The appointment went well. Dr. Clinton was friendly and understanding. Faith got the impression that she truly cared about her health and welfare. She felt comfortable talking to the doctor about her concerns and worries. She listened and didn't judge her about her concerns about being a mother or that the pregnancy was a surprise. There was a small pharmacy adjacent to Dr. Clinton's office. She called in a prescription for prenatal vitamins for Faith.

Faith made another appointment in three weeks for an ultrasound and a check-up. Thirty minutes later, Faith was leaving the pharmacy with prenatal vitamins and a book about women who were expecting for the first time.

She headed to the sheriff's office. Her cell phone rang during the drive. The caller I.D. said it was the home phone at the ranch. "Hello?"

"Faith," Aunt Bea said. "Are you all right? You should have been home by now."

Faith was too busy being in shock half the day that she forgot to call Aunt Bea to tell her she was going to be late coming home. "I'm sorry, Aunt Bea, I got caught up running errands. I'll be home in an hour or so."

"All right, honey, as long as you are all right," Aunt Bea said.

"I didn't mean to make you worry," Faith said. She felt horrible. She knew Aunt Bea was worried sick about the DEA investigation and Joey's legal problems.

"It's all right, dear. I'll see you when you get home. Bye bye."

"Bye," Faith said and clicked off.

She was almost at the station.

****

Faith walked into the station. A girl was sitting at the reception desk. She didn't look older than seventeen. "Hi. Are you Ms. Roberts?" the teen asked.

"Yes," Faith answered.

"The sheriff is expecting you. Just take those stairs." The girl pointed to the right at a flight of stairs going down. "Then, turn to your right. He's in the conference room."

"Thanks," Faith said and headed for the stairs.

Faith took the stairs and turned right. She saw a room with a transparent glass window. The sheriff was in it. The door was open. She walked in. "Hey, Sheriff."

"Faith. Come in, close the door," he said.

Faith closed the door. "I apologize. My appointment took a little longer than I thought."

"Don't worry about it," Sheriff Langford said. "Look, there's a reason why we are talking down here and not upstairs in my office. Normally, I would have approached one of the Matthews boys about this, but I can't be seen doing anything directly that could be perceived as helping them."

Faith's eyebrows rose at his statement.

"I know those guys aren't involved with drugs," Sheriff Langford said. "And it was awfully convenient that the hacker that helped Joey get Adrian off the hook four years ago had come forward. I might be a small town cop, but I'm not stupid. They've been greenlit."

Faith didn't know whether to confide in Sheriff Langford or not. After all, it was his office that arrested Joey and turned him over to the county jail.

"I ran into Mike Scully in town," the sheriff said. "He said something about Rosita Rodriguez setting the boys up out of revenge. My wife and I were arriving at the BBQ when Steve was escorting Rosita off the premises. She was madder than a rattlesnake that had been stepped on."

Faith nodded.

Sheriff Langford gave a little smile. "I don't blame you for being careful about talking to me. Some things I really shouldn't know. But, there is something you should know. I found your hit-and-run driver."

Faith's eyes widened. She had given up hope that the sheriff would catch him.

"He was drunker than hell that night, but he remembers hitting you," Sheriff Langford said. "He and some of his friends were drinking and partying outside of town in the desert. He got scared and kept driving. He's a rich and privileged little punk. He got access to his trust fund this year and bought a condo in Dallas, a

Corvette, and one burgundy Hummer."

The Hummer that Adrian had described.

"Where is he now?" she asked.

"Richard Lewis, who happens to be Rosita's stepson, hadn't been seen since early this morning," Sheriff Langford said.

Faith's mouth dropped open. *No. No way. It's too much of a coincidence.* "Are you sure it's who you say it is?"

"Positive," Sheriff Langford said and stood up. "I did the background check myself. Plus, the little creep kept saying that his daddy was a wealthy man in California who would pay any amount of money for me to drop the matter. I wasn't interested."

"I see," Faith said. "So, he hasn't been seen since early this morning?"

"Nope," he confirmed. "A little birdy told me that he could be in an interrogation room in a police station somewhere. But, no one really knows for sure."

Faith caught his meaning. The sheriff had brought Richard Lewis there, and no one knew about it.

"Word on the street is that he hadn't been formally charged with anything and is under a twenty-four-hour hold," he said. "Something about cutting a deal with him and using him as leverage to resolve another situation."

"I see," Faith said slowly.

"You know much about technology, Faith? We're having trouble with the cameras in our interrogation room down the hall. You mind taking a look?" he asked.

Oh shit, she thought. Faith wasn't naturally crafty. She needed help. She knew enough to know that she couldn't call Adrian. He was too close to the situation.

Something could go wrong. "I don't mind at all, but I need to consult with my brother first," Faith said. "He knows a lot more about cameras than me. Do you mind if I call him before I take a look?"

"Not at all," the sheriff said as he headed for the door. "Take your time. Do whatever you have to do to fix it." Sheriff Langford left her alone in the conference room.

Chapter 39

Four days later…

Cliff had advised Faith on how to handle Mr. Richard Lewis. She had gone to Mike Scully after speaking with Richard. She told Mike her plan. He liked the idea, but he didn't like that they were going to execute it behind the Matthews boys' backs.

Faith had told Mike that she told Adrian that she wouldn't get involved and he would be upset that she was involved. Faith had also reminded the attorney that the DEA was watching the Matthews like hawks and Joey couldn't be associated with a sting that could influence his case. Mike Scully had smiled and said she should have been an attorney. He agreed to keep quiet and helped Faith iron out any possible legal holes in her plan.

Sheriff Langford had slipped her the phone number of an officer who worked in vice on the Dallas PD. Detective Chambers was more than willing to help and gathered a team together.

It was a day before her plan went into motion. She

wanted to be there. She had to see this through. Over the past few months, she had grown to love the Matthews family. She was doing this for them, for the man she loved, and their child.

Because of all the excitement and running around town Faith was doing putting the plan together, she hadn't told Adrian she was pregnant. Once the dust had settled and Rosita got what she deserved, Faith would tell Adrian. With all the drama behind them, Adrian would be happy about the pregnancy.

Faith walked into the den. Joey was in there watching the evening news. Hagar and Chop were walking around the room. Joey was being a trooper. Everyone knew he was miserable because he couldn't go out and work the land and take care of the cattle and horses. He was the outdoors type. However, Joey hadn't complained once. The day after he came home from jail, he tried walking to the stables. The ankle monitor had gone off fifty yards from the stables.

"Hey," she said. "Mind if I watch T.V. with you?" she asked.

"Nope," he said and sipped his beer. "But, I thought you'd be in the stables with Adrian."

Adrian was finishing up some work in the stables' office with a couple of the ranch hands.

"I'll head down there soon. I just wanted to see how you were doing," Faith said. "For living on the same property we haven't seen each other in a few days."

"Yeah, you've been running a lot of errands lately," Joey said. He looked at her. "Is everything all right?"

"Yeah," Faith said. "I just need to get some things squared away since I've decided to make Elliot my home."

"How was your doctor's appointment a few days ago?" Joey asked. He was looking at her like he was studying her.

"Fine," Faith said. "It was just a check-up."

"Hmm," Joey said. "You were pretty exhausted yesterday when you got home. Aunt Bea and Adrian were concerned that you were wearing yourself out."

By the time she got home yesterday evening, she was so fatigued. Faith wasn't sure if it was the pregnancy or the stress of putting together a sting. She was so tired that she grabbed a sandwich and went to bed early. "After I finish my business in Dallas tomorrow, I'll be back to my regular routine. Thanks for letting me drive your jeep."

Joey kept looking at her like he was studying her. "Yeah, what kind of business do you have in Dallas again?"

"Well, I have to go to the DMV to get a Texas license. I wanted to do some shopping. My brother is going to wire me some money to a Western Union, so I have to pick that up," Faith said. She hated lying, but she had to. She couldn't let everyone know what was going on. Faith had to protect the Matthews family. She planned on coming clean after tomorrow.

"You know," Joey began. "Aunt Bea said you looked like you were getting lightheaded at breakfast this morning."

"It was nothing," Faith said. "Just a little fatigued."

"That's what I told her," Joey said and chuckled. "She thinks you're pregnant."

Faith chuckled nervously. "That's…that's

something. Aunt Bea is something else."

Joey smiled at her. "She is, but it's rare that she is wrong when she gets a whiff of something."

"I see," Faith said.

Joey chuckled and shook his head. He gave Faith a Cheshire cat grin. Joey grabbed the remote. "You want to watch 'Deal or No Deal?'"

Chapter 40

It was 3 p.m. Saturday afternoon. Adrian was working in the office in the stables. He had been rushing through paperwork and getting things in order just in case things got worse with the DEA. Mike had said if the DEA got any more evidence against them, they could put a freeze on their accounts. Adrian kept cash in a safe in the house and in a safety deposit box at the bank, but it would only keep them for so long.

He was still trying to figure out how drugs got planted on their property. Out of paranoia, Steve and Adrian checked the barns and stables every day. The last thing they needed was to get caught with drugs on the property.

"Hey, boss," Isaiah said as he entered the office. Ray was with him.

"Hey, guys," Adrian said. "Did you move that head of fifty out to the Southside?"

"Yep," Ray said. "We came to tell you something."

Adrian couldn't take any more bad news. "How bad is it?"

Isaiah chuckled. "Well, it depends on how you look

at it. Lily is pregnant."

Adrian's brows furrowed at the news. "What? How the hell did that happen? I thought her colt baring days were over."

Isaiah smiled. "We did, too, but looks like the old girl got one more left in her."

"How did it happen?" Adrian said. "We still keep the females in a separate part of the stables, don't we?"

Ray chuckled. "Yeah, but a few weeks ago when I was locking up, Blaze was gone. He had kicked his stable door open. I went to the other side of the stables looking for him. He must have jumped the gate because it wasn't tampered with. Anyway, I caught him humping Lily like she was the last piece of ass he would ever see."

"Jesus, Ray, you didn't stop him?" Adrian asked with annoyance.

Ray looked at Adrian like he had gone mad. "Hell no," Ray enunciated. "Blaze was hornier than a teenage boy that night. I wasn't going to get kicked in the face for interfering with something that is perfectly natural. You know how temperamental he can be. Besides, Lily didn't seem to mind."

Isaiah laughed.

"And like you, I thought her colt bearing days were over. So, I let them carry on. When Blaze was finished with her, I took him back to his side of the stables, fixed the door, and went home," Ray said.

Adrian couldn't help but smile. He stood up. "Have you called the vet?"

"No, not yet," Isaiah said.

"Call him," Adrian said. "Ask him to come and give

Lily a look over. She's healthy, but I'm concerned that she might be a little too old to carry a colt to full term."

"You got it," Ray said.

Isaiah and Ray left the office.

Adrian walked out of the office a few minutes after them. He passed two other horses before he got to Blaze's stall.

The black stallion looked over at him.

Adrian knew he was expecting some sugar cubes or an apple. "No treat for you; you bad boy. I know what you did."

Blaze blinked.

"What were you thinking busting your door and going to the girls' stables?" Adrian asked and placed his hands on his hips.

The horse neighed.

"You're old enough to control yourself and to know better, now," Adrian chided.

The horse bowed his head down.

"You knew I was going to take you to that pretty filly two towns over in three months."

Blaze shook his head wildly as he snorted.

Adrian chuckled. "Couldn't wait that long, huh? Oh well, it's done, now. You're going to be a father."

Blaze raised his head. He nuzzled Adrian's jaw.

Adrian laughed and gave the horse two good pats on his long thick neck.

"Steve, come in, Steve, come on back," Joey said over the walkie-talkie.

Adrian listened as he rubbed and patted Blaze.

"Yeah, Joey, what's up?" Steve said.

"You and Adrian need to come to the house pronto,

over," Joey said seriously.

Adrian grabbed his walkie-talkie out of his pocket. "Joey, I'm down at the stables. What's going on?"

"Not sure, but it has something to do with Faith and all the other crap that has been going on, over," Joey said.

Adrian's muscles tensed. If Rosita was messing with Faith, he'd kill her. "I'll be at the house in five minutes, over," Adrian said in a deep tone.

"I'm a ways out," Steve said. "I'll be there in ten."

****

Adrian was approaching the house. A black SUV he didn't recognize was in the driveway. He swore under his breath. What the hell did the DEA want now? They had ransacked the place last week. A few days later, they questioned them and every ranch hand on the ranch. What else could they possibly want? He entered the house.

Adrian stalked into the den. He came up short when he saw a light-skinned black man the same height as him standing next to the bar. He was chunky and his dark hair was in small twists on his head. He wore a pair of jeans that were too big in the legs for him. His shirt was blue and white striped with a collar. He didn't look like a DEA agent.

"Oh Adrian," Aunt Bea said as she went to him. "I'm so worried." She wrapped her arms around Adrian's waist.

Adrian took hold of her. "What's going on?" He

looked at Joey, who was sitting on the sofa. "Who's this?" he asked as he nodded to the black guy.

"I'm Cliff Roberts, Faith's older brother," he said.

Adrian was speechless. Faith didn't mention that her brother was coming.

Aunt Bea let Adrian go.

Adrian walked to Cliff. They shook hands. "Nice to meet you. What brings you to Texas?"

"My sister," Cliff said seriously. "I don't like leaving Miami unless I really have to. I felt like I had to. I came here to make sure Faith didn't get too involved with this thing, but when I got here your brother told me it was too late. She's already in Dallas."

"What?" Adrian asked with confusion. "She went to Dallas to run some errands. Go to the DMV and to do some shopping."

Cliff shook his head. "That's what she told you," Cliff said. "She's trying to protect you and your family. I didn't think she had it in her, but looks like she has a little bit of Daddy in her just like me after all. It just took something serious to bring it out. You better sit down, man. This is one helluva story."

"I'll keep standing, thanks," Adrian said.

"All right, but I warned you," Cliff said and sipped his drink. It looked and smelled like a screwdriver. "A week ago, Faith called me and told me about baby boy's arrest and your DEA problems. I said if you guys were sure it was that Rosita chick that greenlit you, maybe you can get her on tape admitting it. Faith liked the idea, but she didn't know who to get that Rosita would talk to. A few days later, the sky opened and gave Faith her wish."

"What does that mean?" Adrian asked.

"The sheriff in this town caught the asshole who hit Faith on the road that night you found her," Cliff said. "Richard Lewis, who coincidently is the step-son of that Rosita chick."

"Shit," Joey said with wide eyes.

Aunt Bea sat down in an armchair in astonishment.

"The cop didn't book him, though," Cliff said. "He allowed Faith to talk to him first. She called me right in the police station. She asked me to advise her. Hell, I told her to take the phone in the room with her and put us on speaker. She didn't want to, at first, because she was afraid I was going to cuss the guy out and threaten him. I promised to keep my cool and to help her use the situation to her and your advantage."

Adrian's mind churned. "Are you saying that you and Faith talked this guy into helping you get Rosita to admit to setting us up?"

"In so many words, yes," Cliff said. "Turns out the rich boy resents his step-momma for making his future inheritance smaller by marrying his old man and having a baby by him. But, they have a good relationship just the same. They hang out sometimes. As we talked to the rich boy, he admitted that Rosita enjoys white sugar from time to time. Long story short, Faith wouldn't press charges against the rich boy in exchange for his help."

Adrian closed his eyes as he let out a long low breath. *Why didn't she tell me? She didn't have to do this.* "What was the plan?"

"Faith has been working on it all week," Cliff said. "A connection hooked her up with some guy on vice in Dallas. The cop was willing to help her out as long as he got a lead or two on drug dealers. Faith and the rich boy are working with vice to set up a sting to catch Rosita with coke. If Rosita gives up her drug connection and fesses-up to the DEA that she set you guys up, they will let her slide."

"It doesn't sound that dangerous," Joey said.

"I didn't think so either until last night," Cliff said. "Turns out the hacker that turned you in is involved, too. He and Rosita like hanging out with each other and party sometimes. The rich boy tricked Rosita and the hacker into meeting him at his condo in Dallas for a private party. The hacker…he doesn't sound like good people. Lost his job in Silicon Valley because of drugs. The way Faith talked, he sounded a little sketchy. The original plan was for her to be with vice when they caught Rosita red-handed so Faith could talk to Rosita herself. But, I told her to sit it out because I didn't like the sound of the hacker. She said she would, but…"

"But?" Adrian asked with urgency.

"After I got off the phone with her, I kept getting a nagging feeling she was lying to me. I couldn't sleep half the night. I got up early this morning and tried calling her several times. Her cell phone kept going straight to voicemail. I left a message that said that if she didn't call me back in thirty minutes, I was coming out here. Either she didn't get the message or she didn't think I was serious - I don't know. But, what I do know is that I closed the shop for a few days, kissed my wife goodbye, got on a plane, and flew out here."

"How did you know where the ranch was?" Aunt Bea asked.

"Faith gave me the address when she asked me to

send the rest of her things," Cliff answered. "When I got off the plane, I got a rental car and plugged the address in my GPS."

"Surely, the police wouldn't let anything happen to her," Aunt Bea said with a shaky tone.

"Maybe," Cliff said with a shrug and worry in his tone. "But, dirty cops, a hacker with drug ties, a rich hit-and-run driver, and a triflin' ho is a nasty combination. Something could go wrong, and Faith could get caught in the crossfire. And in her condition?" Cliff shook his head. "I told her she had to take care of herself, now."

"What do you mean in her condition?" Adrian asked.

"I was right," Aunt Bea said in a low tone and leaned back on the sofa.

Joey blew out.

Cliff shook his head. "She still hadn't told you. Yo man, she's preggers."

Adrian's brows furrowed. "What?"

"Preggers is another word for pregnant, Adrian," Joey explained. "I just learned that term watching a reality show this week."

Adrian grabbed the edge of the bar. "Pregnant! Faith's pregnant!"

"Faith's pregnant," Steve repeated as he walked into the den.

"You said the sting was going down in Dallas at the guy's condo?" Adrian asked.

"What sting?" Steve asked with confusion. "Now, we're talking about a sting?"

"Yeah, but I don't know where the condo is," Cliff said. "Hell, I didn't even know it was going to go down today. But, I think I know someone that does know where the condo is."

"Who?" Adrian asked with desperation.

"Your legal counsel, Scully," Cliff answered.

"Mike helped Faith with this behind our back?" Adrian asked.

"If it makes you feel any better, legal counsel wasn't comfortable keeping it from you at first, but Faith made him realize that you guys couldn't be directly involved with a scheme that could affect your problems with the DEA and baby boy's hacking case."

"Mike did something behind our back?" Steve asked.

"What are you going to do, Adrian?" Aunt Bea asked.

"It's Saturday, Mike's office is closed, but I bet he's at home," Adrian said as he adjusted his Stetson. "I'm going to find out where Faith is and lock her in the house until the baby's born. Hell, I might keep her locked up after that." Adrian was shocked and angry. How could she not tell him she was pregnant? How could she keep all this from him? Adrian shook his head. He had to focus. The first priority was to find Faith and keep her safe. Faith had a way of getting in life or death situations. She was a lucky woman, but people couldn't always depend on lady luck.

"All right," Cliff said. "We'll take my ride."

Adrian nodded. He looked at his brothers. "Come on guys, let's go."

Adrian and Cliff walked out the den. Aunt Bea, Joey, and Steve followed behind him.

"Go where?" Steve asked. "Will someone please tell

me what the hell is going on?"

"We'll fill you in on the way," Adrian said. He didn't want to waste time standing around the ranch filling Steve in. They had no idea what time the sting was going down, and something could go wrong if the hacker was as shady as Cliff thought he was.

They got outside and started heading for the black SUV.

"Where do you think you're going, Joey?" Aunt Bea asked as she stood on the front porch. "You can't go with them."

Everyone turned to look at Joey, and then down at his ankle monitor.

Adrian couldn't believe he had forgotten about it.

"She right, dude," Cliff said. "You're under house arrest."

"Fuck," Joey hissed under his breath. "She's doing this for me, too. I can't just sit here-"

"You ain't gotta choice, Joey," Adrian said as he walked to him. "You can't go past the driveway without that thing goin' off."

"We'll call you and let you know what we find out, man," Cliff said and opened the driver's side door of the SUV.

Chapter 41

Adrian had filled Steve in on the way to Mike Scully's house. They stood in Mike's living room demanding to know where the sting was taking place.

"Look, we know that it's at Richard Lewis's condo in Dallas," Steve said. "We just don't know where the condo is in Dallas."

"If you boys go barreling in like bulls in a china shop, you could blow the whole thing," Mike said. "Plus, it can be seen as obstruction of justice, possibly witness tampering. Faith is a big girl, she can take care of herself, and the cops aren't going to let anything happen to her. They'll keep her out of harm's way if something goes wrong."

Adrian wasn't trying to hear all this right now. The woman he loved had put herself in the middle of his family's problems, and in the process put herself in a possible conflict.

"If that's the case, what harm would it do to tell us?" Steve said.

Mike scoffed. "I know you boys. You're going to run right in there and ruin everything."

"No, we won't," Steve said. "We'll call the Dallas PD and let them know we want in."

Mike quickly stood up. "You can't do that. It could jeopardize Joey's case. The hacker is expected to show up. It could be seen as witness tampering, and as far as the DA's office is concerned, Joey has a history of that."

"All right, fine," Adrian said. "We won't call the Dallas cops, but for my peace of mind, tell me where she is."

"Adrian-" Mike began.

"Damn it, Mike, she's pregnant," Adrian spat out. "I have the right to know where the mother of my unborn child is!"

Mike was speechless. "I'm sorry. I didn't know. I-" Mike stopped talking and took a deep breath. He looked up at the ceiling. "All right, I have the address written down, but for the love of God, don't interfere."

After Mike gave them the address and door number of Richard Lewis's condo in Dallas, they thanked him and walked out the door.

All three of them stopped dead in their tracks at the sight of Joey leaning against the SUV with his arms crossed over his chest. "So, where are we goin'?" he asked nonchalantly.

"What the fuck?" Steve said with wide eyes.

Adrian looked down at Joey's ankle. The monitor was gone. "I don't know what you did to get that thing off, but go back to the house."

"I'm not a kid anymore, Adrian," Joey said. "You can't send me back home when you and Steve are about to get into some mess."

"I have to say I'm impressed," Cliff said with awe

on his face. "How did you get it off?"

"And where is it now?" Steve asked.

"I can't divulge all my secrets, but I put the monitor on Hagar," Joey said. "As long as the dog stays in the house, the authorities won't even know that I'm gone."

"What did Aunt Bea say?" Adrian said.

"She wasn't happy about it, but she knows how to let a man be a man," Joey said. "Let me be a man today, Adrian."

Adrian didn't have time to argue with him. "Just get in the car before Mike sees you and has a heart attack," he said with exasperation.

The men climbed into the SUV.

"How did you get to Mike's house?" Steve asked. "Faith has your jeep."

"One of the ranch hands gave me a ride," Joey said as he put his seatbelt on.

"I'm going to try and call Faith again," Adrian said as he pulled his cell phone out of his pocket.

Cliff plugged Richard Lewis's address in the GPS.

Adrian got Faith's voicemail again. He clicked off. He prayed that whatever guardian angel that looked after Faith in the past would do it one more time until he got to her.

Dallas was a two-hour drive. The sun was setting by the time they got there. Traffic was horrible. It took them an additional thirty minutes to get to the condo building. They cursed when they saw it was guarded by a gate and a security guard.

Cliff parked a block away from the entrance. "Now what?"

"We need to be in the parking lot at least," Steve

said. “From there, we’ll be able to see when Faith and the cops will show up.”

“What if they are already in there?” Adrian asked with worry. “We gotta come up with a way to get the guard to let us in.”

“Hey, I think I got an idea. It’s a little questionable, but it might work,” Cliff said.

“What is it?” Adrian asked.

“We’ll bribe him” Cliff answered. “Security guards don’t get paid that much. How much cash do you guys got on you?”

Chapter 42

Faith sat in Richard's living room with three vice cops. She watched them do a mic check on Richard. He was going to wear a wire. Vice had also set up a mini camera on the TV. You could hardly see it.

"All right, Richard," Detective Chambers said. "You're all set. Remember, be casual -relaxed. Don't let on that something is amiss." Detective Chambers had dark curly hair and pale skin. His eyes were a strange blue-violet, but they were attractive.

"I understand. I'm not going to screw this up," Richard said. "Rosita and I have drinks and…recreational activities together all the time. She didn't suspect a thing when I invited her here to hang out tonight and to see if she can help me out with my problem. That's why she's bringing the hacker."

"What else do you know about this hacker?" Chambers asked.

"Not much. Rosita said that Andy was an expert hacker, but he ran into some bad luck in Silicon Valley and lost his job. She said he might be able to help me with my problem. Oh, and he loves snorting coke."

"All right," Chambers said. "Try not to get high with them, but if they press, you'll have no choice. Just do enough to make them feel comfortable. Don't get high as fuck, you got it?"

"Yeah, I got it," Richard said.

"Chambers," Officer Murphy said as he came out of the bedroom. "Everything is set. We heard every word you two said and the camera is working perfectly." Officer Murphy was a black man with dreadlocks. He mostly worked undercover for the vice squad.

"Great," Chambers said.

"They'll be here in a few minutes," Richard said. "She's pretty punctual."

"Let's go in the back, Faith," Chambers said.

Faith stood up. "Thanks for doing this," she said to Richard.

"It's the least I can do," Richard said. "I know you think I'm doing this to save my own ass, and technically, I am. But, I'm also hoping this will make us even."

Faith looked at the skinny blonde-headed young man. "If this goes the way I hope, we will be." With that, Faith walked with Chambers to the master bedroom where the equipment was set up. Faith was mad as hell at Richard, but this wasn't about her. This was about Adrian and his family. If she had to sacrifice justice for herself to get justice for them, she would do it. Besides, it's not like Faith died in the accident or got life-altering injuries from it.

Chambers let her walk in first, and then he closed the door behind them. "So, what kind of excuse did you tell them?" he asked Faith.

"I told them that I had a lot of errands to run and I

wanted to go shopping," Faith answered.

Chambers nodded. "So, you really love this guy, huh?" he said.

Faith smiled. "I do."

"That's too bad," Chambers said with a grin. "You're a good-lookin' woman. If it doesn't work out, give me a call."

Faith shyly looked to the side and looked back up at him. "All right, but it's going to work out. I don't care if I have to tie him to a chair and lock him in a room."

Chambers laughed. "All right, but the offer is there."

"Hey, lover boy," Detective Williams said as he approached them with two headsets. He handed one to Chambers and the other to Faith.

As they were getting settled in, the doorbell rang.

"Here we go," Chambers said.

They watched Richard walk to the door on a laptop computer screen.

Chapter 43

Richard Lewis opened the door. Rosita stood in the hallway in a shiny blue wrap with a matching dress with two slits in the front. She had two guys with her. Not one.

"Rich," Rosita purred and kissed him on the cheek.

"Hey, Rosita. Come in," he said with an easy smile.

Rosita and the two guys filed into the vast living room.

"Who are your friends?" Richard asked as he closed the door.

"This is Duke," Rosita said and glided her hand down the man's strong chest. Duke had green eyes and dark reddish-brown hair.

"Nice to meet you," Duke said and offered his hand.

Richard shook it. "And you."

"I hope you don't mind me letting Duke tag along. He lives here in Texas, so we don't get to see each other much," Rosita said as she continued to rub the man's chest.

Duke put his arm around Rosita's waist.

"This is Andy. My friend I told you about," Rosita

said with a big smile.

"Hi," Andy said.

Richard shook hands with the goofy looking four-eyed guy that was carrying a laptop case.

"Sit down," Richard said with a big smile. "You guys want a drink?"

"Absolutely," Rosita said. "I'll help you fix the drinks.

"You guys sit down and make yourselves at home," Richard said.

"Much oblige," Duke said.

Andy walked to a black leather chair and sat down. Duke sat down on the sofa.

"What do you boys want to drink?" Richard asked as he and Rosita walked to the bar.

"I take a beer if you got one," Duke said.

"Jack Daniels and coke, please," Andy said.

"Coming right up," Richard said.

As they fixed the drinks, Richard whispered to Rosita, "So, who's the cowboy? I thought the hacker was the only person you were bringing along."

Rosita gave him a sultry smile as she put ice in the glasses. "Oh, I met Duke four years ago when I lived in Elliot. He's just an old playmate."

Richard rolled his eyes.

"You're not going to tell your daddy, are you? Not that he would care," Rosita said.

"No," Richard said. "But, you know I invited you over here to…help me with a problem."

"Duke is cool," Rosita said as she grabbed a bottle of Jack Daniels. "He's tried to help me in the past. Maybe he can help you, too."

Richard didn't have a choice, but to go with it. Richard had felt ill when Sheriff Langford had told him that the woman in that old four-door car would have burned to death if someone hadn't stopped to help her. He wanted this done, and the slate wiped clean so he and Faith Roberts could go on with their lives. Richard had learned his lesson this time. No more drinking and driving.

Once they got everyone a drink, Rosita sat down on the floor, stretching her legs under the coffee table next to Duke's legs. Richard sat down in the other leather armchair.

"I brought something to help ease your mind," Rosita said to Richard. She pulled a bag of coke and a razor blade out of her purse. She reached for the vase on the glass coffee table and sat it to the side. She grabbed the flat mirror plate that was under it, and emptied the bag of white powder on it.

Duke pulled a dollar bill out of his pocket and started rolling it up.

Rosita started chopping at the white powder with the blade.

"Maybe in a few minutes," Richard said. "I'm hoping we can discuss this, and then if something can be done, I'll celebrate."

Rosita expertly used the razor to put the powder in thin straight lines on the mirror plate. "What's wrong, sweetie?"

"I…I was in a hit-and-run incident," Richard said and looked down. "I hit a woman in a car and kept going. I was drunk. I didn't know what I was doing."

Everyone remained quiet.

"The woman is fine, but there was a witness," Richard said. "I think he got half of my license plate's number. It's only a matter of time before the police catch up with me. I can't do prison time."

Duke leaned down and snorted white powder up his nose.

"You can't pay anybody off to make it go away?" Rosita asked.

Andy stood up and walked over to Duke.

Duke finished a second line and handed the dollar to Andy.

Andy quickly took it and leaned his head down over the coke.

"I'm afraid to try," Richard said solemnly. "If I try to find out who the investigating officer is, it might expose me."

"Ah," Rosita said with understanding. She took the dollar from Andy. "I think my friend can help." She leaned over and snorted a line.

"Oh?" he asked as he fought the itch to partake in the snort fest.

"Yes," Andy said, and then he dug in the front of his nostrils to clear the coke. "I've done things like this before. I hacked the Dallas PD a few years ago for another client. I'm sure I can do it again, but I don't work for free."

"All right, but what would be the purpose of hacking it?" Richard asked.

"I can get into the system and find out who is investigating the case. All you have to do is give me the day and time that you hit the driver. I can run a search on it and find out the name of the witness and the cop looking into it. Then, you'll be able to buy them off," Andy said.

"Andy will also be able to wipe the system clean of any evidence," Rosita said.

"Yeah, the cop you buy off can get rid of any hard copy evidence that the cops have," Andy said. "What condition is the vehicle in? That might be a little trickier. They could get the paint color of your car from it."

"The car caught on fire," Richard said. "The woman got out in time, but the car is a heap of metal now."

Duke had a weird look on his face. Richard couldn't tell what he was thinking. Duke took a long swig of his beer.

"Even better," Andy said. "You won't have to worry about it."

"I appreciate the offer to help, but how in the world did you and Rosita meet?" Richard asked.

"We met in California," Rosita said. "He's my dealer."

Richard was taken aback. "You said he was a hacker."

"I'm both," Andy said. "I only get hacking jobs here and there. The drugs mainly pay the bills."

Duke took a sip of his beer.

"Oh," Richard said. "I heard of hackers getting into payrolls and robbing them."

Andy scoffed. "Too much trouble anymore, and most of the time, it isn't worth it. The payrolls that are open to cyber-attacks don't have much in them. And, I wouldn't even rob a poor sap who is barely making above minimum wage."

"Are you sure you can do it?" Richard asked.

"You're not out of practice?"

"He can do it," Rosita said with a smile. "I don't know about the client that he did the job for in Dallas, but he did hack a courthouse system and a police station in Texas before."

"Oh yeah," Richard said with mild interest. He didn't want to let on that he was needling them for information. "Tell me about it."

"Well," Andy said. "I guess I can tell you about that since I got immunity."

"You got caught?" Richard asked.

"No," Andy said. "I turned the guy who hired me in."

This was it. The information Richard had to get. "Why?"

"Oh, it wasn't personal," Andy said with a smirk. "Not for me anyway."

"Remember the guy that beat your father up four years ago, but didn't go to jail for it?" Rosita asked.

Richard slowly shook his head. "Yeah."

"Andy was the guy who wiped that man's records clean," Rosita said. "Of course, I didn't know that at the time. I just knew that the hotel clerk that witnessed what happened had disappeared and the evidence was gone. That's when I refused to testify. I didn't know what was happening and your father couldn't get any headway in Texas to find out."

"Ah," Richard said. "So, you found out Andy did the job when he became your dealer."

"That's right," Rosita said. "And the guy's little brother hired Andy to clean the electronic files."

"All right, but that doesn't explain why you turned

the guy in years later," Richard said.

"Normally, I'm not a snitch, but I wanted to help Rosita out," Andy said with a smile.

"I went back to Elliot a month ago. I tried to make amends with my family and the man that I left to marry your father. My family spurred me, and if that wasn't bad enough, my former fiancé and his other brother treated me like a tramp when I showed up at their house. Practically threw me off the ranch," Rosita sneered and picked up the rolled-up dollar. "I vowed to get revenge, and I did."

"So you asked Andy to turn your ex-fiancé's brother in?" Richard asked.

"Yep," Rosita said. "But I did more than that. I called in an anonymous tip alerting the DEA that they were trafficking drugs through their property. Of course, one phone call wasn't going to get them moving, so I got Duke and a girlfriend in California to call the DEA, too."

"Are they trafficking drugs?" Richard asked.

"No," Duke said flatly. He took a sip of his beer.

"No, I got Duke to plant some product on their land, but they found it and got rid of it before the agents showed up," Rosita said.

"How did you get on the ranch?" Richard asked Duke.

"Oh, I got my ways," Duke said. "But, I can't plant anymore because now they are on the lookout for it. They do a search every day to make sure more haven't magically appeared."

"I see," Richard said.

"So, do you trust Andy to do the job for you now?" Rosita asked, and then snorted a line.

"Well, as long as he doesn't turn me in later," Richard said bluntly.

"Nah," Andy said and walked back to his chair. He grabbed his glass and took a long swallow.

"He won't," Rosita assured Richard. "Like I said, Andy just did it as a favor to me."

Andy sat back down in the leather chair. "Yeah, I take exception to people who treat my friends like shit."

"How much do you charge?" Richard asked.

"For the job you want, and you are Rosita's step-son, plus Rosita is a good customer, I'll do it for $700," Andy said.

"Deal," Richard said.

"If you got the money on you now, I can get started," Andy said. "I got my laptop with me."

Richard shook his head. "I got cash in the safe in my bedroom."

"Great," Andy said happily and picked up his laptop case. He started opening it.

"Now that your problems are about to slip away, take a line," Rosita said and held out the dollar to Richard.

"It doesn't look like you have much left," Richard said. "I don't want to snort all your supply."

"I got more with me," Andy said as he booted up his laptop. "Have a ball as long as you can pay for it."

"And we can," Rosita said, and then giggled.

"Yeah. It's Saturday, let's party," Duke said and stood up. "Mind if I have another beer?"

"No, help yourself," Richard said and gestured towards the bar.

"Thanks," Duke mumbled and headed for the bar.

"Andy, while you're working on Richard's case, see if you can find out any more information about that girl Adrian is seeing," Rosita said.

"I thought you were going to let it go now," Duke said from the bar. "You got them in knots at the ranch. Isn't that enough?"

"If the DEA would have found the coke you planted, it would be," Rosita said.

"Faith's a nice woman. She didn't do anything to you," Duke said.

"I know, but she's important to Adrian," Rosita said. "He's the one I want to hurt. Looks like I have to go through her to do it."

"I told you that she's clean," Andy said. "Besides, do you really want to hurt a pregnant woman?"

"She's pregnant?" Richard and Duke asked at the same time.

"Calm down guys," Rosita said nonchalantly as she batted her hand in the air. "I don't want to destroy her life. I'm a mom, too, remember? I'm just hoping we can find out if she had a lost love that might want to come back into her life. Perhaps she wants him, too. Perhaps she would leave Adrian for him."

"Hmmm," Andy said. "I can try to find that out, I guess."

"Good," Rosita said with a satisfied smile. "You know I'll pay you."

Andy's laptop started beeping really loud.

"What the hell is that?" Duke asked from the bar.

Andy slammed the laptop closed, reached in his bag, and pulled out a gun. "Nobody fuckin' move!" he said harshly as he pointed the firearm around the room. The gun had a silencer on it.

Everyone froze in place.

"This is a fuckin' setup!" Andy yelled as he frantically stuffed his laptop into the case.

"What the hell are you talking about?" Duke asked.

"Don't play dumb with me," Andy said as he looked wildly around the room. "My alarm went off. It's set to detect listening devices and camera equipment."

Shit.

"The coke has made you paranoid," Rosita said as she slowly stood up. "Put that thing down."

"Shut up, you conniving bitch!" Andy yelled at her. "You brought me here. You're setting me up. Why? You want to blackmail me into giving you free product?"

"No!" she yelled. "I don't know what you're talking about!"

"Screw it. I'm not taking any chances," he sneered, and with that Andy started firing his gun.

Chapter 44

Adrian, Cliff, Joey, and Steve were listening at the door. They couldn't hear a damn thing until a man started yelling his head off. Then, they were startled by a woman screaming.

"No!" a man yelled.

Adrian kicked the door in. A gun barrel met him.

"Get down!" Cliff yelled and dove down.

Steve tackled Adrian to the floor before the man could fire his gun.

"Put the weapon down!" a man ordered with harshness.

Then, two gunshots echoed into the atmosphere.

"Shit!" Cliff yelled.

"Is he dead?" another man asked.

"Oh God!" a man groaned in agony.

"Nope," a man said.

Adrian saw a pair of black lace-up boots approach him. "Get up, you damn fools!" the man said with disgust.

Adrian and Steve looked up to a man wearing blue jeans and a black polo shirt. He had a badge clipped to his belt and a gun holster around his waist. He had the strangest eyes Adrian had ever seen.

"Who the hell are you, and what the hell did you think you were doing?" he asked in a deep tone.

"We heard a woman screaming," Adrian said as Steve got off of him.

"So your first instinct was to kick the door in?" he asked with disbelief. "Are you cops?"

"No," Steve said as Adrian got up. "I'm Steve Matthews, and this is my brother, Adrian."

The man scoffed. "Well, fuck."

"You shot me, you fuckin' pig!" a man yelled from inside.

The cop who was talking to them looked over his shoulder. "At least you're alive," the cop sneered. "The woman you shot isn't."

"Shit!" Cliff said and pushed his way past everyone.

"Hey!" the cop said.

"Faith!" Adrian said as he followed Cliff inside.

"She's fine," the cop said as he went to the entryway of the hall. "Faith! Come on out, it's safe!"

The door down the hall opened, and Faith emerged.

"Faith," Adrian said as he opened his arms to her.

She quickly jogged down the hallway to him, and they embraced.

"What the hell were you thinking?" Adrian asked against her ear.

"I wanted to help you," she answered. Her voice was muffled against his chest.

"Do you enjoy making me worry like a damn woman?" Cliff asked as he approached them.

Faith's head shot up from Adrian's shoulder.

"Cliff?"

"Yeah, remember me?" Cliff asked and pulled Faith out of Adrian's arms.

The siblings hugged.

"What are you doing here?" Faith asked.

"Making sure you were all right," Cliff answered. "I started getting a bad feeling about all this. I tried calling you a dozen times, but your phone kept going to voicemail. So, I got on a plane, and here I am."

"You paid for a round-trip plane ticket for me?" she asked with shock. "And you left Florida?"

Cliff smiled down at her. "If those two things don't say I love you, I don't know what will."

They hugged again.

"Where the hell is Lewis?" a black cop asked.

"Here," a man said in a shaky voice. The man who owned the voice slowly emerged from behind an armchair. He was trembling like a leaf in the wind, and holding on to the top of the chair for dear life.

"Did you get hit?" a cop asked.

"No," he breathed. "But, I pissed on myself."

"Holy shit," Joey said.

Cliff, Adrian, and Faith turned to look at him. Steve was standing beside him gawking at the same scene Joey was. They followed their eyes to Duke, one of the Lone Wolf's ranch hands. Blood was seeping from his shoulder, but he didn't seem to be concerned about it. He was on his knees with his hands balled into fists next to Rosita. A bullet hole was in Rosita's forehead. Her brown eyes were open and lifeless.

Duke snapped his head over at a man who wore glasses. The man was sitting in the floor. His hands were behind his back. His shoulder and leg were bleeding.

"I'm going to kill you for this," Duke said with simmering rage.

"You ain't going to do shit," the cop with the strange eyes snapped. "Murphy, take this guy to the back and take his statement."

"Yes, sir," Murphy said.

Adrian stared at the body of his former fiancé'. Rosita's ways had finally caught up with her.

"Well," the man with the glasses said. "Fancy seeing you here, Joey."

Adrian looked up.

Joey and the man, who Adrian assumed was the hacker, were staring each other down.

The cop with the strange eyes and dark hair seemed to know who Joey was. He walked over to him.

Adrian's gut clenched. He was going to take Joey into custody for violating his bail.

"Hey, kid," the cop with the strange eyes said. "You better get out of here before the ambulance, coroner, and backup gets here. Matter of fact, all of you should go."

Adrian looked at Cliff. "Take Faith to the car."

"What are you going to do?" Faith asked with wide eyes.

"I'll be along in a minute," Adrian said. "I want to talk to these nice officers."

"I'm staying with you," Faith said.

"No, you're not," Cliff said as he took her elbow in hand.

"I'm not a child," Faith said.

"Angel, please go with your brother," Adrian said and kissed her on the forehead. "I'll be along shortly."

Faith nodded and left the condo with Joey, Steve, and Cliff.

"Um officer, um," Adrian said to the cop with strange eyes.

"Detective," he corrected. "Detective Chambers."

"Detective Chambers," Adrian said. "The man that your officers took in the back is one of my ranch hands. What the hell was he doing here?"

Chambers exhaled. "No offense, Adrian, but you should be more careful about who you hire. He was the one that planted that coke on your property for the DEA to find."

Adrian rocked back on his heels. "Did he say why?"

"Not yet, but judging by how he reacted to Rosita being dead, I take it he did it for her."

"I want to talk to him," Adrian said.

"Not now," Chambers said. "This turned into a shit show. This was supposed to be a simple off-the-book sting. We weren't expecting Duke to show up. We got to get a statement, and then get him to the hospital. I don't think the bullet went straight through."

"I'll be meeting you at the hospital," Adrian said with conviction.

Chapter 45

Adrian and Steve were at Duke's bedside in the ER. Joey was in the hospital parking garage in his jeep. They didn't want to take the chance of a cop seeing him. Adrian had given Cliff some cash and asked him to get two hotel rooms. Adrian, Faith, and Cliff would go back to Elliot in the morning.

Faith had protested in the condominium's parking lot. She wanted to stay with Adrian. However, Adrian had hushed her with a kiss and sent her off with Cliff.

Adrian and Steve stared down at Duke. His shoulder was in a sling. The ER doctor gave him something to numb his shoulder so he could get the bullet out. It was only a flesh wound.

"Why, Duke?" Steve asked. "Why did you betray us?"

Duke looked down. "It wasn't about betraying you. Ya'll treated me well, but I loved her. After Rosita told me how you two treated her when she came to the BBQ to make amends, I got hot. She wanted to teach you guys a lesson. She asked me to plant the coke and I did, but that's all I did. I didn't meet Andy until later on. I didn't even know he was her dealer until last night."

"You were in love with her?" Steve said. "Didn't you know that was a fool's cause? She was married."

"She was going to leave her husband to be with me," Duke said. "We were going to raise little Carlos together."

Adrian shook his head. Rosita hadn't changed. She had spilled the same crap to him at the ranch.

"You fool, she didn't love you," Steve said. "She peeled her clo-"

"Steve," Adrian interrupted. Duke was a dumb snake, but he didn't need to hear how Rosita tried to seduce Adrian in the barn.

Steve kept quiet.

"I take it that I'm out of a job," Duke said solemnly.

"Yeah," Adrian confirmed. "You're out of a job."

Duke exhaled. "I can't say I blame you."

Steve and Adrian left Duke to simmer in the mess he had helped to create. They went to the ER lobby. Detective Chambers was there talking to two officers.

Chambers gave them their marching orders, and they left the lobby. He turned to look at the brothers. "Hey, did you find out what you wanted to know?"

"Yeah," Adrian said. "Thanks for letting us talk to him."

"No problem," Chambers said. "Do you want to press charges?"

"Against Duke?" Steve asked. "Didn't know we could."

"We got him dead to rights," Chambers said. "He admitted on tape and camera that he planted coke on your property, called the DEA with a false tip, and would have planted more coke if you guys hadn't become so vigilant about someone setting you up."

"If we pressed charges against him, it could help get the DEA off our backs," Steve said.

"Sure would," Chambers confirmed.

"All right," Adrian said. "Let's do it."

"It's late," Chambers said. "You can come down and make a statement in the morning, but we have enough evidence to arrest Duke tonight and place him in custody."

"That's fine," Adrian said.

"Here's my card," Chambers said and handed it to him. "I'll be at the station by 10 a.m."

"What about Andy?" Adrian said. "Do you think him being arrested will help Joey's case?"

Chambers shrugged. "If you have a shrewd lawyer, it might. Depending on what the DA in Wichita wants to do. He might be able to get a fair plea deal. Hell, the guy that ratted him out was a drug dealer, a hacker, and now a killer. A jury would give him the side eye."

"Let's hope," Steve said.

"Where are Faith and her brother?" Chambers asked.

"They went to a hotel for the night," Adrian said.

Chambers said, "She's one helluva woman. Treat her right."

"I will," Adrian said.

"Congratulations on the baby," Chambers said.

Adrian's eyebrows shot up. "She told you?"

"No. Andy checked into Faith at Rosita's request. Rosita wanted to find out if Faith had an old boyfriend she could use to lure Faith away from you," Chambers said.

"Damn. Momma used to say we shouldn't speak ill of the dead, but I think that only applied to humans," Steve said and shook his head. "Oh, well, she's a wild hyena in hell now."

"Since you are going to press charges against Duke, I'm going to place him under arrest," Chambers said.

Chapter 46

Cliff had texted Adrian on his cell phone to let him know which hotel and rooms they were in.

Faith had taken a shower and put on a complimentary hotel robe. She was hungry, so she ordered room service.

There was a knock at the door.

Faith walked to the door and opened it.

It was Adrian. "Hey, Angel," he said with a small smile.

They hugged each other.

Faith was relieved to see him. Not only was she worried about him, but she also missed him. "Come in," Faith said. "I thought you were room service."

"Hungry?" he asked as he crossed the threshold.

"Yeah, a little," Faith said. "I just got some fruit, cheese, and sparkling cider."

"Sounds like a nice light snack," Adrian said and took off his black Stetson. He placed it on the dresser. "Where's Cliff?"

"He's in his room across the hall," Faith said. "Cliff was tired. He said he didn't sleep well last night then he got up early to catch the plane here."

There was a knock on the door.

"Sit down," Adrian said. "I'll get it."

Faith sat on the edge of the bed.

Adrian opened the door. It was a waiter with a cart. "Come in," Adrian said. He opened the door wider for the food service worker to enter.

"We have sparkling cider and a fruit and cheese tray, correct?" the waiter asked.

"That's correct," Faith said.

"Just leave it there," Adrian said as he dug in his pocket. He pulled out his wallet and gave the boy a tip.

"Thank you," the waiter said. "You folks have a good night." The waiter left.

Adrian wheeled the cart closer to the bed where Faith was sitting. He grabbed the sparkling bottle of cider and started opening it.

"Where's Steve and Joey?" she asked.

"Steve and Joey rode back to Elliot in the jeep. We didn't want to take the chance of Joey being discovered."

"How in the world did he get that ankle bracelet off?" Faith asked with intense curiosity.

"Joey wouldn't say, but I told him before they left that he better get it off Hagar and back on himself before I get home tomorrow," Adrian said flatly.

"What happened at the hospital?" Faith asked.

Adrian popped the plastic cork on the bottle. "Well, Andy was attended to. He got one in the shoulder and one in the leg. He'll spend the night at the hospital for observation then the police will escort him to jail." Adrian poured the cider into two champagne glasses on the tray.

Faith removed the covers off the trays.

"Steve and I spoke to Duke. He was in love with Rosita. She had told him that she came to the ranch to apologize to me. She had also told him that we threw her off the ranch for no good reason. Duke felt that the woman he loved was insulted, so that's why he agreed to plant the drugs in the stables." Adrian shook his head as he sat the bottle down on the food cart. "It was obvious she was using him. Duke lost his job and is probably going to jail for a year or two over a woman that didn't give a rat's ass about him."

"And she's dead," Faith said. "Are you okay?" Faith popped a piece of cantaloupe in her mouth.

"Yeah, but Duke's betrayal was hard to swallow. He had been working at the ranch for four years."

"I wasn't talking about him," Faith said. "I know you don't love her anymore, but you did at one time. You had to feel something when you saw Rosita on the floor – dead."

Adrian sat down on the bed next to her. "I did. I felt pity for her. I also felt that her duplicity came back and bit her on the butt. If she would have continued to go on with her life instead of coming back to Elliot for God knows what, she would be alive. Now, she's dead and there's a three-year-old boy out there somewhere that has to grow up without a mother."

Faith shook her head. She ate a strawberry.

"We're pressing charges against Duke," Adrian said. "The cops got him on tape admitting that he planted drugs on the ranch and he called in one of the phony tips into the DEA. It will go a long way in ending the DEA investigation against us."

"That's good," Faith said. "That's what I wanted out of all this. I wanted to get Rosita on tape admitting that she set you guys up. I had hoped that we could get something against the hacker, too so he would recant his statement to the DA's office in Wichita."

"Joey might get out of this still," Adrian said. "Chambers' theory is that the DA might offer Joey a good deal since the star witness in the case is a drug dealer and a murderer."

"Let's hope," Faith said and popped a grape into her mouth.

Adrian took a sip of sparkling cider. "Faith, why didn't you tell me you were pregnant?"

She knew that question was coming ever since Cliff admitted that he spilled the beans to Adrian when he had arrived. "I wanted to wait until after the sting. I thought you would see it as good news once your troubles were behind you."

Adrian sipped from his glass again and placed it on the food cart. He looked at her. "You didn't think I would be happy about it?"

Faith glanced away. "We've only been seeing each other for a little over a month at the most."

Adrian put his finger under her chin and turned her head to face him. "I think I've made it clear how I feel about you," Adrian said. "And that I want a future with you. You are designing a house on the property we just bought."

Her heart warmed as she smiled. "I feel the same way, but this is all happening so fast. I…I wasn't planning to have children this soon."

He grinned. "Well, it's not like I gave you a chance to use precautions."

Faith laughed. "Yes, I went to Dr. Green to get birth control pills. You can imagine my surprise when he said that it was too late."

"Is everything okay? I mean, is the baby healthy?"

"As far as we can tell, yes," Faith said. "I'm only a few weeks pregnant. I have an appointment for an ultrasound in a week and a half. I'll know more then."

"We'll know more then," Adrian corrected. "I'm coming with you."

Faith smiled. "I would like that."

Adrian lifted her chin a little higher. He leaned down and kissed her. The tip of his tongue slowly traced the outline of her mouth. Then, he sultrily lapped at her lips. He didn't stop until she let out a yearning moan.

She gazed up at him.

He looked down at her under heavy lids. "Tomorrow morning, I'm going to ask Cliff for your hand in marriage."

She gasped. "Oh Adrian," she whispered. "I think Cliff would appreciate that. He will see it as a sign of respect."

"And what about you?" Adrian asked. "How would you see it?"

"I'm going to save that answer for when you officially ask me to marry you," Faith said with a smirk.

He chuckled. "I love you, Faith."

"And I love you," she whispered.

Adrian kissed her again as he leaned her back on the bed.

Epilogue

Three months later...

Faith was upstairs in the main house at the Lone Wolf Ranch. She stared at herself in the full-length mirror. Her wedding dress was white satin with a ten-inch train. Three white roses were pinned on the side of her auburn hair.

She was fourteen weeks pregnant, and she was barely showing. They had started building the house, but it wouldn't be ready for another two months. Until then, Adrian and Faith would live in the house with Steve, Aunt Bea, and Joey.

The DEA had dropped the drug investigation against the Matthews family. The DA offered Joey a plea deal. Chambers was right. The DA didn't want to take a chance at trial, despite the computer disk Andy had given him proving the crime. Since Andy was a criminal of the highest order, the DA was afraid that a good defense attorney could argue that the disk was forged to make Joey look guilty. The DA believed a jury would take that under consideration. Joey got two years' probation and two hundred hours of community service.

Andy was sentenced to life in prison with the possibility of parole in twenty years. Duke was sentenced to onc year in jail. Faith kept her word and didn't press charges against Richard Lewis. The truth was, if Richard hadn't hit her that night, Faith and Adrian never would have met.

Since Richard's father was too old and sick to take care of a three-year-old boy, Richard took Rosita's son and brought him to Dallas. It was evident that a near prison and death experience had matured and changed Richard. He had contacted the Rodriguez family and had said that they were welcomed to visit Carlos whenever they wanted. The family took Richard up on his invitation.

The wedding guests had arrived. They were having the ceremony and reception inside since it was cool in Texas this time of year.

Aunt Bea, Cliff, and Tenika, Cliff's wife, entered the bedroom.

Aunt Bea was smiling like a proud mother. "You look beautiful," she said.

"Thanks," Faith said.

"It's time," Tenika said. "Are you ready?" Tenika was Faith's maid of honor.

"I'm more than ready," Faith said with a big smile.

Tenika handed Faith her bouquet that was filled with lilies and greenery.

Cliff stuck his arm out. "Let's do it, little sister."

Faith took her brother's arm so he could escort her to her future as Mrs. Adrian Matthews.

Thank You

Thank you for purchasing The Rancher. I hope you have enjoyed Faith and Adrian's journey of love. May you find peace and love in your own life.

Olivia Saxton

The Billionaire's Proposal

Calvin Michelson needs to get married and produce an heir so his fly by night cousin won't inherit the family legacy and fortune when he dies. This is business for Calvin. He has every intention of resuming his playboy life after marriage so he needs a woman who is willing to bear a child and can put up with his ways. After a quick conversation with a family member, Calvin realizes that the perfect bride was right in front of him all along.

Yvonne Moore has worked for Mr. Michelson for ten years. He was a good boss and he had never expressed interest in the efficient assistant with dark framed glasses who always wore her hair in a bun. So when her billionaire boss asked her to marry him, she laughed her head off– until she realized he was serious. Yvonne wants time to think about it. Calvin is not a patient man. He's in hot pursuit in convincing Yvonne to marry him and have his child. What Calvin and Yvonne didn't bank on was falling in love.

Garvey's

Biracial twin sisters, Jodi and Jackie, are two inches away from filing for bankruptcy and losing their heritage. The twins' grandparents started Garvey's Hotel and Bar. The business was solvent until the 2008 crash.

With eminent ruin on the horizon, Jodi comes up with a radical idea to revitalize Garvey's; hosting orgies in the bar on the weekends. Jodi convinced her conservative twin, Jackie, to try the new business plan on a trial bases.

However, things come to a screeching halt when local law enforcement shuts them down. Jackie and Jodi must team up with other citizens in the small Arizona town to keep the Orgy Bar alive.

CPSIA information can be obtained
at www.ICGtesting.com
Printed in the USA
BVHW081502160619
551129BV00001B/51/P

9 781796 770971